To the Oregon gals –
Never stop reading on the beach or laughing about the Tetons

A Love Connections Sweet Romcom

THE
RUSE OF
ROMANCING

HILLARY SLAUGHTER

CHAPTER I
Dani

Herriman, Utah

WAS IT *TECHNICALLY* AVOIDING someone if you happened to be intentionally unavailable every time they called? Or texted? Or stopped by? I mean, I typically talked to my older sister, Avery, every day, multiple times a day. But lately, I didn't want to hear what she had to say, so I'd found creative ways to be too busy to answer the door. Or the phone. Or my texts.

Right now, I was fairly certain Avery was calling to tell me to finish packing before she got here to take me to the airport, but I needed both hands for that and my earbuds were already in my carry-on. Avery hated speaker phone, so not answering the phone was really a favor to her.

Of course, I'd never admit that her call had startled me mid-social media scroll, about to read the comment section on a post by The Starlit Review. Reading comments as an author was always a terrible idea, but Starlit had just posted a review of my book, and I couldn't help myself despite knowing the majority of the comments would just amplify the imposter syndrome that had become my constant companion of late.

In my defense, it wasn't every day one of the biggest romantasy social media accounts shared their thoughts about my debut novel, a novel that had, according to several news outlets, taken the fantasy world by storm. An unexpected storm that had, for the most part, been a positive one, with thousands of five-star reviews and dozens of features of my book on news sites and book blogs. Unfortunately, as with all storms, there was also a not insignificant amount of collateral damage, but I tried not to think of what the more negative reviews had said.

Of course, this post from Starlit Review was less review and more speculation about my upcoming novel and what was next for "promising young debut author Danielle Baldwin."

I wish I knew.

What I *did* know was that I was struggling to write.

Sure, I had words on the page, but they were... less than impressive. A fact that had been made painfully obvious when Sadie, my cousin, editor, and best friend, sent me feedback on the few chapters I'd emailed her a couple of weeks ago. Her comments had been... disheartening, to say the least.

I hadn't written a single word since then, and my publisher was understandably nervous.

I haven't missed my deadline yet. I reminded myself. That was why I was flying to Oregon in just a few hours. The change of scenery would be good for me, help me disconnect from life and really dig into the story. Assuming I could get the characters to speak to me again. And assuming the words they said to me weren't complete garbage.

Sadie, along with our other female cousins, who were essentially bonus sisters, assured me in our "Cheaper Than Therapy" group text, that my writing would start flowing again soon. But growing up they also thought Max from *A Goofy Movie* was the epitome of sexy, so what did they know?

That was why I needed to go on this trip. If anywhere could snap me out of my writing funk, it would be the Oregon coast with its tree-covered mountains and misty beaches that seemed to ooze creative energy from all the photos and videos I'd scrolled online. I'd never visited Oregon before, but the pictures I'd seen of my vacation rental looked cozy and welcoming, if a bit dated. Not to mention the owner of the rental was a complete doll, messaging me regular updates and low-key trying to set me up with her grandson who she assured me was "very single and attractive, underneath all the hair." I appreciated the thought, but I had neither the time nor desire to look for romance while I was in Oregon. As much as my hopeless romantic heart hated to admit it, I needed to focus on writing, not the possibility of meeting a bearded Oregon man.

I just had to get to Oregon first then let it work its magic.

Shaking my head to clear it, I set my unanswered phone on the nightstand and recommitted to packing. I could do this!

I reached for the remote and turned up the volume on the TV mounted on my wall. Doris Day and Rock Hudson bantered on screen, their commentary keeping me company as I worked. There was something soothing about having my favorite movie, *Pillow Talk,* playing in the background. It was so comforting that I sank onto my bed, hugging a pillow to my chest, and stopped packing, getting completely sucked into the story. No matter how many times I watched it, it never grew old.

The sound of my front door banging open startled a scream from me, and I hurried to stand and look busy, throwing my pillow back onto the bed and reaching for a shirt to roll up and place in my suitcase. I knew exactly who was storming through my front door and it would be better for me if Avery didn't catch me procrastinating. Again.

"Are you seriously screening my phone calls?" She asked from the living room of my townhouse, her voice drawing closer as she approached my bedroom. The clack of paws on the tile floor outside my room told me Hercules, my black 75-pound giant schnauzer, had decided to leave his spot in the living room to greet my sister. From the moment I'd pulled out my suitcase, he'd retreated to his dog bed, moping because he knew I'd be leaving soon, and he wouldn't be coming with.

For all his appearances of a giant, intimidating defense dog, Hercules was the world's biggest softy. He hated when I left, which had been happening a lot lately thanks to my recently completed book tour. If I thought Avery wouldn't have a conniption, I would have tried to bring him with me on this trip, but I knew he'd just serve as a distraction from what I was supposed to be doing: writing another *New York Times* bestseller. No pressure.

I raced to the dresser and pulled out some clothes, hurriedly stuffing a few more shirts into my luggage in hopes of disguising just how little progress I'd made. If Avery was here, it meant she was ready to drive me to the airport, which meant more time had passed than I'd realized. Good thing the airport was only thirty minutes away and Avery had insisted we leave significantly earlier than necessary in case of traffic.

"Should I even ask how many times you've watched this movie?"

Avery was leaning against my bedroom door frame in her usual blouse and slacks, her hair slicked back in a tight bun that emphasized her cheekbones. Hercules sat at her feet, his whole body vibrating with excitement at having one of his favorite people in the house. As she took in the scene, her hand resting on Hercules's giant head, Avery's lips tipped up into a small smile that emphasized the freckles on her cheeks. My sister and I were nothing alike in coloring, but we had similar facial features, our cheekbones and noses clearly indicating to the world that we were related despite the difference between her gorgeous auburn locks and my average brown hair cut into face-framing layers. We did have the same brown eyes, but people tended to miss those. Especially when Avery was dressed to the nines for a day at the office while I sported leggings and a well-loved t-shirt in anticipation of my flight.

"There is literally no such thing as watching *Pillow Talk* too many times," I said, walking over to give her a hug. Just because I was avoiding her and the pressure I felt to write every time I was in her presence, didn't mean I wasn't happy to see her.

That was the one downside to being represented by a publishing house that was run and co-owned by your sister and her ex-fiancé. The pressure was always there, even if you didn't want it to be.

Avery returned the embrace, allowing me to hold on a little bit longer than normal, seeming to sense that I needed the hug.

And I did need the hug. I couldn't tell her that after receiving Sadie's feedback, I'd deleted the few chapters I'd written of the book Avery's been waiting for. Or that I was one more frustrating writing session away from deleting my outline too. What she didn't know wouldn't kill her. And it wouldn't add to her already overflowing plate of stressful things.

"There is when you owe your publisher another novel," Avery said. "By the way, I hate to add pressure, but have you given any thought to design suggestions for the cover for this book? The designer who did the last cover is dealing with a family emergency and I sent you a list of potential designers—"

I squeezed her a bit tighter, making the air whoosh from her lungs.

"I've been a bit focused on trying to make sure there will be a book to create a cover for. As soon as I have a solid draft going, I'll give the cover more thought, I promise," I said, stepping out of the embrace so I could get back to packing.

One of the pros of publishing with my sister's publishing house: I had more say in my book covers than the average author. This meant I adored the cover for my first book, *Of Curses and Pomegranates*, because I'd been part of the design process. Unfortunately, this was also one of the cons, since it added one more thing to my never-ending list of author to-dos for book two.

When I'd decided to publish my debut novel with Rose & Quill Publishing, I was simply grateful to finally have someone interested in my book. I'd worked on it for years and, after navigating rejections from agents and larger publishing houses, and determining self-publishing wasn't the right fit, I was starting to doubt my book would ever see the light of day.

What none of us had anticipated was just how well *Of Curses and Pomegranates* would perform. My gender-swapped, magic-packed retelling of Hades and Persephone galloped up the best-seller charts as audiences fell in love with Hypatia and Petros's enemies-to-lovers vibe, witty banter, and insane chemistry. Which wouldn't be a problem if I hadn't ended the book on a cliffhanger.

And while I'd technically outlined book two before we published book one, now that it was time to follow the outline, the words wouldn't come. Which was especially rude since I'd quit my day job based on book one's success, adding a level of pressure to book two that was nearly suffocating.

"You ready to head to the airport?" Avery asked, ignoring the open suitcase on my queen-sized bed that contained three shirts, a pair of joggers, and one tennis shoe.

"About that," I said, walking to my dresser and pulling out more clothes. I wasn't sure how long I would be gone so it was next to impossible to know what and how much to pack, but I made sure to grab a swimsuit and a couple sweatshirts for good measure. On the way back to the bed, I stooped down to pick up the missing tennis shoe from the floor before putting my armload into my suitcase. "I was thinking. I don't feel good about leaving, not with you and Mr. Wet Blanket so recently broken up." At this, I turned to gauge her reaction. "Who's going to help you cancel wedding things? And what about—"

Avery held up a hand, cutting me off. I tried not to notice her empty ring finger, something that was harder to do than anticipated. The garish heirloom engagement ring from her ex-fiancé's family had sat on her hand for over a year and, while the ring had never fit Avery and her personality, it still felt weird not seeing it.

"First of all," Avery said, giving me a stern look and holding up a single finger, "you know very well his name is Eric."

"Doesn't change the fact that he's a wet blanket," I muttered under my breath, adding socks to my suitcase.

Avery shot me a scolding look but didn't acknowledge my comment. Instead, she continued her list, holding up another finger.

"Second of all, you need space and time to write. You are *not* canceling this trip."

I stepped toward her, clutching a ratty sweatshirt that really needed to be retired but was too comfy to get rid of. "But you need—"

"I need you to write a killer book to finish your duology and establish Rose & Quill as *the* up-and-coming publishing house. Mom and Grandma Sue can help me with cancellations," Avery said, lowering her hand and sitting on the bed next to my suitcase. Hercules took advantage of her change of position, settling his head in her lap, looking like a stern elderly man agreeing with her point.

"Are you sure?" I asked, handing the sweatshirt to Avery so she could add it to my bag as I went to retrieve toiletries from the bathroom.

I needed this trip. I knew I did. I needed a change of pace, a change of scene, a change of *something* if I was going to write this book. But I didn't feel good about leaving my older sister home alone to deal with her recently broken engagement and canceled wedding by herself.

"I'm sure. Besides, if you finish the book fast enough, you can be my plus one on my no-longer-honeymoon trip to Italy." Avery tossed me a wide, conspiratorial grin I didn't trust. I knew she was hurting more than she was letting on, but I also knew she'd share her pain when she was ready.

"Fine," I conceded, depositing my toiletries before returning to my dresser and pulling out the remaining hodgepodge of items I'd need for my trip.

My phone dinged from the nightstand, drawing both of our attention.

"Cousin chat or a flight reminder?" I asked as I worked, knowing Avery had my passcode and could check for me.

"Neither. Looks like last-minute instructions for the rental."

"More instructions? What else haven't they told me?" I moved to my closet and stooped to dig through my shoes, looking for a specific pair of sandals that were ideal for the beach.

Avery snorted a laugh that carried into my closet and made me grin. It had been too long since Avery had laughed easily.

"Just a warning that if you run into a gruff, bearded gentleman when you arrive not to be alarmed. Apparently, he's the grandson she's been trying to set you up with and he also works as the property manager. There's a note about how he refuses to shave, even though she tells him he'd have more dating success if he was clean-shaven."

While I'd never met either the owner or her grandson, it was the kind of comment I could picture our Grandma Sue making and it made me smile as I finally found my sandals and surfaced from the closet.

"I don't know. Tall, dark, and bearded holds a certain appeal." I mused.

"And it can hold all the appeal in the world you want, *after* you've written me an award-winning sequel," Avery said pointedly. "Are you almost done packing? We've got to leave soon if we're going to make it to the airport on time."

I pivoted on my heel and did a quick sweep of my bathroom and closet. I knew from experience if I forgot anything, I could buy it when I got there, but it would be so much easier if I could just remember everything I needed the first time.

"What do you think are my chances of making it to my gate and onto my plane without Poppy pulling me into her shop to sign more books?" I asked as I came back into the room with a final pile of items to add to my suitcase. While I adored my cousin, I wasn't really in a headspace to navigate her enthusiasm.

Avery snorted, taking my clothes from my arms and adding them to my suitcase. "I think you have a better chance of winning the lottery."

"I was worried about that."

I sat at my gate, waiting for my flight and feeling absolutely ridiculous with my hair tucked up into a black baseball cap and a pair of oversized sunglasses perched on my nose. While the light coming through the many windows of the Salt Lake City airport was bright, it wasn't exactly bright enough for sunglasses inside. But if the basic disguise worked for major celebrities traveling, I hoped it could help hide me from Poppy for another ten minutes until my flight started boarding. There were many perks to flying first class and boarding first was one of them.

With Avery's help, I'd made quick work of packing. She'd driven me to the airport in record time, Hercules riding in the back seat, his head out the window the entire drive. I'd passed through security quickly, to the point where I almost wished one of the security guards would need to search through my carry-on, anything to reduce the amount of time I'd be stuck waiting at my gate. I was flying out of the A terminal, which normally wouldn't have been an issue if it wasn't for one fact: the store where Poppy worked was directly across from my gate, a near-guaranteed formula for her facilitating an impromptu signing. It was almost as if the universe was trying to thwart my efforts to keep a low profile.

Most people didn't recognize authors when they weren't sitting at a signing table with a poster declaring who they were next to them, but writing the current top-selling romantasy book in the country increased chances of being recognized exponentially. Typically, I could keep a low profile, but the handful of times I'd flown to out-of-state signings and talk show interviews had quickly taught me staying under the radar only worked when Poppy wasn't standing next to me proudly declaring to the entire airport that "*the* best-selling author, Danielle Baldwin, was in the store right now!"

I'd almost missed several flights thanks to her exuberance leading to multiple spur-of-the-moment signings and question and answer sessions.

I loved Poppy like a sister and could never repay her for the amount of publicity she'd created for me. Honestly, Avery probably owed Poppy some kind of compensation for the number of books she'd single-handedly sold. But I was already nervous enough about this trip without adding in the self-doubt that plagued me every time I stepped into the limelight as *author* Danielle Baldwin.

I glanced up to find a middle-aged man in business attire studying me a bit too closely for my liking. I slouched down further into my seat, lifting the book I was pretending to read even higher to cover more of my face. I glanced at my smart watch, only nine more minutes until boarding, assuming they started on time.

"Whatcha reading?" An all too perky and familiar voice asked from my left.

I gave a startled squawk, turning to find Poppy grinning like the Cheshire Cat in the seat next to me. Her brown curls tumbled down her back, her flowy floral dress looking like it had come straight from the sixties. She wore a large, amethyst pendant around her neck, with matching crystals hanging from her ears.

"Poppy," I said, lowering my book and pressing a hand to my pounding heart, "you scared me."

She gave a carefree shrug, propping her chin in her hand as she rested an elbow on the back of her seat, the gesture sending the scent of a unique, but lovely combination of essential oils my way. I was always impressed by her ability to combine different aromas. If I tried my hand at essential oils, I'd most likely end up smelling like an old lady who got lost in a swamp.

"I thought it was you sitting here when I walked past earlier, but then I thought there was no way my *dear* cousin Dani could possibly be in the airport right now without stopping to say hi to me before settling in at her gate. After all, the shop has books she could sign and so many customers who would love to share how they met *the* Danielle Baldwin while traveling. But sure enough, it's you," Poppy said sweetly, each word twisting the knife of guilt deeper into my stomach.

I winced, fighting back the urge to shush her as she said my name louder than everything else. The businessman across from me was no longer pretending not to study me. He was full-on watching our exchange, though I wasn't sure if it was because he recognized my name or because a picture of Poppy could have been placed in the dictionary next to the term *flower child*.

"I'm sorry I didn't stop, Poppy. You looked busy when I walked by." Which was only a partial lie since there had been people in the shop when I'd ducked past. "And I don't have time to sign books today." This was more of a lie since I'd been hiding at my gate for twenty minutes, hoping to avoid this exact circumstance, but Poppy didn't need to know that. While I loved my fans and was grateful for their support, I wasn't exactly feeling extroverted enough to really engage with strangers right now. I was too stressed about my next book and how much writing I needed to do over the next several days.

"I'm just glad I caught you. I've been thinking about your trip since you texted in the cousin chat you were headed to Oregon today, and I have a gift for you!" She patted her sides, trying to find her pockets in the many folds and layers of her dress. "I made it last night, hoping to see you today."

"You didn't have to make me anything!" I rushed to say. The last time Poppy had made me a gift, she'd given me a tea blend to reset my digestive system. Based on the events that followed drinking a single cup, it had done its job and then some.

"Found it!" She declared proudly, withdrawing a bracelet of crystals from her pocket. The piece of jewelry was far from my style, consisting of a combination of heart-shaped green crystals and oval-shaped reddish-orange stones. I had no doubt there was someone out there who would immediately fall in love with the bracelet and the bold statement it made. Unfortunately, that person wasn't me.

"Wow, Poppy," I said, forcing enthusiasm into my voice. "Those stones are something else."

Poppy beamed, snagging my hand and slipping the distinct bracelet around my wrist, the cool, smooth stones against my skin causing my arm to break out in goosebumps.

"It's the perfect combination to cure your writer's block! The green stones are amazonite. It connects to your heart chakra and is ideal for positivity and resilience, which we both know you need with this book." She tapped one of the heart-shaped stones, her words coming out fast in her eagerness to explain her gift. "The other stone is carnelian, which is kind of obvious since you're a Virgo."

I *hmm*-ed in acknowledgment, having no idea what the reddish-orange crystal had to do with my zodiac as an August birthday.

"I promise it's more than your birth crystal. Carnelian promotes—"

A voice came over the speakers, announcing the first round of boarding for my flight and I shot to my feet, hurrying to stuff my book and sunglasses into my carry-on. I straightened, giving Poppy a wide smile.

"That's so sweet Poppy, but I've got to board. Don't want to miss my flight!" I bent to give her a quick hug, not giving her time to stand and return the gesture. While I loved Poppy's interest in crystals, I knew from experience that once she got going explaining different stones and their abilities, it was difficult to get her to stop.

"Travel safe, Dani! And don't forget you owe me signed books when you fly home," she called as I hurried away.

I gave her a wave over my shoulder, the giant bracelet weighing down my wrist. I would be slipping it off as soon as I settled into my seat, not that I'd ever tell Poppy. She had the world's biggest heart, and I would hate to hurt her feelings.

I pulled up my boarding pass on my phone and waited for my turn to board, counting down the minutes until I'd arrive in Oregon. Nerves danced in my stomach as the gate agent scanned my ticket and waved me down the jetway. My laptop in my backpack softly bumped against my back with each step, seeming to remind me of the work ahead. I'd find my inspiration there. I had to.

CHAPTER 2
Mason

Cascade Harbor, Oregon

THE GROCERY STORE DOORS opened with a whoosh as I glanced down at the list in my hand. It included an odd assortment of items, all things my grandparents insisted I needed to purchase for the rental half of the duplex I lived in and managed for them. While the last-minute shopping trip wasn't how I'd originally planned to spend my Saturday morning, it was a small price to pay for living on the Oregon coast rent free. My grandparents had purchased the duplex as an investment property years ago and, when they were no longer able to keep up with the maintenance, I was more than happy to help in exchange for a place to live, even if it meant running random errands on the weekend and getting weekly comments from my grandma about how much she disliked both my beard and my long hair.

This time around, the vacation rental had been rented by a long-term guest, our first since my grandparents had completed their ill-advised renovation. Somehow, Grandma had gotten it into her head that thrift store chic was a good idea, transforming the slightly dated rental that looked like it was from the early 2000s into something straight from one of her old movies, complete with bright color-blocked rooms, silky couch pillows, and bulky gold lamps.

I'd thankfully convinced her not to repeat the same renovations on my side of the duplex. The colors would have most definitely interfered with my creative process as an artist and graphic designer.

I pictured trying to work on my commissions in a pea-green room and shuddered. I was quite happy with my clean white walls and furniture that hadn't been pre-owned by at least five people before me.

I grabbed a cart and started my trip up and down the grocery aisles, snagging instant coffee and bargain-brand bottles of shampoo and conditioner. Just because my grandparents had added it to the list, didn't mean I had to purchase top of the line products. The duplex looked like it was a time capsule from the fifties, no reason for it to have fancy coffee or shampoo bottles that cost as much as a tank of gas.

Though I made sure to grab the shampoo that did not smell like vanilla. I'd had my fill of female tourists who smelled like vanilla to last a lifetime. Strawberry was a nice, safe aroma. Strawberry didn't spell trouble and heartbreak.

"Mason, I thought that was you." A cheery female voice called as I started making my way to the checkout line.

I looked up to find the local baker and my favorite person in the entire coastal town waving at me from the pharmacy area. Joane had the physique of someone who enjoyed her own baking, meaning she gave the best hugs of anyone I knew, with the exception of my own mother, who lived several states away in Utah. Add to that the hint of mischief that always lurked behind Joane's glasses, and exchanges with her were guaranteed to be entertaining, making them some of my favorite conversations when I was in town.

"Joane! How is the prettiest lady in all of Cascade Harbor?" I asked, giving her my biggest grin as I pushed my cart over to her so we could chat more easily.

Joane blushed as she reached up to smooth back some gray hairs that had escaped from her ponytail before returning her hand to her cart.

"Oh, you flirt! Don't think I don't know just how you use that smile, sir. You could weaponize that thing." She swatted my arm, but there was no sting in the motion. It was more an affectionate pat.

"This smile," I smiled wider and stroked my chin, the soft yet slightly coarse feel of my beard reminding me I'd skipped my bi-weekly barber visit last week and needed to stop in tomorrow morning. It was probably time to trim my hair as well, touch-up the ends so my grandma couldn't claim it was getting unruly and unkempt. "How do I use this smile? If you ask my mother or grandmother, it's too deeply buried behind stubble to be visible."

While I kept my beard well-groomed, my mom was convinced any facial hair was too much. She regularly lectured both me and my brother Grey on our need to shave.

"The long list of leggy blondes, brunettes, and redheads I've seen you chatting up at the beach tells me exactly how you use that smile. And if Spencer is to be believed," she raised an eyebrow at this, "those interactions don't stay exclusive to the beach."

"Now Joane, a gentleman doesn't kiss and tell," I said. I was going to have to have a chat with my best friend about not sharing all details from my personal life with his mother.

"Who said you were a gentleman?"

I placed a hand on my chest in mock outrage. "Are you saying I'm *not* a gentleman?"

"We both know the answer to that question," Joane said, pushing her cart a couple of steps away before turning to add, "but that doesn't change the fact that you're my favorite customer. Make sure to stop by the bakery this afternoon. I'm trying a new white chocolate cranberry sourdough recipe, and I need your feedback."

"Joane, you're killing my physique," I called to her retreating back with a chuckle. I was going to have to make a second trip to the gym today if I added a visit to Sugar and Sea Bakery to my plans.

Joane just waved at me over her shoulder, knowing full well I would be stopping by. No one said no to Joane's baking, at least no one with functioning taste buds.

As I walked away, I tried to dismiss Joane's comments about my not being a gentleman but her words continued to play on a loop in my mind. Normally comments about my flirting ways didn't bother me, but something had shifted lately, and I wasn't sure what to do about it. When I'd first moved to Cascade Harbor, I'd been young and naïve, opening myself to heartbreak each time a tourist caught my eye. That summer, I'd let one tourist too close. I could still hear her laughter in my ears when I'd asked if we could stay in touch when she left and she'd told me about a boyfriend who was waiting back home, ready to propose the second she landed.

Now I kept exchanges with women casual, be they locals or tourists. And it worked for me, chasing away the loneliness that lurked around the corners of my life. Or at least, it had until the last few months, though I'm not sure what triggered the change.

Shaking my head, I pushed aside thoughts of relationships and loneliness from my mind, refusing to look too closely at my emotions, knowing they never led anywhere good.

I quickly finished my shopping, reaching the checkout line right behind three women in their early twenties who were laughing and gesturing animatedly as they talked about their plans for the day. Their wardrobes were a combination of cutoff shorts and long-sleeved tops that hinted they'd come for the beach but knew Oregon beaches and California beaches were not the same thing. One of them looked my way, her flashing smile contrasting with her dark skin and drawing attention to her dancing green eyes. Her expression filled with interest as we made eye contact.

Joane was right about one thing, my skills weren't limited to the beach. And this woman looked like the perfect distraction from thoughts of self-reflection and memories of women who smelled like vanilla and left my heart shattered in a million pieces.

"Hello, I couldn't help overhearing, it sounds like you ladies could use a lunch recommendation." I gave them my biggest smile, grateful my hair was currently pulled back into a bun and that I was wearing one of my many flannel shirts that hugged my arms and chest. Women loved their lumberjack fantasies, and I was more than happy to provide it for them with my appearance. As a bonus, my career meant I also had the sensitive, artist angle covered.

Women came to Cascade Harbor looking for an escape and distraction, two things I was more than happy to provide.

The woman who had made eye contact turned her full attention to me, cocking a hip and brushing her long black hair over her shoulder. "And you're confident you have one that we'll all enjoy?"

"Sugar and Sea Bakery has an amazing lunch offering. I've yet to meet someone who doesn't enjoy it," I said. The least I could do was use my smile to send some business Joane's way. If I played my cards right, we both could benefit from this exchange in the checkout lane. "Their sourdough sandwich bread is legendary."

Just thinking of the thick slices of soft, tangy bread Joane used as the base for her sandwiches had my mouth watering.

"What if we need something with gluten-free and vegan options?" This came from one of the green-eyed woman's friends, an Asian woman wearing cutoff overalls with a cardigan, whose voice carried a slight accent.

"Still Sugar and Sea Bakery. I haven't tried their allergy-friendly menu, but Joane's an expert in the kitchen."

"I don't know..." The woman who'd initially captured my attention trailed off, biting her lip and drawing my gaze to a mouth I wouldn't mind getting to explore up close and personal with my own lips. "We were planning to drive into Portland to try this restaurant with amazing potatoes that a friend recommended."

"You're going to drive two hours for potatoes when the world's best sourdough is within walking distance?" My voice held a note of incredulity, hopefully just enough to pique their interest without putting the trio on the defensive. "If you don't find something that instantly makes you fall in love with Joane's food, lunch is on me." If I knew one thing, women loved confidence. And if I could disguise a date invitation as a confidence flex, all the better.

"Is that so?" I could tell from her tone that I'd captured her attention. Now to reel her and her friends in. That was the other lesson I'd learned living on the coast and flirting with the many tourists who chose to grace Cascade Harbor with their presence every summer: If I wanted to woo a woman, I had to win her friends over too.

"Absolutely. I was just headed over there myself. I'd be happy to show you the way if you don't mind a local temporarily crashing your girls' trip." I looked to her friends, knowing their buy-in would be essential if I was going to get beyond making a lunch recommendation. "The bakery is right next to our local bookstore, which is definitely worth a visit."

This snagged their attention, their eyes lighting at the mention of a bookstore. Books and bread, the perfect combination to capture a woman's interest.

"I'm down for a free lunch. You know how picky I am about food." The third friend, this one a blonde with a nose-ring and pixie cut, chimed in. "And I've been wanting to pick up a copy of that one romantasy book after Lynette raved about it at book club. The title had something to do with pomegranates."

The other women nodded their agreement, chiming in with their desire to visit the bookstore, and one corner of my mouth tipped up in victory. I was one step closer to getting some one-on-one time with the green-eyed beauty.

"I'm Mason and it looks like I'm the luckiest guy in all of Cascade Harbor." I offered a hand to the green-eyed member of the group and held on a moment longer than necessary when she accepted my hand-shake.

"I'm Veronica," she said, her voice containing a husky quality as her hand lingered in mine.

My lopsided grin shifted into a full wattage smile, even as I missed her friends introducing themselves.

"Veronica, has anyone ever told you that you would make an excellent model? I could sketch you every day for a year and I'm still not sure I'd capture the fire in your eyes or the exact shape of your bone structure."

The blonde rolled her eyes over Veronica's shoulder, but I ignored her, channeling all of my charm into my exchange with her friend. I was laying it on a bit thick, but my instincts told me that was exactly the right move for Veronica.

"I haven't heard that before," she said, tossing her hair over her shoulder in a flirtatious flip. "Are you an artist or something?"

"Or something," I said, reaching for some well-timed humility as I gave a small shrug and began unloading my groceries onto the conveyer belt as the cashier finished ringing up her group's purchases. "I'm a graphic designer. Though there's still nothing like drawing a live model. It brings a level of challenge I can never get enough of."

"Sounds interesting," Veronica said, grabbing her bags and turning to leave the grocery store.

"I can tell you more about it over lunch," I offered, stepping up to the card reader as the teenage cashier rang up my purchases.

"I'd like that."

I resisted the urge to do a fist pump, instead appreciating the view as Veronica walked away with her friends. I'd have to thank my grandma for sending me on this last-minute grocery trip later. It looked like my Saturday plans had just taken a turn for the better.

CHAPTER 3
Dani

Cascade Harbor, Oregon

IF I'D REALIZED HOW much of a hassle it was going to be to get from Salt Lake City, Utah to Cascade Harbor, Oregon, I would have canceled the trip before I stepped onto the plane. It was like the universe was punishing me for avoiding Poppy or something.

A medical emergency had delayed take-off, I'd tried and failed to write, my seatmate had spent the entire flight humming something out of tune, and, due to the take-off delays, I'd had to use the plane bathroom, which everyone knows should be avoided at all costs. The bathroom trip had also resulted in an unfortunate run-in with a flight attendant who hadn't found my accidentally bumping into her when I came out of the restroom at all funny.

By the time we landed in Portland it was well past dinner, and my stomach was ready to stage a full-fledged revolt. I stopped at a fast-food joint in the airport to snag a quick meal, catching up on texts and emails while I waited for my food. There was a text from Avery making sure I made it safely and another from my mother wishing me a safe trip. There were also a couple of texts in the "Cheaper Than Therapy" cousin chat, most of them dealing with the family reunion Sadie was headed to with her other side of the family and the drama that was guaranteed to follow.

There was also a message from Poppy:

> Dani, did you use the essential oil blend I made for you? It has clary sage, lavender and peppermint. Those will aid in relaxation and help with your overactive bladder. Which is really just your body telling you your chakras are not aligned. You need to find some balance in your life.

I snorted as I read. Was there a bladder chakra? I'd have to ask Poppy when I got home, not sure if I really wanted to know but also genuinely curious.

The final text waiting for me was from Grandma Sue, my mom's mom. She was the type of grandma I hoped to become someday: elegant, sassy, and involved in her grandkid's lives. Though she did have a tendency to overshare about our cousin Kaden. As the spoiled only child of Grandma Sue's only son, Kaden got away with murder. Based on her description, he walked on air and farted rainbows.

Grandma Sue:

> Kaden just finished his degree at Harvard and will be moving back to Utah in a couple weeks. Can't believe we'll have an Ivy League man in the family! LOL [kiss emoji] Cordially, Grandma Sue.

While our family had tried explaining to Grandma Sue that she didn't need to close every text with her name, she didn't listen. Though I wasn't sure anyone had explained to her that "LOL" didn't stand for "lots of love." The cousins had discussed having someone tell her, but no one had followed through. After all, what was family for if not moral support and the occasional, non-life-threatening prank where you didn't intervene when someone was saying something ridiculous?

Deciding I'd respond to Grandma Sue and text the cousins about the latest Kaden update later, I quickly finished my food and headed to grab my luggage and rental car. An issue with my reservation was the icing on the cake for my day, further delaying me so that it was well after 8:00 p.m. before I was finally on the road driving to my vacation rental over two hours away. Unfortunately, this left me navigating the winding roads to the Oregon coast in the dark.

"I'm pretty sure this is how most slasher movies start," I mumbled to myself as I followed the car's GPS instructions up a tree-lined road that looked deserted. The rental listing had mentioned the duplex was secluded, which had sounded like a major selling point when I'd been booking it for my writing retreat. I hadn't thought about the fact that I would be staying in a strange house, in a strange place, surrounded by strangers, alone.

The music I'd been listening to on a spotty local radio station decided to call it quits, plunging me into complete silence as I drove, the GPS indicating the duplex where I was staying was at the very end of the road.

"It's fine. Just don't think about all the true crime podcasts you shouldn't have listened to, but couldn't help yourself."

Unfortunately, saying the words out loud didn't seem to help. Instead, it just conjured images of flannel-bedecked bearded men wielding chainsaws and chasing me through the woods. Having a writer's imagination came with distinct disadvantages. Though maybe Avery would accept the first chapter of a thriller. If I couldn't get the characters of *Of Curses and Pomegranates* to talk to me, maybe it was time to try a different set of characters.

At that moment, a deer darted into the road, making me screech as I slammed on my brakes. The animal froze and watched me for a moment, illuminated in my headlights, before darting into the woods. It reminded me of the opening scene in *Twilight,* and now I was picturing sparkling vampires lurking in the woods, ready to drain me of my blood.

Having an overactive imagination really was the worst.

Keeping my foot firmly on the brake, I leaned my forehead on the steering wheel, taking deep breaths as I tried to calm my pounding heart.

"It was just a deer," I said under my breath. "Just a stupid deer. It wasn't a serial killer or bigfoot or a vampire or anything else. Just breathe."

After a few more deep breaths, I eased my foot off the brake, allowing myself to continue inching up the road. I had to be getting close. All I wanted to do was unload my luggage and go straight to bed. I'd worry about less important things like writing bestsellers and finding food in the morning.

The headlights continued to illuminate my path until, finally, I reached the duplex, a ranch-style building with two garages in the middle. I knew from the match-making messages with the owner that half of the unit was occupied by their grandson and caretaker of the property, Mason, which left the entire other half to me. While I loved Avery and Hercules and my entire host of meddling cousins and family members, having some distance from real life would be a good thing.

It had to be. At this point, I didn't really have a choice. It was either make this writing retreat work or go back to my day job, disappointing millions of fans worldwide and bankrupting my sister, which would result in Sadie's business also taking a hit, since she was contracted as my editor. So really, no pressure.

The scene revealed by my headlights as I approached the driveway made it clear Mason wasn't the only one currently enjoying the duplex. Leaning against the door of a small car parked in the driveway, two people stood locked in a very tight embrace. And while I could only see the back of the man's head, a man I was assuming was named Mason, I was fairly certain their lips were very occupied. Occupied enough that they didn't even look up at the lights and sounds from my car.

Of course, there was always the chance this man wasn't Mason and there was a serial make-out artist on the loose in Cascade Harbor. Was that a thing?

Pressing on my brakes, I evaluated my options. The driveway was clearly large enough for two vehicles, but the make-out car currently sat in the middle of the driveway, leaving me without anywhere to park. Additionally, it made it so I couldn't access the garage for my side of the duplex, which was how I'd been instructed to enter the building using the last four digits of my phone number as the garage code.

Rolling down the window, I winced at the chill in the air. I hadn't thought to put on one of my jackets when I'd left the airport. I'd been too focused on getting to my rental before it got too late.

"Um, excuse me?" I called, not really sure the correct protocol for interrupting a make-out session in front of your vacation rental after ten at night. Sadie would know exactly how to handle this situation in a way that they'd all be best friends after. I was more likely to offend and embarrass everyone involved.

The couple continued their activities, oblivious to my presence and discomfort. It was just my luck that I was going to be living next door to some kind of flannel-wearing Fabio for the foreseeable future. Another point in the universe's favor for making this one of my top five worst travel experiences ever. I'd learned my lesson: avoid Poppy at the airport at my own peril because karma was after me for dodging her instead of getting over myself and just signing some books.

"I'll wear her bracelet everyday I'm in Oregon if it means the bad luck will stop," I said to myself as I tried to remember which pocket of my carry-on I'd slipped it into while on the plane.

I put the car in park along the side of the road and climbed out, not wanting to honk and disturb any unseen neighbors this time of night. Since politely keeping my distance and calling to the enamored couple didn't seem to be doing the trick, it looked like I'd have to resort to more drastic measures.

"Excuse me!" I called again, this time louder as I walked toward the couple, gravel crunching under my shoes. I wrapped my arms around myself in an ineffective attempt to stay warm, goosebumps breaking out over my arms. "I need you to move your car."

The couple finally stopped their activities, seeming to notice they were no longer alone, just the two of them and a host of wildlife like the deer I'd almost run over. Now that I thought about it, that deer was probably running away from this couple and the sight of them thoroughly enjoying themselves in broad... night light.

"I'm sorry, but I think you're in the wrong place," the man said, turning to face me fully, his deep voice coming out gruff and a bit frustrated. He had a beard and dark hair pulled into a bun, though that was about all I could make out of his features in the dark, reminding me of the serial killer I'd been imagining earlier. Why the duplex didn't have something as simple and helpful as porch lights, I had no idea.

I'd pass along the suggestion to the friendly owners, if I ever made it inside my rental.

"I beg to differ. My vacation rental agreement says otherwise," I said, holding up my phone as if it proved anything. Realizing my lockscreen wouldn't help in this moment, I quickly unlocked the screen and opened my email, certain the email confirmation would clear up any confusion, only to find I had no service. Not even a single bar.

I waved the phone around, hoping to pick up a signal.

"There's no reception out here. Besides, I'm the only one who lives here. This," he waved behind himself in a dismissive gesture, "is my place."

Looked like I was right. This bearded jerk was Mason, who, despite his grandmother's comments to the contrary, was doing just fine wooing the women with his overabundance of hair. Glad he'd clarified that. It made me feel better that there wasn't an unidentified, strange man making out in random driveways in Cascade Harbor. But only slightly better.

"That may be true," I said, slipping my phone back into my pants pocket and taking a step closer to the couple. The woman had remained silent through this exchange, hiding a bit behind Mason, the man who his grandmother had assured me would be "happy to help with my every need" while I was staying here. I had a feeling the owners had exaggerated his helpfulness. "But one side of this house is my home for the next several weeks. I'm the new renter."

Mason groaned, massaging his temples. "The new tenant. Give me just a minute."

He turned back to the woman who had been standing behind him. From what I could tell in the dim headlights of my car, she was gorgeous with dark skin and long hair, though how she wasn't freezing in her mini skirt and form fitting, sleeveless blouse, I had no idea. I was wearing leggings and a t-shirt and was trying to fight back the chill in the air. Utah and Oregon had very different definitions of "summer" when it came to temperature.

"I'll see you tomorrow at the bakery for breakfast?' The woman asked hopefully, biting her lip.

Mason smacked his forehead. "Oh man, I forgot I have a meeting with a client tomorrow in Portland. I won't be around for a couple of days."

The woman pouted, resting her hands on his chest. "Are you sure? We leave tomorrow afternoon, and I was really hoping to see you again. It's not every day a woman meets such a talented artist. This sketch is truly amazing!" She held up a paper I hadn't seen her clutching. It was crumpled, probably during the make-out session I'd interrupted. "I wouldn't mind modeling for another."

The way her voice purred at the word "modeling" made it clear she was hoping to do more than just model for the man.

"It's not every day a man gets to work with such a pretty subject for his sketches. You know if I could, I'd spend all weekend sketching you, give you a whole collection of drawings to take back home with you to Missouri." He leaned in closer with this pronouncement, like he was ready for make-out session round two. Or at least, round two that I had witnessed. I had a sinking suspicion they hadn't limited their activities exclusively to modeling earlier in the day. "You are my inspiration, Veronica."

I wanted to gag. I didn't know either of the people in front of me, but based on his confidence as he spoke, I had a feeling he'd just given her a line he'd used many times and she was falling for it hook, line, and sinker. This was why I preferred my men to be fictional. They were less cringe-worthy and much easier to navigate.

I cleared my throat loudly, hoping to cut the exchange short before I had to witness more making out.

Mason didn't bother looking my way, instead he wrapped the woman in a final embrace, planting a kiss on her lips before opening her car door and helping her get settled inside.

"Drive safe, Veronica! I hope the rest of your stay in Oregon is just as magical as tonight." He closed the door and stepped back, waving as she called her goodbyes and drove away.

I snorted and he looked up, his mouth pinching in a scowl.

"Do you have something to say?" His voice was a growl that I'm pretty sure my cousin Lucy would call "sexy." I just found it off-putting after my long day of travel.

"Nope. Just surprised you could keep a straight face when delivering that line," I said, as I walked to the garage door and entered the door code, the door opened to reveal a dark, empty space where I could now park. I could vaguely make out a door into the duplex on the side of the garage.

My headlights continued to be the only source of light, telling me the garage light was either out or not automatic. Another piece of feedback to pass along to the owners in the morning. As soon as I got all my belongings inside, I was going straight to bed. It had been a long day, and I was exhausted. All my feedback as a renter could wait.

"Who said it was a line?" Mason asked from where he still stood in the middle of the driveaway, arms crossed over his chest.

Dang, the man had muscles. It really wasn't fair that the men with some of the best assets ended up being tools and players.

"Just a gut feeling," I said with a dismissive wave, stopping a few feet away from him on my side of the driveway.

"Sounds to me like you're jealous. Maybe you could use a modeling session." His eyes tracked up and down my form. "I'm sure I could squeeze you in sometime during your stay."

Gag me with a spoon.

"I'm not here for any squeezing," I said, flinching as the inane words registered. I really was better at arguments in writing.

"Shame, I'm very good at squeezing and... other things." Somehow his voice had grown even deeper and gravellier.

Where did men like him get the audacity?

"I'm good thanks." I turned on my heel, prepared to climb into my car and forget about this mildly unpleasant exchange when his mumbled response stopped me in my tracks, my anger making me so heated I was no longer wishing for a sweatshirt.

"Maybe if you had a good squeeze, you wouldn't be so uptight."

I whirled around and stomped over to him, jabbing a finger into his firm, overly confident chest. The gesture didn't seem to faze him. If anything, he found it humorous as his mouth ticked up into a lopsided smirk.

"I'll have you know I've had a terrible travel day on top of work stress and having to deal with your over-inflated ego. So, forgive me if I'm not all rainbows and butterflies at the moment."

"You're forgiven."

I wanted to squeeze the smirk right off his face, but that was probably the exhaustion talking.

I closed my eyes and took a handful of deep breaths, counting each inhale and exhale until the sharpest points of my anger had dulled.

"Just kindly ask your next squeeze-buddy or model or whatever you want to call her to please park on *your* side of the driveway," I said through clenched teeth, forcing a smile in an effort to appear civil. "I really don't want to have to park my car on the side of the road again when I'm paying for a garage."

This seemed to bring him up short and he straightened, dropping his hands to his sides.

"Are you an early riser? Because if not, you might want to keep your car—"

"Do you seriously have another 'model,'" I did air quotes for emphasis, "on their way planning to spend the night?"

"No. The la—"

"Did you tell her she's also 'your inspiration'?" The nerve of this man.

"I'm just trying to be a good neighbor." He called as I walked to my car. I just wanted to put this night and this obnoxious man behind me.

"Because good neighbors historically block your parking space and host make-out sessions in your front yard moments before hitting on you." I muttered to myself as I pulled into the garage and climbed out of the car. My temporary neighbor watched me for a moment before taking a hesitant step my direction.

"Can I help?" He offered, his tone begrudging as he approached the garage entrance. Apparently the man did have at least some semblance of manners, even if they were too little too late.

I popped the trunk and pulled my wheeled suitcase from the vehicle, slinging the backpack I'd brought as a carry-on over my shoulder. I held up a hand, stopping his advance.

"I've got it. I wouldn't want you to strain yourself after so much... physical activity." I knew my remark was harsh, but after the day of setbacks I'd experienced, I just wanted to be left alone to my rental and the wifi password so I could update my cousins in the group thread about my adventures.

He gave a small huff.

"I have plenty of stamina for any and all *physical activity*."

"You say that like it should impress me." I called over my shoulder as I walked to the door into the house. "News flash, it doesn't. Though remember that line the next time you see Veronica or another one of your *models*."

With that, I hit the button on the garage door opener attached to the wall of the garage, allowing the door to close on my obnoxious neighbor and his womanizing ways.

As the door closed, it sounded like he was trying to tell me something, but I was so tired I didn't care what he could possibly be saying. I needed sleep.

CHAPTER 4
Dani

I FUMBLED IN THE dark, attempting to find a light switch. When my fingers finally made contact with the switch and the light flickered on, I was charmed by the space in front of me, an assessment that only grew as I explored the different rooms, the quaint space quickly causing my frustration with my neighbor to dissipate. The space was small, with only two bedrooms and one and a half bathrooms, but it was perfect for my needs. Everything except for the kitchen appliances looked like it had come from the fifties and sixties. While dated in appearance, it looked cozy and welcoming. In many ways it reminded me of *Pillow Talk*.

I could just picture Doris Day's character, Jan Morrow, lounging on the sofa or doing her makeup in front of the vanity in my bedroom.

A quick search of the space revealed the welcome binder sitting on the coffee table in the living room. I located the wifi information, quickly logging in so I could message the cousin chat an update on my adventure so far, almost certain no one would be awake this late in Utah. Or in Chloe's case, North Carolina.

Dani:

Made it to my rental! I need you to know I got "ma'amed" twice by the world's orneriest flight attendant. Do I look that old?

> Also, my neighbor/landlord is a bearded wom-
> anizer and I'm pretty sure we just became ene-
> mies thanks to his flavor of the night blocking
> the driveway.

And his overconfident propositioning, but they didn't need to know that part.

I tucked my phone into my pocket but was surprised when it vibrated almost immediately with a reply.

Avery:

> 1. If you're old, what does that make me? 2. Are
> you sure you vetted this place before booking it?
> Do I need to find you a different place to stay?

Why was I not surprised Avery was still awake? Sometimes I wondered if she'd somehow figured out how to survive on books and coffee alone.

Lucy:

> Hi, travel agent here... why didn't *I* book your
> place??

> But also... is he cute?

Dani:

> Lucy, I booked it while you were dealing with the
> whole Finn situation. (Which clearly worked out
> for the better! [Winky face emoji]) Trust me, I've
> learned my lesson and will not be booking my
> own accommodations in the future.

> Also, it was too dark to see him clearly, but I'm
> pretty sure he looked like Fabio and a lumber-
> jack had a baby.

Poppy:

> Oh, please don't tell me he's a Capricorn or a Scorpio!

Lucy:

> So... he IS cute *eyebrows wiggling*

I snorted. Leave it to Lucy to find the romance in the situation. As a romantasy writer, I tended to see relationship potential in a variety of situations, but Lucy took that skill to a whole new level.

Lucy:

> But also, say the word and we'll get you a new place. Between me and Avery, we can get it done in a heartbeat, I'm sure.

Dani:

> Thanks for being willing to come to my rescue! I'm too tired to even consider alternative accommodations, but I'll let you know if I change my mind in the morning.

> By the way, it's late here in Oregon. Do I even want to know what y'all are doing up at this hour in Utah? *raised eyebrow*

I leaned against the wall, my exhaustion hitting me hard but not feeling quite ready to end the exchange yet. It was nice to have the cousins here with me in a sense. It made the duplex feel a bit more homey.

Poppy:

> I've got a test tomorrow. Why do I need to know about supply chain logistics, bottleneck analysis, and lean systems???

Lucy:

Anne of Green Gables marathon.

This travel back and forth from Canada has my internal clock screwed up.

Keep us updated! And good luck on your test, Poppy!

Poppy:

Thanks! I'm diffusing grapefruit and orange to keep my energy up!

Dani:

Good luck, Poppy!

Also, I need you guys to have more exciting night lives! I live vicariously through my more extroverted family members.

Avery, I sure hope your reason involves a tall, dark, and handsome man and not some ridiculous deadline set by He-Who-Shall-Remain-Unnamed.

Lucy:

I promise to improve my nightlife when my boyfriend can walk unaided again. [saluting emoji]

Avery:

> Eric doesn't give me deadlines...

> And no, of course there's no man involved. Unless you count Mr. Darcy. I was reading and didn't realize how late it was...

Lucy:

> Avery! Pride and Prejudice marathon—you and me and a big bowl of popcorn. You in?! We can give Dani a play-by-play... does that count as exciting nightlife??

Knowing the chat would continue in this vein for a while, I acknowledged my need for sleep and dragged my bags into the bedroom, pulling out the essentials. I plugged my phone into the outlet next to the dresser, changed into a sweatshirt and fresh leggings, and brushed my teeth before collapsing into bed. I had a million things to do if this trip was going to turn into the productive oasis I needed. But all of that could wait until morning. For now, I just needed sleep.

The next morning I woke to the sound of a lawn mower. I did my best to ignore it, but the persistent sound combined with my growling stomach forced me from the bed. Peeking through the blinds, I noticed a lanky man riding a lawn mower around the small yard. Based on the pictures I'd seen, I wouldn't have thought the yard was big enough for a riding lawn mower but decided not to question it. Shuffling into the kitchen, I opened the cupboards praying I would find some food to tide me over until I could get dressed and head into town. All that greeted me were a couple of expired condiments in the fridge and a tin of instant coffee.

"Looks like I'll be making a grocery store run sooner rather than later," I muttered to myself.

I got ready quickly, showering, running a brush through my hair, and applying some mascara. Scrounging through the odd mix of clothing I'd packed, I finally settled on a pair of shorts and a tank top, snagging a sweatshirt to throw over the top just in case.

I was pondering what I wanted to purchase for breakfast when I opened the garage door only to find the flaw with my plan: a giant white truck with the words "Scooter's Lawn Service" on the side parked in the middle of the driveaway and blocking both garages.

I stood dumbfounded, my stomach growling in protest as I processed what I was seeing. Apparently, Veronica wasn't the only one in this town with the inability to choose a side when parking. A bright green piece of paper on the garage floor caught my attention.

Picking it up, I found a note written in a blocky, masculine hand that had been slipped under the garage door at some point during the night.

> *Dear neighbor,*
> *I tried to warn you last night, but Scooter comes every Sunday at eight in the morning to mow. He is incapable of parking anywhere other than the center of the driveway. If you'd listened to me, this note would be unnecessary. Hopefully you don't have any squeezing or modeling to do this morning. Don't feed Scooter or he'll never leave.*
> *- Mason*

I snorted, not loving the condescending vibe of the note. Mason definitely could have tried harder to warn me last night, maybe even encouraged me to park on the street. Then his words from the night before came back to me, and I smacked my forehead. He *had* tried to get me to park on the street, but I'd been too busy assuming it was to accommodate his next conquest. In my defense, it was an assumption he hadn't done much to correct. He still could have tried harder, maybe even knocked on my door this morning, but it was too late to do anything about it now. I was trapped.

On the plus side, there was no danger of me accidentally feeding Scooter. I couldn't even feed myself at the moment. I glanced at my watch. It looked like Scooter had been mowing for about an hour. He had to be close to finishing. The yard was tiny. I was genuinely surprised he'd been going for as long as he had. Best guess he'd be done soon, and I'd be on my way to the grocery store followed by a trip to the beach. I'd read somewhere that working in and around water could cure creative blocks, and I was more than happy to test that theory.

Maybe reading through my outline while listening to the sound of the waves would be the magic cure I'd been searching for.

Pleased with my plan, I closed the garage and headed back into the house. Figuring I might as well use the time to settle into the duplex, I quickly unpacked my luggage, dismayed to realize I'd packed way too many t-shirts and skimped on the underwear for some reason. Unless I was going to spend all day every day on the beach in a swimsuit, I was going to need to remedy that ASAP. While I worked, the mower gave a small stutter, giving me hope Scooter was almost done, but it soon revved back to full volume, creating a monotonous soundtrack while I worked.

Eventually, the sound of the lawn mower faded, but I hadn't heard Scooter's truck drive away. Opening the front window blinds, I looked out to find the truck still in the driveway, no Scooter in sight.

Deciding it wouldn't hurt to make a shopping list, I found a pen and some paper in the desk of the bedroom I wasn't sleeping in and got to work on my list. After adding the essentials, primarily more underwear and snack foods to keep me fueled while I worked, I was ready to go.

Except Scooter's truck was still there. Maybe I could ask him nicely to move his truck. The lawn mower was loaded into the back, so he must be working on another project somewhere else in the yard.

I slipped on a pair of sandals and stepped out onto the front porch, breathing in the crisp, pine-scented air. Glancing around, I couldn't see Scooter anywhere. After circling the entire duplex, Scooter remained elusive, though I did find a cut cable next to my side of the duplex. I hoped it wasn't anything important, though I had no way of knowing. I'd also managed to startle several birds and squirrels, but hadn't spotted the lanky man wearing a baseball hat and t-shirt.

My frustration grew as I realized two things: One, Scooter was nowhere to be found and there was no way to know how soon he'd be moving his truck. And two, Mason had known Scooter was coming and hadn't sufficiently warned me how long it would take him to complete the yard work. The next time I saw the not-so-helpful caretaker, I had a few thoughts to share, some of which might be accompanied by expletives if I didn't get food *soon*.

I pulled out my phone to tell the cousins my plight, only to find I once again didn't have service. Figuring I must have ventured too far from my side of the duplex for my phone to reach the wifi, I went back inside. But the phone remained disconnected.

"That's odd," I muttered to myself. I pulled out the information binder to see if it said anything about the wifi being spotty. All it said was to unplug the router if it was having difficulties.

When that still didn't fix the problem, the cut cable outside came to mind and dread pooled in my stomach. Was it possible Scooter had cut the internet cable while he worked? Surely, if the man did yard work here weekly, he'd know to avoid any cables, right?

I shook my head to dispel the possibility. I wouldn't jump to conclusions just yet. Hopefully, there was another, easier explanation.

When I got to town, I'd send the owners a message about the issue. Hopefully it was a quick fix. While I could write without internet, I'd definitely need it to do research once the story really got flowing.

Resigned to my fate, I pulled my laptop from my bag and dragged a kitchen chair over to the window that overlooked the driveway. It looked like I was being forced to work sans internet while I waited for Scooter to leave. But I'd be ready to follow right behind him the second he climbed into his truck and drove away.

And if I added sticky notes to my shopping list so I could write my own very helpful notes to my neighbor that wouldn't be found until it was too late for them to actually be any help at all, no one could really blame me. Right?

CHAPTER 5
Mason

THE BELL ABOVE THE door into Ed's jangled as I stepped inside, greeted by the familiar sight of a trio of retired men lounging around, reading newspapers and shooting the breeze. If anyone accused the women of Cascade Harbor of being town gossips, they clearly had never stepped foot inside the town barbershop on a Sunday. The old men occupying the seats lining the storefront windows wearing matching button up shirts knew more about what was going on in this town than anyone else, and they were more than happy to share if you asked the right questions. I'd used their information to my advantage on more than one occasion, especially when it came to wooing the many single female tourists who passed through town. Through the various shop owners around town, they had an impressive network of informants that was borderline scary if I thought about it too hard. Though I still had yet to figure how exactly they collected all of their information.

The only thing these men didn't know: who originally started Ed's. Town legend ranged from a mountain man who got tired of the fur trade to a fugitive on the run who changed his name and appearance, using the barbershop to hide from his crimes.

Davie, the shop's current proprietor, never so much as hinted at the true story. Instead, if you ever posited a theory, he just grunted and responded simply by saying, "Could be," before returning to his work.

Only one of the barbershop chairs was occupied by a client as Davie finished a beard trim for a hipster I'd never seen before. That was one

thing to be said for Ed's. While the shop's faded brick facade wasn't
much to look at from the outside, Davie's skill with a razor was
legendary, attracting clientele from as far away as Portland. Though
Davie had a policy that Cascade Harbor residents took priority,
making any out of towners wait while Davie serviced the locals first.

Davie's nephew and apprentice, Charlie, sat in the other barbershop chair, staring up at the ceiling as he rocked back and forth.
While Davie was a behemoth of a man with tattoo sleeves and
bulging muscles that hinted at his life in the military before purchasing the shop, Charlie was a skinny kid who, despite being old
enough to have completed all of the necessary coursework to become
a barber, perpetually looked like he was skipping class thanks to a
certain dreamy quality in his expression.

"Well, look what the cat dragged in!" Art, a man who was at least
ninety years old, called from behind his newspaper. A newspaper
that, if I was a betting man, he couldn't read thanks to cataracts
and old age, but it didn't change the fact that he clutched one in
his age-spotted hands every Sunday morning I stopped in for my
bi-weekly trim.

"I'm surprised we're seeing you this early," Marty said from Art's
left. While Art was slim and stooped, Marty was rotund with a belly
laugh that carried through a crowd. He claimed to be twenty years
younger than Art, but I didn't buy it. He looked to be at least in
his eighties. "Heard you had some company last night." Marty's
eyebrows danced as he waited for my response.

"Double company, if Benny's to be believed. He said he saw a car
headed up your road after ten and a different car coming back down
right after." This came from Clyde, a bald man who'd only recently
retired as principal of the local high school. From what I could tell,
Clyde was spending his entire retirement situated at Ed's and using
his divorced insomniac son as an information source.

"Benny should mind his own business," I said, leaning against the wall next to Clyde. "Doesn't he have anything better to do besides watch outside your windows late at night?"

Clyde shrugged. "Wasn't too late for you to have *two* lady friends come calling."

I snorted, thinking of my second "lady friend."

"That second visitor was my grandparents' long-term summer renter. She didn't get to town until after dark." I shrugged, pretending nonchalance even as frustration at what my new temporary neighbor had interrupted filtered into my mind.

While Veronica couldn't sit still long enough to really model for a drawing, she was a *very* skilled kisser. I'd almost felt bad lying to her about having to go into Portland for a few days. I wouldn't have minded having her back for a second "modeling" session. But if I'd learned anything about flirtations with the visiting tourists that flooded Cascade Harbor every year, it was that everything was easier if interactions were kept to one, two days max.

Keep things casual and fun and no one got hurt.

Which was why it was probably for the best that my new neighbor had so thoroughly rejected my invitation the night before. I'd completely misread her, something I was blaming on the darkness and my make-out addled brain. Thankfully, summer brought plenty of tourists and opportunities for other modeling invitations with women who'd be more than happy to spend commitment-free time with me. Women who I might encourage to park in the middle of the driveaway, keep my neighbor on her toes.

"Benny said she was easy on the eyes. That true?" Clyde asked.

Both Art and Marty trained their full attention on me, not even pretending to read their newspapers anymore.

I shrugged, pretending like I hadn't noticed her curves in the dim light of her headlights. "Don't know. It was too dark to really see her last night. I haven't seen her yet today. I left early this morning so I didn't get trapped by Scooter's truck."

I'd tried to warn my new neighbor about our landscaper and his inability to park anywhere other than right in the middle of our driveway, but she'd closed the garage door so fast you would have thought a bear was trying to break in. After moving into the duplex, I'd quickly learned to vacate the premises before eight every Sunday morning if I wanted to leave home before noon. How it took Scooter four hours to mow the duplex's postage stamp yard, I'd never know, but I wasn't going to question it too closely. Scooter charged a set rate, no matter how long it took him to finish, and his mowing meant I didn't have to do it.

At this point, Charlie had stopped rocking back and forth in his barbershop chair, training his eyes on me in a way I didn't like. He had been trying to convince me to let him do my bi-weekly trim for months, despite the unspoken rule between barbers that you should leave each other's clients alone. Davie had always been available to come to my rescue. Not so much right now as Davie was engrossed in discussing some kind of beard cream with the man in his chair. The fact that Charlie's eyes were twinkling with mischief behind his glasses told me he'd just come to the same realization, and I no longer had the ability to hide behind Davie.

"You ready for your trim, Mason?" Charlie asked, his voice filled with far too much enthusiasm.

"Yep. Just as soon as Davie's available." I hedged. I'd seen Charlie's first attempts at cutting hair, I wasn't letting him anywhere near my long locks.

"Come on, Mason! You said once I had more practice, you'd let me give it a go."

I winced, knowing I promised as much back when I was convinced Charlie's desire to take over the barbershop one day was simply a passing fancy. I'd made a bet with Marty that Charlie's efforts would last less than a month. Not only had that bet cost me twenty bucks, but it looked like it was about to cost me today's appointment with Davie as well.

"I did say that..." I trailed off, trying to buy myself time. If I stalled long enough, maybe Davie would finish with the hipster in time to help me.

Unaware of my turmoil, Davie continued chatting with his current client, clearly in no rush. I hesitated a moment longer. Charlie had been working with Davie for six months now. I'd even seen some of his clients walking around town with both ears and a decent haircut. What was the worst that could happen?

Taking a deep breath, I nodded, climbing into Charlie's barbershop chair. The Gossip Gang laughed at my predicament, Art and Clyde taking bets on how badly Charlie would mess up. I clenched my fists, not about to back down with an audience.

I settled into the chair, allowing Charlie to wash my hair before beginning the cut, the chair turned away from the mirror as he worked. I slowly began to relax at the familiar motions. While his technique wasn't identical to Davie's, it was close enough that I could see myself using Charlie again if Davie was having a busy day.

Davie finished up with the hipster, ringing the man up at the cash register before settling in to chat with the group of men lining the window. The conversation shifted from my haircut to speculation about my new neighbor and how long she'd be in town.

"Oops," Charlie said, just as I felt the last bit of tension ease from my shoulders.

I stiffened, reminding myself not to make any sudden movements with Charlie holding a pair of scissors near my head. I closed my eyes, not ready to see the damage.

"Charlie, what do you mean by 'oops'? Oops is not a word you use when trimming a man's hair," I said through clenched teeth.

The Gossip Gang guffawed, and it took everything in me not to look their way to see their reactions.

"I just... took a bit more off than intended in one spot," Charlie said, hesitantly.

The sound of footsteps followed this declaration, indicating Davie had come over to examine Charlie's handiwork.

"Boy, in what world is that 'a bit'?" Davie's voice rang through the quiet shop, and I pinched my eyes closed tighter. All hope was lost.

"My hand just kind of slipped and—"

"If your hand slips, you cut off an inch at most. That is not an inch."

The laughter from the Gossip Gang rang through the shop, punctuated by Marty's distinct, deep belly laughs.

"How bad is it?" I asked, my eyes still closed. I really should just open them, take a peek at the damage. It couldn't be that bad, right?

"Depends," Davie said, his voice deep and calm, though I could hear a level of hesitation. Davie never hesitated.

"On?"

"How much you like your man bun."

Deciding I couldn't put it off any longer, I opened my eyes, turning in the chair to see the damage. Charlie stood to one side, looking sheepish, his scissors dangling awkwardly from one hand. Davie stood next to Charlie, arms crossed over his chest as he waited for my reaction.

A large chunk of hair had been cut from my head, decorating the floor like the world's saddest confetti. The hair next to my right ear, which had reached past my shoulders, was now only an inch or so long.

"How—" I broke off, realizing the question wouldn't do any good as Charlie ducked away from me. I pinched the bridge of my nose, counting to ten as I breathed in and out slowly.

"Can you save it?" I finally asked, already knowing the answer but needing to ask anyway. I remembered the awkward stage of growing my hair out and there was no amount of product or styling that made this particular length look flattering on me.

"Only if you don't mind having a matching mullet with Mrs. Prescott for a few months," Davie said, fingering the cut strands.

He was right, of course, but I still hesitated just a moment before nodding.

"Then I guess you better cut it off, Davie. Just be gentle," I said. I knew it was just hair, but it had become a part of my identity. My long hair was integral to my persona as a beach-loving artist. It had also helped transform me from the punk, ignorant kid who attempted to have a relationship with a visiting tourist into the strong, grown man who knew better.

"Uncle Davie, I can fix it! No need for you—"

I held up a hand, cutting Charlie off. "I think you've done enough, Charlie."

Charlie deflated, and I only felt a little bad for crushing his dreams.

"What do you want to do about your beard? The usual?" Davie asked as he got to work fixing my hair.

I bit my lip for just a moment, hesitating. I'd grown the beard to go with the long hair. If I was being forced into a fresh start, I might as well go all in. My beard grew fast enough that, if I hated being clean-shaven, I could always regrow it.

"Might as well shave that too. Looks like I'm getting a fresh, summer look."

Davie got to work, gently lecturing Charlie as he did about respecting client's preferences and needing to rein in his enthusiasm.

"Charlie, I know you just want to do a good job, but if you don't stop acting like an overeager puppy, you're not going to make it far in the business. You're lucky Mason's handling this so well."

A snort from Art sent the Gossip Gang into another fit of hysterics. They really were worse than a group of middle-aged women. I could only imagine how they'd be recounting this episode to everyone who stopped by the shop today. Fingers crossed a group of kids decided to spray paint a building or Mrs. Olsen hit another fire hydrant with her car, anything to shift the gossip away from me and onto another subject.

CHAPTER 6
Dani

I WAS GOING TO murder Mason.

Scooter had stayed at the duplex until well after noon, doing who knows what to the property. I had never been so excited to watch someone leave as I was when Scooter climbed into his truck. I didn't even bother backing up the document I'd been attempting to write in, recognizing every single word on the page was the result of hunger and anger, which was not a great combination when trying to write sizzling chemistry and other worldly magic.

Not wanting to risk getting trapped at the duplex by yet another visitor who didn't know how to park, I'd quickly snagged my car keys and left, cursing Mason the entire way as my stomach attempted to consume my internal organs.

I pulled onto Main Street, certain it would take me to the grocery store, when a cute shopping complex with a bakery, thrift shop, bookstore, and barbershop caught my attention. My stomach growled at the thought of fresh-baked bread, and I pulled into the parking lot on a whim, nearly cutting off the car behind me in my haste. I'd get lunch first and then grocery shop. And maybe I'd visit some of the other stores in the complex.

Food, books, and thrifting, it was like the universe was rewarding me for putting Poppy's bracelet on this morning.

I glanced at the accessory that hung from my wrist, still wincing slightly at the color combination that really wasn't my style and did not match

my blue sweatshirt. I was most definitely ascribing too much power to
the inanimate object, but I wasn't willing to risk another karma attack
like yesterday by taking it off. And maybe it would help me write. I mean,
it hadn't helped when I was back at the duplex, but maybe it needed time
to warm up or something.

Entering the bakery, I was greeted by the incredible smells of fresh
bread and coffee. This was clearly the right decision as I stood in the
bright, happy space with pink walls, surrounded by baked goods, home
decor, and framed beach scenes created by local artists. The bakery name,
Sugar and Sea Bakery, was written on the wall in pink looping neon lights
that added to the welcoming ambiance.

"Hello and welcome to Sugar and Sea Bakery! I'll be right with you."
A cheery female voice called from the back of the shop.

I took the opportunity to consider my options, quickly scanning the
glass case containing pastries and the shelves of bread behind it. Above
the bread shelves was a chalkboard menu boasting lunch items. I salivat-
ed at the offerings, certain my stomach was about to start eating whatever
remained of my internal organs if I didn't eat real food soon.

My phone was vibrating incessantly in my pocket, telling me I'd found
a patch of service. I would respond to messages as soon as I had food. I
was worried any responses I sent now would have an unhinged amount
of snark and frustration that my cousins and sister definitely did not
deserve.

While I could acknowledge that my emotional state was primarily due
to hanger, it would not prevent me from slipping a very long, very sharply
worded note under Mason's door when I got back to the duplex. He
should have tried harder to warn me about Scooter. Not to mention how
my inability to communicate with the outside world all morning as a
single woman staying in a remote location had added to my stress. There
had been some odd noises, supposedly created by Scooter, that I hadn't
been a fan of.

I was tempted to share some of my thoughts with the landlords about their caretaker grandson, but I'd give my food a chance to kick in before messaging them. I'd learned from experience that I did *not* handle setbacks well on an empty stomach.

Lucy's offer to help me find new accommodations played through my mind but I hesitated. I could only imagine how much a last-minute rental located this close to the beach would cost, assuming she could even find anything. I'd give the landlords a chance to fix the wifi before calling Lucy.

A woman in her sixties stepped into view, her dark hair peppered with gray and pulled back into a ponytail. She wore a bright pink apron dusted in flour with the words Sugar and Sea Bakery scrawled across the front. She reached up to nudge her hot pink glasses back up her nose, leaving a streak of flour.

"I'm Joane and welcome to my bakery. How can I help you?" Joane gave me a wide smile. I instantly liked her, something about her reminding me of my Grandma Sue and her ability to make any situation brighter. Even if Grandma Sue would never be caught dead in a flour-dusted apron.

"I'm Dani and you can help me by recommending something for lunch. I'm starving." My stomach gave an angry gurgle at the statement.

Joane chuckled and waved to the menu above her head. "Sounds like it! You came to the right place. Do you prefer soup or a sandwich?"

"Yes," I said, the combination of a rich soup with a hearty sandwich sounding heavenly. "I'll also probably need a dessert and loaf of bread."

"Well, obviously! Can I recommend the tomato basil soup with the sourdough grilled cheese? The cheese comes from a local dairy, and I can personally attest that the sourdough is the best in all of Oregon." She peeked at me over her glasses, waiting for my response.

"Oo, yes please! And can I add..." I scanned the rows of bread and treats, quickly making my decision, "a peanut butter bar and a loaf of cinnamon swirl bread? Oh, and an iced coffee."

My taste buds still flinched when I thought back to the instant coffee I'd drunk earlier. I needed good caffeine stat if I was going to stand any chance of writing today.

"You got it." Joane rang up my purchases, handing me my receipt and waving me over to a nearby table.

I settled at the worn round table, enjoying the faint sounds of a song I'd listened to regularly in high school. If I'd brought my laptop with me, this would be the perfect place to write, especially if Joane's baking tasted half as good as it smelled.

The promise of food seemed to ease my hanger, so I took the opportunity to catch up on my messages, ignoring a handful of pointed texts from Avery asking about my word count and wanting to see a first chapter. I hoped she'd take my silence as a sign that I was in the groove and making progress.

Going on a trip to Oregon made it exponentially easier to avoid her.

I also typed out a quick email to my landlords explaining the internet situation, though I abstained from making any comments on their grandson's terrible behavior. I'd give Mason one more chance before throwing him under the bus. Now that I was getting food, I was feeling less murdery and could acknowledge he'd tried to warn me about Scooter last night. He hadn't tried nearly hard enough, but he had tried.

"Careful, soup's hot," Joane said a few minutes later, setting a bowl of soup and a plate with a grilled cheese sandwich cut into two triangles in front of me. "I pre-sliced your bread and put your dessert in a to-go container, just in case." She raised a brown paper bag with the bakery's logo and settled it on the table as well.

"Thank you! This looks wonderful."

Not quite sure where to start, I reached for one of the sandwich triangles and dipped it in my soup. As I took a bite, flavors exploded on my tongue, and I groaned. I wasn't sure if the sandwich was really that good or if I was just that hungry, but I decided it didn't matter as I swallowed, dipped my sandwich again, and took a second bite. It was a good thing I was the only customer in the bakery, otherwise I'd be scaring away anyone in my immediate vicinity.

"Slow down and chew, hon. The food isn't going anywhere," Joane said with a laugh, watching me as if she was afraid I'd choke.

"Sorry," I mumbled around another bite of sandwich, lifting my hand to cover my mouth while I chewed. "I haven't eaten much today, and this is literally the best thing I've had since landing in Oregon."

"Where are you visiting from?" Joane asked, settling into the seat across from me.

"Utah. I just got here yesterday."

"Well, you picked the best place in Oregon to visit. How long are you staying?"

"Hard to say," I said, slowing down in my rush to eat now that the first few bites had hit my system. I paused to take a drink of coffee, content now that I was getting fed and caffeinated. "I'm working on a project and hoping a change of scenery will get my creative juices flowing."

"Oh, you're an artist?" Joane asked, her eyes lighting with interest.

"Not exactly." I shook my head with a laugh, picturing my terrible attempts at illustrating my own covers back when I'd considered self-publishing. "I'm an author on deadline for my next book."

"Really? Have you written anything I would have heard of?" Joane propped her chin in her hands, leaning across the table as she listened. Her expression was inviting, the lines around her mouth and eyes clearly from laughing and smiling.

"Maybe," I hedged, not sure if I wanted Joane to be familiar with my book. Life would be so much easier if I could fly under the radar while I worked here. "It's a romantasy, you know, romantic fantasy."

"Those are my favorite!" Joane gushed. "My son runs the bookstore next door, and he can't get the latest romantasies in fast enough. I keep asking him when the next Danielle Baldwin book will be in. That woman knows how to write a story! The way Hypatia and Petros clash, but secretly pine for each other," she leaned back into her chair with a dramatic sigh, pressing one hand to her ample chest, "it's simply the most divine torture. Have you read it?"

I gave a small half smile, deciding to trust Joane with my identity and project.

"'Divine torture' is a great way to describe it. I'll have to pass that wording along to my marketing team. Maybe they can use it in the next round of promotions," I said, watching her reaction. If the team couldn't use it, I definitely could when I got around to paying attention to my much-neglected social media accounts. While I was very good at scrolling through various videos and comment sections, I wasn't the best at posting, much to Avery's chagrin. Maybe I'd finally get around to posting while I was here.

Joane blinked at me blankly for a moment before her face lit with realization.

"Wait, you're saying *you're* Danielle Baldwin?"

I nodded.

"*The* Danielle Baldwin? The author of literally the swooniest book in the history of romantasy?" Joane reached across the table, grabbing my arm as if to confirm I was in fact real and currently sitting in her bakery.

"I don't know that I'd go that far, though I'm flattered you think so," I said, rubbing the back of my neck and ducking my head. I wasn't the best at receiving compliments, though I loved hearing how much readers enjoyed my book. If only I could channel all of their enthusiasm into writing book two and pushing back the imposters syndrome that niggled at the corners of my mind when I thought about my book's popularity too much.

"Wait until I tell Spencer! He's never going to believe it. *The* Danielle Baldwin ate lunch in my shop." She leaned back in her chair, grinning.

"Maybe we could keep who I am between just the two of us," I said, flinching as I watched Joane's face fall at the suggestion. "It'll make writing in Cascade Harbor easier if no one knows who I am."

"I guess that makes sense," she said with a nod, though I could still see disappointment in her eyes.

"If it helps, I'm hoping to eat lunch here again tomorrow, if you don't mind. I like the vibe. It's welcoming and bright. Might even be the perfect place to write, assuming you have wifi?" I could only do so much writing without the ability to research as I went. And while I was hoping the internet back at my place would be fixed soon, it would be nice to have a few writing location options.

"Mind? I'd love it! It would feel like I was living in my own fantasy. Danielle Baldwin writing her next book here in my shop. I'm going to have to ask someone to pinch me. This is unreal!"

"You can just call me Dani, and I'd be willing to pay to use the space. I don't want to impede business or anything." I looked around the shop, certain its empty tables were a fluke based on the amazing lunch I'd eaten.

"If it means the sequel to *Of Curses and Pomegranates* will be releasing sooner rather than later, you can move into my shop. I'll even provide you with all the coffee and pastries you can eat." She waved at the display case.

"I hardly think that's necessary," I said, my cheeks heating at her enthusiasm. "Though I'd be happy to give you an advanced reader copy, once they're available, to say thank you. Oh, and sign a copy of *Of Curses and Pomegranates,* if you have one."

While she professed to be a fan, I made no assumptions about her owning a physical copy. Maybe she was a major library patron or an ebook reader. Though I'd be willing to sign her ereader. I'd done that several times on my book tour.

"If I have one? Dani, my dear, I own at least three. I've got the original hardcover, the special edition hardcover, and the paperback with sprayed edges." She ticked off each edition on her fingers. "I just wish I could get my hands on the UK special edition. That cover is gorgeous!"

I nodded, knowing the exact edition she was talking about. "If it makes you feel better, I don't even have a copy of that edition. They were supposed to send me one, but apparently it got lost in the mail. Though I wouldn't put it past my sister to have screened my mail and snagged the copy for herself. She's my publisher and, honestly, she probably deserves that copy more than I do after all the negotiating she did on my behalf."

Avery denied taking my copy, but she'd been dog sitting for me while I was on book tour so often that it was the only reasonable explanation.

"Wait until I tell Phyllis and the other ladies in my book club you'll be writing in my bakery. They're going to be so jealous," Joane said with a sigh of contentment, clearly picturing her friends and forgetting my request she not tell anyone. "I might have to get a regular paperback too, complete my collection and have you sign every one. My personal library is going to be the envy of Cascade Harbor."

Listening to her list off the different editions of my book still felt unreal. How was it possible that this was my life? And how was I possibly going to follow up my debut with a book even half as good to finish the duology with expectations so high? Maybe running away to Oregon wasn't far enough. How hard was it to get to Alaska from here? I'd go keep Sadie company at her family reunion. Or maybe I could find an Alaskan mountain man and hide away from the world, ice fishing and doing my best to avoid hypothermia for the rest of my life. I hated fish, but that was beside the point.

Shaking myself out of my melancholy thoughts, I forced a smile for Joane. "I'd be happy to sign all of your copies when I come back tomorrow. Just please, don't tell anyone else who I am. I'm trying to keep a low profile."

Joane's eyes widened behind her glasses, and she smacked her forehead. "I forgot about that part."

She mimed zipping her lips and throwing away the key.

"Your secret's safe with me," she whispered, reaching over to pat my hand. "Though fair warning, my son owns the bookstore, and he'll probably recognize you on sight. Your book has been his top seller this year. In fact, he'd probably die of excitement if you went over and signed a few copies."

I hesitated, wondering if I was about to surrender my anonymity, but also recognizing the town was only so big. It was probably better I met Spencer now when I could ask him not to disclose my identity before he started a rumor circulating around town. I was from suburbia, but if watching *Gilmore Girls* had taught me anything, it was that small towns loved their gossip, and a visiting author was prime fodder to make the rounds.

"I could probably do that, if Spencer promises not to blow my cover," I said. The last thing I wanted to do was venture into a bookstore and declare who I was, but if it meant Joane would let me write in her space, I'd take the risk.

"I'll call him and tell him the deal. He'll keep your secret, I promise." Joane pushed up from her chair and hurried into a backroom behind the counter.

I settled into my seat, returning my attention to my lunch. I'd eat quickly and then head over to the bookstore. The sooner I could get this book signing over with, the better. Then I could return to my plans for the day: thrifting, grocery shopping, and writing. Maybe I'd even pick up a book or two while in the bookstore, for reading in the evenings after I'd hit my word count goal. After all, successful writers needed to hone their craft and what better way to perfect my writing than to read a book or three? Really, it was essential author research. And if it happened to take place on the beach, all the better.

CHAPTER 7
Mason

I RUBBED MY JAW as I crossed the parking lot of Ed's, heading to Seabreeze Reads. I was not used to the smooth texture of my skin. Davie had done a good job with my haircut and shave, my hair longer on top and shaved close to my head on the sides. Given that Charlie had been the reason for my shorter-than-planned haircut, Davie hadn't charged me. He claimed he owed me for the ribbing I'd experienced at the hands of Art, Marty, and Clyde for trusting Charlie with my hair, and I wasn't about to argue. And while I'd miss my less fussy, long hair, I'd still get my bi-weekly gossip update if I was going to maintain my new short hair. Though I would need to invest in a razor for shaving in the mornings.

If Spencer hadn't told me to stop in to discuss a possible commission, I would have driven straight home to hide from the world as I let some of the sting of the day wear off before I had to face the town beardless and man-bun-less. I now had more sympathy for Samson than ever before.

Charlie, your name is Delilah. I thought with a snort as I stepped into the bookstore, a perky chime greeting me and contrasting sharply with my mood.

"I'll be right with you," Spencer called from somewhere tucked behind bookshelves.

"Take your time," I said, shivering at an unexpected chill inside the shop. I now understood why so many men in Oregon perpetually wore beanies. Not having my hair to keep my neck warm was going to take some getting used to, especially if I visited my mom over the holidays. Just the thought of a Utah winter had me breaking out in goosebumps.

I wandered the store, certain I'd find Spencer tucked into a corner restocking shelves, his glasses sliding down his nose and his blond hair sticking up in random spikes around his head. Honestly, if things were slow enough, he might even be curled up in one of the striped armchairs reading a new release.

The bookstore was cozy with dark wood bookshelves lining the walls and angled in places to create little reading nooks. When Spencer's grandfather had passed away, leaving behind a large inheritance, Spencer had spent several years exploring different career options as a self-proclaimed entrepreneur. When he'd finally come to me with his idea to open a bookstore, I'd laughed, convinced he was joking. But he'd made the shop work, using its location near the coast to attract authors for signings that also enticed tourists to visit.

Spencer's biggest coup to date was hosting a signing for the hottest thriller author in the country, attracting readers from several hours away for the event. I still wasn't sure how he had convinced the author to visit when Powell's Books, the world's largest independent bookstore, was nearby, but his results spoke for themselves.

Spencer had been trying to convince some fantasy romance author to visit, but he was having a hard time persuading a stick-in-the-mud guy at the publishing house that the event would be worth it. But if anyone could make it happen, it was Spencer. He'd recently completed an addition on the back of the store, creating an event space that hosted a variety of events in addition to signings. Though I doubted any signings would outshine the chaos and magic that was Cascade Harbor's monthly bingo night, which Spencer had started hosting almost immediately after finishing the space.

"Welcome to Seabreeze Reads! How can I help you?" Spencer asked in his best customer service voice as he rounded the corner with a stack of books in his arms and a welcoming grin on his face.

"I feel like I should be asking how I can help you, since you set up this meeting," I joked back, surprised when Spencer blinked back in confusion.

"I set this..." He trailed off, recognition finally settling in as his mouth dropped open. He stood there for several seconds gaping at me before words came spewing out. "Dude! What happened to you?"

I flinched at the shock in Spencer's voice and expression, tempted to shush him like we were in a library, even though, as far as I could tell, I was currently his only customer.

"My hair shrunk in the wash," I said, not wanting to discuss my encounter with Charlie and his scissors.

"And your beard just vanished? I can't remember the last time I saw you clean-shaven," he said, shaking his head. "How are you possibly going to attract the ladies now? You look more like a golf-course junky tourist than our resident lumberjack." Spencer nudged me with his elbow as he walked past me to his office at the back of the shop.

I followed him, ready to be done with his teasing, discuss the commission, and then head home. I was more than happy to call it a day. If I was lucky, my new neighbor would be nowhere in sight so I could enjoy some peace and quiet before jumping into Spencer's commission. At least my tablet and graphic design program wouldn't judge me for my lack of hair.

"Laugh it up, Chuckles. I bet I'll still have more luck with the ladies than you," I grumbled, trying to find my confidence and swagger, hoping I hadn't left it on the floor of Ed's along with my beard and dignity.

Spencer abruptly stopped in front of me, blocking my way into the office as I nearly ran into his back.

"Is there a reason you're following me?" he asked, his voice coming out oddly strained. There was no way that stack of books was heavy enough to be causing him issues. If it was, I needed to get him to the gym more often.

"Yes," I said slowly, confused at his question. "You asked me to stop by to talk about a commission."

If it was anything like Spencer's last commission, which he'd framed and proudly hung behind the cash register, this project would bring in some good money and help build my clientele. Last time he'd asked me to create a print that depicted several children from different backgrounds, with different abilities disappearing into the pages of a book for an epic adventure involving a castle, dragon, and pirate ship. It had turned out so well that he sold smaller copies and bookmarks based on the print with his bookstore logo on the back, splitting a part of the sales with me. I'd lost track of the number of commissions I'd received thanks to that particular piece of art because people saw it in the shop and loved the style enough to reach out to me. This new commission wasn't something I could really afford to miss out on. While I was established enough as a graphic designer that I had a steady stream of customers, I wasn't making enough money to move out of the duplex and support myself fully. Not that I was looking to move anytime soon, but I couldn't live off my grandparents' charity forever.

"About that," Spencer said, turning to face me and shifting his posture to take up more space. While Spencer wasn't the most socially adept person in Cascade Harbor, he was acting weird even for him. "I still want to talk about a commission, but today isn't a good day. I've had... something come up."

"Something 'come up?' Spencer, you were the one who insisted we had to meet today. You said it was urgent," I said, thrown off by my friend's behavior.

"I know, but I've thought about it and realized I need to... sleep on the project some more."

Spencer was a terrible liar. His face did this funny scrunching thing. His mom, Joane, said it had always been that way since he was little, making her job as parent infinitely easier. According to her, if she ever suspected him of lying, she just had to wait to see if his expression made him look like a pooping toddler. The description was remarkably accurate as I watched Spencer's face contort now. He was hiding something.

"Sleep on the project? You slept on it last night," I said, stopping to lean against the wall near the checkout counter to watch him. I waved at the last commission I'd done for Spencer where it hung on the wall behind his head. "You know I love doing this kind of work. I don't understand—"

"Hey, Spencer," a warm female voice called from the office behind my friend, "were you able to find those other copies? I really need to finish signing so I can head back to my rental. My sister's going to flip if I don't make some progress with my writing today."

I arched an eyebrow as the pieces fell into place. Spencer was trying to keep me away from the woman in his office. Which of course meant meeting her was exactly what I was going to do. It was what best friends were for.

Looking from me to the office and back, Spencer pivoted quickly on his heel, stepping into the office and depositing the books on the desk.

"Here you go! Let me know if you need anything else." He hovered for a moment, clearly wanting more from the woman.

She briefly glanced up from the stack of books that was already in front of her, muttering a brief thank you as she leaned away from Spencer, tucking a strand of chestnut brown hair behind her ear and returning to her task.

Spencer hesitated for a second longer before remembering I was there. He quickly shuffled out of the small room, closing the door slightly to try to block my view. Unfortunately for him, I could still see the woman in his office, and I was very much interested in learning more about the gorgeous brunette bent over his desk, pen in hand, signing a large stack of books and ignoring Spencer's clear interest in her.

Her hair cascaded over one shoulder, creating a waterfall that I wouldn't mind running my fingers through. I wondered how she'd feel about modeling for a sketch. I needed to test out my new look some time and this moment was starting to feel perfect. Women liked the clean-cut look too, right?

Spencer grabbed my arm, pulling me further away from the office. I shifted, making sure I could still see the woman through the partially open door. Not in a creepy way. Just in an "appreciating the scenery" kind of way.

"That one's off limits," Spencer said, waving aggressively toward the woman in his office.

"First of all, you can't refer to a woman as 'that one.' She is a living, breathing, functioning human, and your mother would be appalled to hear you talk about a lady that way." I crossed my arms over my chest, feeling confident in my assessment of the situation. "Second of all, you're not the boss of me." That last part sounded better in my head. It came out like I was a small child in an argument with the school bully. But my argument still stood.

"Do you even know who that is?" Spencer asked, stepping into my personal space and arching an eyebrow. While Spencer was only a couple of inches shorter than me, he felt particularly small in this moment as he tried to intimidate me away from this woman, his slim frame contrasting with my gym-honed muscles. "Also, weren't you here yesterday with *three* women? For once in your life, leave some for the rest of us."

"Again, she's a woman, not the last scoop of ice cream in the container. And I was here with *one* woman yesterday who happened to be visiting with two of her friends, both of whom you could have tried to woo. None of them are in town anymore, so I don't see the problem in pursuing someone new. I've got to test drive the new look at some point and you have a very promising lady currently sitting in your office who has yet to experience all that this," I gestured at myself, "has to offer." I ran a hand through my short hair, flexing my bicep with the gesture to emphasize my point. I was going to save a fortune in shampoo with my haircut, but it was going to take some serious getting used to. Also, all that saved money would be going back to Davie to maintain said haircut, even with the generous locals discount he gave me.

Spencer watched me for a moment, seeming to consider what I said.

"How do you keep all these women straight when they text you later?" He asked after a moment, probably looking for the secret to my success with the women who visited town.

I shrugged. "First rule of interacting with the tourists, you don't give them your phone number." I wouldn't repeat the real first rule to him: never get attached. I'd mentioned it to him before, and I knew it wasn't what Spencer wanted to hear. He wasn't the kind of man to do casual, which is why we differed dramatically in the dating arena. As soon as you took emotions out of the equation, everything got much simpler for everyone involved. It was a lesson Rebecca taught me quite thoroughly my first summer here, and I wasn't about to forget it any time soon.

Besides, who needed emotions anyway? It wasn't like I was looking to settle down with someone. I was just looking for a good time to combat the loneliness that lurked in the corners of my life if I looked too closely. Luckily for me, most tourists were searching for fun, which was my specialty. And if they weren't, I was more than happy to move on to the next woman who visited.

"But what if it's a relationship you want to last past the summer?" Spencer continued, looking over his shoulder to where the brunette worked.

For a moment, I considered backing off and letting Spencer pursue the mystery woman without competition. And if she'd seemed interested in him, I would have. However, I'd read loud and clear the vibes she was giving him when he'd been in the office, and she was far from interested. Some men could come back from that complete lack of interest. Spencer was not one of those men.

"Spencer, my friend," I said, resting a comforting hand on his shoulder, "that's your first mistake. The tourists aren't here for long-term relationships. They're here for vacation fun and you're just here to amplify that experience."

Spencer sputtered, his face turning bright red. I thought I'd lost the ability to shock him when it came to dating. Good to know I still had a few tricks up my sleeve.

Spencer's guest chose that moment to leave the office, carrying a paperback copy of one of the books she'd been signing. It had a cover I'd seen around. In fact, I was fairly certain Spencer had had an entire table full of this particular book earlier this year.

The cover had the silhouettes of two people turned away from each other, a mix of deep red pomegranates and twisting green vines framing the scene, the title written in a looping cursive script: *Of Curses and Pomegranates*. The artist had done a good job. I'd designed a handful of indie book covers for people who'd found my art on social media and reached out, so I knew designing the perfect cover took a fair amount of work and finesse. But looking at the cover, I saw small adjustments I'd make to make it pop more, maybe add a hint of silver mixed in with the vines and fruit or a slight adjustment in the posture of the characters to up the chemistry and tension between the man and woman.

"Do you mind if I buy this copy in addition to the books I picked out earlier? I owe your mom a signed paperback." She held up the book, looking back and forth between me and Spencer, clearly not wanting to interrupt but also wanting to move on with her day. As her eyes met mine, they lingered an extra heartbeat, a spark of interest in her eyes that I could definitely work with.

I noticed a small stack of books sitting next to the cash register, presumably the books she'd already picked out. I wanted to study the titles, see what I could learn about the woman before making my move. I also wouldn't mind studying the cover designs, see what had spoken to her. The woman was an author and maybe she could help open some cover design opportunities for me, if I could find a way to leave our interaction on friendly terms.

Spencer snorted, his face stretching into a crazy-eyed smile that would make children cry. Maybe I should help him impress this woman, give him some much-needed flirting tips, number one being: *Calm down.*

"Of course! Though she really owns enough copies of your book." He laughed, but it wasn't a laugh I'd ever heard before, coming out high-pitched and overly aggressive, almost like a donkey bray.

I shifted away from him, not wanting to be associated with whatever craziness was currently manifesting itself in my best friend.

The woman registered the movement, looking at me again with a slow, interested smile. Or at least a friendly smile. I may have imagined the interested part, but I was certain I could win her over if I could get her away from Spencer for a moment.

As Spencer rang up her purchases, asking small-talk questions, I took in her appearance. She was dressed casually, but even under her sweatshirt and shorts, I could tell she had curves I wouldn't mind exploring.

"Will that be all?" Spencer asked quirking an eyebrow, his voice coming out oddly deep now.

"Oh, actually I did want to wander and maybe pick up a couple of writing craft books." She turned to take in the store. "Which way..." She trailed off, waiting for Spencer to direct her.

"If you'll follow me." Spencer all but climbed over the checkout counter to lead her to the correct section. Dude had no chill and now I understood why he hadn't had a second date in the years I'd known him.

Just as the pair was about to leave the checkout counter to disappear among the bookshelves, the chime above the door sounded, followed almost immediately by a call from the new customer, the voice shrill and familiar and one that instantly sent chills down my spine.

"Spencer! If the sequel to this book you recommended last week isn't out yet, I'm going to murder you. You know how I feel about cliffhangers."

Spencer and I both flinched as we registered who had just walked in: Joyce Campbell. We looked at each other, knowing what would ensue if Joyce felt like she was being ignored. There was a reason her husband, Clyde, spent most of his time hiding at Ed's now that he was retired. Joyce was never happy, and she was a force to be reckoned with when she was on a war path. I'd heard rumors she'd made the entire high school football team cry with a single look. I personally had seen her make both Clyde and their son Benny cry on multiple occasions, though, to be fair, Benny was only a few months post-divorce and Joane had also made him cry when she handed him a cup of coffee "on the house" the first time he'd visited the bakery after signing his divorce papers.

"I'll be right back," Spencer said to the author, glancing between her and me before disappearing around the corner to deal with Joyce.

"But what about..." The woman trailed off, seeming to register that there was no point protesting. If she thought she was leaving the bookstore any time soon, she was sadly mistaken.

Recognizing an opportunity to introduce myself, I leaned against the checkout counter and pulled her into a conversation.

"Welcome to Cascade Harbor: the prettiest little town on the Oregon coast and the one with the quirkiest residents. Trust me, it's better for everyone in the bookstore if Spencer helps Joyce now," I said, nodding in the direction of the entrance. "Otherwise, we'll all be recipients of a lecture about 'kids these days' and how no one understands the meaning of true customer service." I wished I was joking, but I'd witnessed that lecture one too many times around town and was not in the mood for a repeat.

The woman snorted. "Seriously? What about customer service for the person he just left abandoned at the cash register?"

I shrugged. "Joyce has a very narrow, specific definition of customer service. Essentially, she's *the* customer and you exist to serve her."

The woman shook her head, glancing around the shop. "I guess I might as well wander, see if there are any other books that catch my attention. Not that I'm here to read."

"What are you here for?" I asked, curious. There was something vaguely familiar about the way she stood, one hip cocked to the side, one hand on her waist. Maybe I'd seen her on the beach recently.

"I'm here for work." The response came out terse and clipped, as if she'd practiced it multiple times but it still felt uncomfortable to say out loud.

I nodded. "Not the typical response for someone visiting Cascade Harbor in the summer. Usually, people come here to escape work. What do you do?" Given that she'd been signing books, the answer was obvious, but it made for easy conversation to get her talking.

She bit her lip, debating what to say next. I was very much a fan of that lip. I wouldn't mind giving it a little nip, after I'd convinced her she wanted to see me again outside of the bookstore. Though kissing her might not be conducive to leveraging a connection to help with my book cover design efforts. I'd have to play the romantic angle of things by ear. Right now, I was more interested in learning about just how well-connected she was in the publishing industry.

She exhaled, her shoulders slumping as she seemed to make a decision. "You'll probably figure it out, if you haven't already." She gestured to the paperback on the counter next to her stack of books, resigned. "I'm an author. I'm here to write my second book."

I reached around her, picking up the book. *"Of Curses and Pome-granates* by Danielle Baldwin."* I read the title out loud before flip-ping it over to read the back. It only took me a moment to realize this was the book every woman I'd interacted with this summer had raved about. It was the kind of book that made careers, for authors and cover designers.

"Please don't read the synopsis while I'm standing here," Danielle said, covering her face with her hands. "I never know how to react when people are judging my book baby in front of me. It's okay if it's not the book for you, I just don't need to know that."

I quirked an eyebrow. "What makes you think it's not for me, Danielle Baldwin?"

"It's Dani. And probably because it's very much a romance and you don't strike me as the romance kind of guy."

I pressed a hand to my chest in mock offense, continuing to hold the book with my other hand. "I feel like I'm being judged and coming up short. How do you know I'm not a romance kind of guy? I'll have you know, I can be very romantic. I've even read at least one Jane Austen novel."

I'd read it in high school, and I didn't remember which Jane Austen novel, but that was beside the point. *Jane Eyre* was by Jane Austen, right? Or was that *Wuthering Heights*?

"It's just... um... I... uh," she stuttered, clearly thrown off by my response.

"If nothing else, I am a design guy, and this cover," I held the book up for her to see, as if she wasn't familiar with her own book cover, "is very well designed."

"Thanks! I wish I could take credit for that, but my publishing house hired this incredibly talented designer and—" She broke off with a groan, smacking her forehead as if just remembering some crucial piece of information. "The cover." She muttered.

"The cover?" I asked, curious how my comment could have led to this response. I felt like it was a good, solid compliment, but her reaction said otherwise.

"I forgot that, in addition to writing the second book in the series, I need to send in suggestions for the cover design. And with my cover designer on an unexpected hiatus, I'm supposed to be reviewing a few alternative artists my publisher is considering." She continued muttering to herself, patting her pockets, likely in search of her phone.

Her comments had my interest further piqued. If her publisher was considering a new artist for her cover, could I possibly get myself on their radar? It would mean shifting this interaction firmly away from anything romantic into something professional, but I had no issues with that. There would be more tourists. There was no guarantee I'd get another shot like this to get my work in front of a publisher. And even if they didn't use me for this book cover, maybe they'd consider me for other books.

I couldn't fully hear what Dani said as she pulled out her phone, something about "Avery" and "murder" and "run away to Alaska," but I got the sense that her stress levels had just skyrocketed. Maybe, if I played my cards right, I could help with that stress level and do a bit of networking.

I looked around, trying to come up with some way to redirect the conversation when I registered the sounds around us. Specifically, the sound of a very loud, very angry Joyce Campbell getting closer to the cash register, and Spencer's quieter, placating voice attempting to calm her. It sounded very much like Joyce was gearing up for the aforementioned customer service lecture and Dani and I were about to become unwitting audience members.

Panicked, I glanced around the bookshelves for an escape, not certain which aisle the unwelcome pair were coming down but certain they'd arrive soon. Spencer's open office door caught my attention, offering the only viable escape route.

"Quick, hide!" I snagged Dani's arm and pulled her into the office with me, flipping off the lights and closing the door behind us.

CHAPTER 8
Dani

THERE WERE SO MANY things wrong with my current predicament, starting with the fact that I'd followed a stranger into a dark, confined space without question and ending with the fact that I didn't hate it.

When he'd pulled me into the office, I'd stumbled a bit, so his hands were on my arms, steadying me, and I wasn't necessarily eager for him to let go. The man smelled amazing, something woodsy and sweet, kind of like a lumberjack and a bakery had a baby. Not to mention his hands communicated a level of strength that 90 percent of women would find attractive. At least according to the totally unbiased, peer-reviewed fictional assessment I'd made in the brief moments since he'd tugged me into Spencer's office with him.

"Why are we hiding?" I whispered the question as the man released me, and I immediately missed the contact and the zing it sent down my spine, even as I took a step back from him. He was a stranger, after all. Even if he smelled and looked like the man of my dreams. Honestly, I'd pictured a man like this when writing Petros, though Petros's hair was longer and darker, and he had a bit of scruff.

"Joyce Campbell."

I let out an exasperated huff. "You say that name like it means something."

"That's because it does mean something." His voice was deep and earnest. It held a familiar quality that I couldn't quite place. Maybe he sounded like an audiobook narrator I'd listened to recently or something.

"Joyce Campbell is the kind of woman nosy busybody stereotypes are based off of."

I shrugged, not sure if I should be intimidated or impressed by the woman. "So, she's a strong flavor. I still don't understand why that means we have to hide in the bookstore office in the dark."

"If I can delay your first run in with Joyce Campbell, I'm going to do it. Trust me, the longer you can go without meeting her, the better."

"While I appreciate your heroics, I think I can handle one opinionated person."

"Famous last words." He muttered. "I've seen Joyce make grown men cry by just looking at them. Those grown men were her husband and son, but still."

I snorted a laugh, not sure what to think of the man in front of me. I could just make out his features thanks to the light coming from under the door and I could tell he had defined cheekbones. Maybe I needed to reevaluate Petros's scruff. There was something to be said for an attractive, clean-shaven man.

"Shh, you don't want to give away our location," he hushed, though I was fairly certain his lips were quirked up in a teasing smile with that assertion.

"Sorry, I wouldn't want to risk bringing down the wrath of Joyce Campbell on us," I said, getting a bit caught up in this ridiculous game of ours. Why was I playing along? And why was I enjoying it so much?

"Trust me, it's for the best. She's genuinely the worst citizen of this town, and I'd hate for her to scare you away when we're just getting the chance to meet." His voice radiated charm, and I fell for it, just a little. The guy was definitely giving off friendly vibes, though I couldn't decide if they were of the flirtatious or just nice variety. But I didn't hate it. He was the kind of person I'd go out of my way to avoid back home, but I wasn't home, and part of my reason for this trip was to do things outside of my norm in hopes of finding writing inspiration. Maybe a romantic interlude with a stranger in a bookstore office could do the trick.

"She can't be that bad. Currently, my neighbor is my least favorite person in Cascade Harbor," I said, not thinking before the words escaped. I clapped a hand over my mouth. I didn't know the man in front of me. For all I knew, he and Mason were best friends. "Sorry, I didn't mean that. I just..." I trailed off, not sure what to say. While much of my frustration with Mason had been hanger-fueled, I clearly had some lingering frustrations. Though, that didn't mean I had to say as much to the attractive man I was currently trapped with.

The man snorted a laugh. "And what has your neighbor done to earn such disdain?"

I bit my lip, considering what to say before deciding I might as well share it all. We had time to kill, and it wasn't like I'd have to see this guy again.

"I'm renting out part of a duplex for the next couple weeks, maybe even the rest of the summer, and the guy who lives on the other side," I paused, shaking my head in frustration as I remembered the make-out session I'd interrupted the night before followed by his attempt to proposition me. I'd give him grace for the Scooter thing, but I was still unimpressed by the man. "He's inconsiderate and a player. I've been here less than twenty-four hours, and I'm just not impressed by the bearded man next door. So, while it's not impossible for Joyce Campbell to supplant him, I'm also not putting her in the bottom spot just yet."

CHAPTER 9
Mason

WELL, THAT HADN'T BEEN what I was expecting. Dani's words sank in, and I knew instantly who she was: my grandparents' long-term renter and my new next-door neighbor. And I was currently her least favorite person in town. Not exactly the kind of impression I wanted to give to someone I was hoping to connect with further.

But it was too late now.

My mind scrambled, trying to think of some way to salvage the situation. It sounded like I was firmly in her black book, something I was kicking myself for. It was just my luck that the woman I'd managed to tick off last night could help me grow in my career, potentially giving me the boost I needed so I could finally support myself and succeed in a dream I'd been chasing since my dad died.

Then her words fully registered. She'd called me a "bearded man." I ran my hand over my smooth, naked chin. I wasn't bearded any more. For the first time since Charlie said "oops," I saw a bright side to this whole new-look situation.

Was it possible I could use my appearance to gain a second chance?

I knew most authors had little to no say over what happened with their covers, but even if she could facilitate an introduction for me with her publishing house, it could be a game changer.

I cleared my throat, hoping this woman wouldn't suddenly recognize my voice as being the one she'd bickered with the night before. "What makes you hate him so much?"

"Several things, but he was totally leading this woman on last night. I guess he's some kind of artist and used that to lure her to his house. He tried something similar with me,' but I saw straight through it. Then he trapped me in my rental all morning and most of the afternoon without food."

I winced, realizing her assessment was fair based on her experiences with me so far, though I wouldn't say I was worse than Joyce Campbell. Dani just hadn't seen me in the best light last night, or really any light for that matter.

"I think he did try to warn me about Scooter, the lawn guy who was the reason I got trapped. Mason should have tried harder, but the sticky note he left indicated he did at least *try*." Her tone told me she was less than impressed with my note. I wanted to defend myself, explain that I hadn't wanted to wake her up if she was sleeping, but knew doing so would likely destroy any chance of this exchange ending in a positive place.

"Anyway, you don't want to hear about my crummy neighbor." She gave a self-conscious laugh, and I wished I could flip the light on to read her expression, though at the same time I was grateful for the dark and how it allowed me to hide my reactions from her. "I really should know better than to vent to random strangers in bookstore offices. I can only imagine what you must think of me. After all, I don't even know your name."

It was the perfect opportunity to introduce myself. Maybe I should introduce myself as Mason, clear up any misunderstanding from the night before. Start fresh with an apology and the promise of buying her dinner. But I hesitated to come clean. I didn't like not being liked.

An idea started to niggle in the back of my brain, something I probably should have immediately dismissed. It was ridiculous. Yet, there was something about this woman that made me want to try my hand at befriending her, see if I could get to know her and convince her to introduce me to her publisher.

Unlike my usual tourist interactions, this wasn't something romantic, though she was gorgeous and, if my career wasn't hanging in the balance, I'd have no qualms about shooting my shot with her. This was about my career and the dreams I sometimes worried would never fully materialize as I scraped by on Etsy store orders, Spencer's commissions, and my grandparents' generosity.

I'd also been warned that the publishing world was small, with people connected to each other in ways you'd never expect. One misstep could cause irreparable damage to a career, especially for someone just starting to dip their toe into the waters. However, once I'd found my way into the publishing industry, I could only imagine the opportunities for me as a cover designer. By attaching my name to a book as big as the sequel to *Of Curses and Pomegranates,* I'd have enough commissions to buy the duplex from my grandparents and live on the Oregon coast permanently if I so chose.

As long as Dani never found out I was Mason.

Thinking quickly, I extended my hand, praying I wasn't about to regret this decision but knowing I needed to take my chance with the woman in front of me. Designing a cover, or even just doing character art for her, could be a gamechanger for my future.

"I'm..." I scrambled for a name that I'd remember but that was different enough from Mason that she wouldn't come close to connecting me with the jerk I'd been the night before. "I'm Bradley, well actually, Allen. Allen Bradley."

I winced. Allen? Really? It was my middle name, and I'd always hated it, but for some reason it was the name that sprang to my lips in this moment. If there was a less attractive name in the world, I'd yet to find it. And to make things worse, I'd introduced myself like I was in some kind of really awkward Bond movie. She'd remember me all right, for being even more socially-inept than Spencer.

"Nice to meet you, Allen Bradley." She shook my hand, seeming to hold on a little longer than necessary, though that might have been wishful thinking on my part. Normally, I had all the swagger and confidence with women, but my deception had me on shaky footing and I wasn't sure how best to move forward. Especially when I was hoping for was a connection of the just friends, professional variety.

I was good at flings, not so good at long-term relationships, even if it was just as friends. I was still amazed at Spencer's continued friendship, though I had a feeling that was more due to his nerdy awkwardness getting in the way of him making other friendships than it had to do with any true attachment to me.

I wasn't the kind of guy people stuck around for and stayed connected to, something Rebecca had taught me all too clearly. And I was perfectly fine with that. Life was easier without lots of messy attachments.

"You know way more of my life story than you probably bargained for, so tell me about you. How long have you been in Cascade Harbor? Are you a local or a tourist like me?"

"I'm a tourist," I said, thinking quick to build my backstory in a way that I would hopefully remember. "Well, sort of. I'm staying with my grandparents a few towns over but like to come here for the..." I scrambled to think of something Cascade Harbor offered that the other nearby towns lacked, "bakery and bookstore. I visit most summers, which is why I'm so familiar with the town. It only takes one summer to learn to stay away from Joyce Campbell." I forced a laugh, hoping Dani bought my story. "She's worse than any of the meddling middle-aged ladies back home in... Rexburg."

I winced again. Rexburg, Idaho? Really? I mean it was a town I was very familiar with, thanks to it being where my dad had grown up, but it wasn't exactly somewhere exciting. Not only did I give myself the worst name but now I was from one of the most boring states in the country. What was next, telling her I collected stamps for fun?

She seemed to take what I said at face value, though I again wished I could flip on the light to read her expression. Not that I'd given her any reason to doubt what I was telling her, but I kept waiting for her to see right through me and call me on my lies.

Note to self: Never become a secret agent. I wasn't built for deception.

"Makes sense. I'd visit Cascade Harbor every summer just for Sugar and Sea Bakery. Joane's baking is going to be very dangerous for my waistline."

I'd lost track of how long we'd been hiding in the office, and I didn't register that the voices near the cash register had faded until Spencer opened the door. The sudden brightness from the bookstore surprised us for a moment but by the time my eyes adjusted I could still see the hurt and disappointment on Spencer's face. Even though Dani clearly wasn't interested in him, I would still owe my friend a giant apology when all of this was over.

But first I needed to make sure he didn't blow my cover. Another piece of the deception I hadn't considered: how to keep my secret without anyone revealing I was Mason. And of course I had to start with the man who couldn't lie to save his life. What could possibly go wrong?

"I see you two have met. Why are you hiding in my office? I could have really used your backup with Joyce, Mas—"

I stepped from the room, cutting him off with a hand on his chest and a mostly gentle nudge out the door.

"I wanted to save Dani the pain of Joyce's customer service lecture. Didn't want to give her a bad impression of Cascade Harbor on her first full day here." Or at least, not a worse impression after I apparently bungled things so royally.

"From what I understand, it was the heroic thing to do." Dani gave me a shy smile and a delicate shrug, as if we now shared our own inside joke. It was good to know I hadn't scared her off completely with my antics.

Spencer cleared his throat, obviously trying to regain Dani's attention.

"The writing craft books are this way. If you'll follow me?" Spencer waved toward the nonfiction section of the bookstore before disappearing between the shelves.

Dani made to follow him, but I snagged her arm, stopping her for just a moment. I was about to break one of my summer tourist rules but, if this thing was going to go beyond hiding in bookstore offices and lead to a career opportunity for me, drastic measures needed to be taken.

Dani turned to me, her eyebrow arched in curiosity. I released her arm and gave her my best smile. Hopefully it still worked without the beard and didn't come across as trying too hard. Knowing how this day was going, I probably looked like a grinning fool. I was going to have to double check all my go-to moves in the mirror now that I was working with different assets.

"Before you disappear with Spencer, can I get your number? I would love to show you around the area, introduce you to the magic of the Oregon coast."

She paused, pondering my request, and it took everything in me not to reach up to stroke my non-existent beard or find some other way to fidget.

Finally, she gave a sheepish shake of her head before softening her rejection with a smile. "No, but not because I don't want to. This is going to sound ridiculous and like I'm full of myself, but since publishing my book, I've had to be careful about who I give my number to."

I felt a twinge of disappointment but could understand where she was coming from. Based on how some of the women I'd interacted with earlier this summer had talked about Dani's book, I could only imagine the types of messages she'd received. Not getting her number did put a damper on my plan though, and I scrambled to figure out a way to salvage our exchange. Maybe she wouldn't give me her number, but maybe I could get an email or something. That was the professional thing to do, right? Exchange emails. Or was it business cards? Did people still use business cards?

Though giving her a business card would not only reveal my name was Mason but it would also tell her what I did for work before we'd gotten to know each other. While I was hoping to use this exchange as a networking opportunity, she didn't need to know everything just yet. I didn't want her to think I was only using her for her connections. That would hardly lead to the industry introductions I was hoping for.

"I guess that makes sense," I said, taking a step back. There was a fine line between accepting a woman's rejection while also trying to pivot and figure out a plan B. Not chasing a woman for a quick fling was new territory for me. If I assured her my interest was not romantic, would that make things worse or better? "I just figured you could use a friend, someone who knows the area."

Now it was her turn to grab my arm and stop my retreat.

"I'm saying no today, but," she bit her lip, hesitating for just a moment before continuing, "if you were to ask me the next time I see you, my answer might be different."

She smiled at me and then seemed to realize her boldness. "From a purely friend perspective, of course." She rushed to tack on.

And before I could react, she released my arm and slipped between the shelves to follow Spencer, leaving me staring after her.

My heart gave an unexpected thump of excitement at her parting words. It was a sensation I wasn't used to, and I told myself it was because this was a step forward in my career, nothing more. However, a part of me worried it could be something more. I tried so hard to keep all women at arm's length, but I had a sinking suspicion Dani could be a different story, and I had no idea what I was going to do about it.

Shaking my head, I disappeared into the bookshelves in the opposite direction of Spencer and Dani. I still needed to talk to Spencer, assuming he'd still give me the commission after I'd disregarded his wishes and made a move on Dani.

If I told Spencer it was for professional reasons and nothing more, would he believe me? I'd never hidden what I was doing with tourists in the past, but telling him about my hopes for my time with Dani felt weirdly vulnerable. Not to mention if I told him, he'd likely blurt the truth to her the first chance he got. Best to keep the details to myself for now.

I settled into one of the bookstore's armchairs to wait for Spencer, pulling up the official social media pages for *the* Danielle Baldwin. If I was going to try my hand at designing her next book cover, I might as well do some research, so I'd be ready for our next exchange. And there would be a next exchange. As her next-door neighbor, I'd make sure of it. I just had to make sure she never figured out I was her actual next-door neighbor.

As if conjured by my thoughts, an email notification popped up on my phone. While my grandma still served as the primary contact for the duplex, she forwarded me all maintenance requests. As I read the request I silently groaned. Looked like fate was throwing a small wrench in my plan: Dani's internet was down, and I had to figure out a way to make the repair without her seeing me. What could possibly go wrong?

CHAPTER 10
Dani

I'D STAYED IN TOWN longer than I should have, wandering the bookstore for a bit before making it to the grocery store. And I'd be lying if I said I hadn't been hoping to run into Allen again, have our second exchange so I could give him my phone number.

It was a silly rule, not giving my number to someone after a single interaction, but one I was adamant about after some uncomfortable texts from past acquaintances who suddenly wanted to reconnect when they saw my name attached to a book on the bestsellers list. I'd lost track of the number of phone numbers I'd blocked this last year. It was amazing the things people would send you when they thought you had a bit of money and influence.

By the time I'd finished at the grocery store, my stomach was growling, and clouds had moved in, bringing a cool, drizzling rain. Feeling guilty for considering eating out again when I'd just bought a ton of food, I'd driven back to the rental determined to fix dinner and settle in for an evening of writing. I was also hoping the internet would be working. I'd gotten a message from the duplex owner that Mason would get to work on my wifi issue immediately. Though when I got back to my temporary home it quickly became apparent that he hadn't managed to fix it while I was in town, which would make research difficult but would drastically reduce my tendency to avoid writing by scrolling social media. I was in the middle of putting the groceries away and pondering on what I wanted to make when there was a knock on my door.

Pausing the audiobook on my phone, I ventured to the front door and looked through the peephole to see who waited on the other side. While I hadn't told any of my new acquaintances in town where I was staying, I had a feeling it wouldn't take much effort in a town this size for someone to figure out the address of my temporary home.

An unfamiliar, willowy blonde woman stood on the other side of my door wearing a short, low-cut dress that wasn't exactly weather appropriate, the rain having shifted from a slight drizzle to a full-on downpour. She was huddled close to the door, her arms crossed over her ample chest in an effort to stay warm and out of the rain.

"Hi. Can I help you?" I asked as I opened the door and greeted the woman. I noted her car parked in the driveaway, a posh red sportscar currently occupying the middle of the space. What was with people in this town and their inability to park on one side of the drive, or even in the street? I was just grateful I didn't have plans to leave the duplex again until morning, otherwise she'd have me trapped again.

If I didn't know better, I'd suspect Avery of paying the good people of Cascade Harbor to keep me contained and focused on writing. When I had reception again, I'd have to ask her if she'd stooped to such dastardly levels.

The woman's eyes swept over me, as if taking my measure before she spoke, her pinched expression telling me she was unimpressed by my ponytail, leggings, and worn sweatshirt that I'd changed into to combat the dip in temperature that came with the rain. Her voice carried a faint southern drawl as she spoke. "Well, hello. Is Mason around?"

Of course, she was here for my ladies' man of a next-door neighbor.

"I'm sorry, but he lives on the other side of the duplex. I have no idea if he's home or not," I said, doing my best not to sound put out by this exchange. What was I, the man's secretary?

Relief flickered across the woman's face. "Oh, I should have known you were one of his renters!" She looked me up and down, her lip curling in disgust. "He doesn't really go for the," she seemed to search for the right word, "homey type. I'm Tiffany."

She extended a well-manicured hand to shake, and I wondered what her reaction would be if I told her Mason had asked me out within minutes of meeting me, and I'd rejected him.

"I'm Dani," I said, giving her hand as brief of a shake as I could manage while still being polite. Her hand was cold, and I could see goosebumps breaking out over her skin. I was very grateful for my sweatshirt and to be safely inside in this weather.

As if reading my mind, Tiffany glanced over my shoulder into the duplex, taking a step forward.

"Do you mind if I come in while I wait for Mason? I hadn't counted on the rain, and he didn't answer when I knocked." She gave what was probably meant to be an inviting smile, but it looked far too fake and practiced. "Rain wreaks havoc on my hair." She tossed her curls over her shoulder, and I noted the slightest traces of frizz.

I was amazed at the woman's boldness, but if I didn't give out my phone number the first time I met someone, there was no way I was letting a complete stranger into my temporary home. Especially one who judged me and clearly found me lacking, making me think even less of Mason if this was the type of woman he normally dated. I crossed my arms and stepped forward, doing my best to block any chance of entry into my rental. While I felt for the woman's predicament, there was no way I was playing hostess while she waited for my bearded neighbor.

Also, I needed the man focused on my internet issues, not another romantic interlude.

"I'm sorry. I'm just getting ready for dinner," I said, making a show of glancing down at my watch. My stomach growled, as if underscoring my words. It wasn't a lie. She just didn't need to know that I wasn't actually planning on leaving the duplex to eat. "But you can park your car on *his* side of the driveway and wait for him."

She deflated.

"Of course you are. Tell Mason I stopped by. I'm in town just for today and would love to catch up." Her words were laced with innuendo, leaving little question in my mind as to what "catching up" entailed. She'd no doubt "modeled" for him as well. I could just imagine the stream of women who'd graced the halls of the neighboring duplex unit and been dubbed Mason's "inspiration."

"I'll be sure to let him know," I said through clenched teeth with what I hoped resembled a smile more than a grimace. "Bye bye now."

I slowly closed the door, forcing Tiffany back out into the weather. I watched her through the front window for a moment as she wandered over to the neighboring duplex one more time, assumingly to try knocking again. When her knock remained unanswered, her shoulders slumped further and she slunk back to her car, sitting in it for a moment before driving away.

I gave an audible sigh of relief at her departure, and the grumbling of my stomach drew me back into the kitchen. I got to work pulling together ingredients to make one of my favorite go-to meals: fettuccine alfredo from a jar with a side salad. As I worked, my mind once again wandered to my neighbor.

I wanted to believe I was misjudging him, but so far I was less than impressed. And he hadn't even stopped by to check out my internet issue.

My eyes snagged on the neon orange sticky notes I'd purchased at the grocery store. I'd selected the color partially because orange was my least favorite color but also because there was no way someone could miss a note in that particularly vibrant hue.

Pausing my meal preparation, I retrieved a pen from the spare bedroom and set to work telling Mason exactly what I thought of his nonexistent caretaking skills and my unexpected visitor. Though I'd hate to give up Joane's baking so soon after discovering it, if I didn't get internet soon, I would have Lucy book me a new rental.

CHAPTER II
Mason

WAS I PROUD OF the fact that I was currently hiding in my front room with the lights off doing my best not to be visible through any of the open windows in my home? Absolutely not. But at this point, it was a matter of survival.

After meeting my new neighbor the second time, I was hopeful, counting down until the moment when I'd see her again and get her number. Short of women who were married or in a committed relationship, I'd found very few straight women who could resist my charms, with the exception of Dani the first night we met, of course. Having officially met her today, I could clearly see where I'd gone wrong that first night, and now I could course correct.

I just needed to play my cards right and I'd have Danielle Baldwin eating out of the palm of my hand, begging me to become her cover designer.

Figuring I could help my case in a roundabout way by putting her in a better mood by fixing her internet issue, I'd come home following the meeting with Spencer determined to get to the bottom of the problem. The wifi was working on my side of the duplex, making it clear there was something wrong on Dani's side. Thinking quickly, I'd pulled on a hoodie and a scarf, overkill for the weather to be sure, but necessary to keep up my ruse, and knocked on her door. When she hadn't answered, I'd let myself in, knowing my grandma would have communicated to her that I'd be stopping by to check out the problem and would let myself in if she wasn't there to answer. When it was clear the router was plugged in and should be working, I'd wandered outside and quickly identified the problem: Scooter had cut the cable for internet on her side. Again.

This was only the second time it had happened, but I'd thought this was the kind of mistake a landscaper only made once. Given that our landscaper was Scooter, I should have known better.

I'd headed back to my side of the duplex and quickly called the internet provider, knowing they wouldn't answer this late on a Sunday, but leaving a message. Last time, they'd been able to make the repair fairly quickly. Fingers crossed it would be the case this time too.

Guessing Dani would be headed back to the duplex soon and wouldn't be able to check her email without internet, I'd been searching the living room for the sticky notes I'd used the night before to communicate with my neighbor when I'd spotted an unwelcome visitor through my open window: Tiffany.

As soon as I spotted her, I ducked to the side of my window where I could watch her but hopefully she couldn't see me.

The woman had been one of my biggest mistakes since I'd moved to Oregon, and it looked like she was back to make my life miserable.

Tiffany had come here last summer on a bachelorette trip to celebrate one of her friend's upcoming nuptials, and the Texas beauty had immediately caught my eye. It hadn't taken much to convince her to come back to my place for a bit of modeling. Unfortunately, I'd spent the rest of her stay in Cascade Harbor fighting off the woman's advances because the word "no" apparently wasn't in her vocabulary. I'd finally had to spend a couple of days at my grandparents' house on a "business trip" to get her to take the hint and leave me alone. Even then, I'd been worried every time there was a knock on the door that I'd open my grandparents' door to find her standing on the other side with bleached waves and her unnaturally white smile telling me she'd just happened to be in the area.

Now it looked like she was back, and I had no idea how I was going to avoid her. Maybe it was time to go visit my mom and brother in Utah. That would put a damper on my plans to woo Dani, but I wasn't sure I would survive another summer visit from Tiffany.

I'd hoped she would have forgotten about my existence by now. Clearly, my luck had its limits.

After knocking on my door, Tiffany walked down the front porch steps, and I held my breath, watching to see if she climbed back into her car. Instead, she moved past her car and turned toward the front door on the other side of the duplex. While I couldn't see or hear anything, I could guess what she was up to. The woman was persistent, I'd give her that much.

With Tiffany out of sight, I quickly grabbed my phone, which contained notes from my meeting with Spencer, and sprinted down the hall to my bedroom, regretting the necessity of leaving my blinds open for Tiffany to come back and peer in if she desired. If I closed them, she'd be well aware I was home and I couldn't guarantee she wouldn't try to do something crazy like let herself in. Tiffany wasn't exactly the kind of woman who accepted rejection, a quality I'd initially found attractive until it came back to bite me. Repeatedly.

Settling onto the floor by my bed, I snagged my tablet and pulled up my design program. If I was trapped at home, I might as well make the most of the time. Usually, I worked in my studio with music playing, but the blinds in that room were also open and I wouldn't put it past Tiffany to walk around the house, peeking in all the windows just to be certain I wasn't home. Thankfully, I typically kept the blinds in my bedroom closed, though to be safe, I stayed on the floor and made sure to keep my bed between me and the window on the off chance she could see the glow of my screen through any of the gaps in the blinds.

While my bedroom, with its white walls, poor lighting, and aged carpet wasn't my preferred workspace, I quickly lost myself in my work as I sketched out design concepts for Spencer's art piece. It had taken some coaxing, but I'd convinced him to still meet with me to discuss the commission. After repeatedly assuring him my interest in Dani was purely professional and promising him I'd help him impress a different woman this summer, he'd lost himself in describing the commission.

He was redoing the children's section of the bookstore and wanted several prints to add to the space. He wanted a triptych series of images focused on books and reading. He'd said he'd leave it up to me to decide what direction to take things, but he'd talked me through a few ideas he'd had based on popular book series. He wanted whatever I drew to be bright and inviting, illustrating the magic of reading for children of all ages in the same style as my first commission.

Sketches of superheroes, princesses, mermaids, and dragons bursting from the pages of books quickly filled my tablet. I particularly loved the rough sketch I'd done of a little girl reading on a toadstool, surrounded by mythical creatures reading over her shoulder and a castle in the background.

Sometime later, the grumbles of my stomach convinced me to set down my work to make food. I hadn't dared turn on any lights for fear of Tiffany noticing and I attempted to rub away the strain from my eyes after staring at the blue light of my tablet for so long.

Standing and stretching, I cautiously made my way down the hall to the front room, confirming Tiffany's car was gone before closing the blinds and flipping on the lights. Realizing I needed to put out the trashcans for pick up tomorrow morning, I slipped on my jacket and cautiously opened the front door, pausing when I spotted a series of bright orange sticky notes covered in feminine handwriting stuck to my door.

At first, I thought they must be from Tiffany, though she didn't strike me as the kind of woman to carry sticky notes in her purse. Upon closer inspection, I realized the notes were from my temporary neighbor.

I bit back a chuckle as I read:

Mason –
I did not come to Oregon to play secretary. Please keep your lady friends to yourself.
Also, in case you were unaware, my internet still isn't work-ing. If it's not fixed soon, I may need to vacate the premises for a vacation rental with reception, internet, and a helpful caretaker. In which case, I will expect a refund for the re-mainder of my stay.

Dani

It appeared I had ruffled my neighbor's feathers even more than I'd realized. I could just picture her, her eyebrows pinched in concentration as she tried to fit all of her frustrations onto the tiny pieces of paper.

Looked like it was time for me to do a bit of damage control, even if I found surprising humor in her frustration. If she only knew the amount of power she currently held over my actions. If it would improve my chances of an introduction with her publisher, I'd offer to switch duplex sides with her until her internet was fixed.

I stepped back inside and grabbed my pad of green sticky notes and a pen. I jotted down a quick note and stopped to place it on her door before taking care of the trash cans. Hopefully, my note would appease her. It would do me no good if she moved to a different rental before I could secure her phone number. There were no other available rentals in Cascade Harbor, so her moving would spell disaster for me and any chances of breaking into the publishing world with Dani's help.

CHAPTER 12
Dani

"THIS ISN'T WORKING," I growled under my breath as I slammed my laptop closed and pushed it away from me. I'd been attempting to write at Sugar and Sea Bakery for several hours with mixed success. Last night, I'd actually written several chapters, veering away from my initial outline and allowing my characters to guide me. It was rough and I knew Sadie would have a field day tearing it apart with edits, but it was *something*. When I'd started writing today, words had been flowing, up until now when I'd slammed headlong into a plot hole that had me completely stumped.

I could just see the negative reviews now: "Author Danielle Baldwin, a one hit wonder" or "*Of Curses and Pomegranates* sequel not worth the paper it was printed on."

Nothing was working. My original outline was all but useless with the changes I'd made last night. Neither Hypatia nor Petros were talking to me, which made writing their book more than a little bit difficult. Add in the periodic, well-meaning texts from Avery asking for progress updates, and the pressure was on.

I knew Avery was throwing herself into work to distract herself from the breakup with Mr. Noodles-for-Brains, but I wouldn't be offended if she turned some of her attention on a few of her other authors.

The weight of Poppy's bracelet on my wrist was slowly driving me insane with each word I typed and deleted. I was about ready to chuck it and my laptop across the bakery and ask Joane if she was hiring, make my hiatus in Oregon permanent. I'd just have to sell my townhome and figure out a way to get Hercules out here, but both were doable with the right motivation.

What if I couldn't write a solid sequel? What if this book flopped? What if I wasn't cut out for this author gig?

Maybe I'd quit my day job too soon. No, I hadn't had the PTO needed to go on book tours, but that job had at least served as a safety net against failure, a safety net I wouldn't mind having at the moment.

I groaned, massaging my temples as I tried to decide what to do next. Maybe I needed to go back to the rental, try a change of space. Though if I did that, chances were very high I'd wrap up in a thick, fuzzy blanket on the couch with the young adult fantasy I'd picked up at the bookstore yesterday. The book description had sucked me in, and I had a feeling that if I started it, I'd stay up way too late reading.

My gaze snagged on a green sticky note that I hadn't noticed was stuck to my laptop. It was the note I'd found from Mason this morning as I'd pulled out of the garage into the driveaway. The note had been stuck to my door and, while I couldn't explain why, it had annoyed me the instant I laid eyes on it.

It appeared my neighbor had responded to my notes from the day before.

I'd tromped up the stairs to the front door, curious to see what the bearded ladies' man had to say that he couldn't just knock on my door to tell me in person.

> *Dear Dani,*
> *I'll take your notes on my caretaking ability under advisement. By the way, Scooter was kind enough to cut your internet cable yesterday. I'll call the provider first thing tomorrow and see if we can't get someone out ASAP to get it fixed. Also, my apologies for Tiffany, though to be fair, I*

be fair, I had no idea she was in town. Now that I know she's here, I'll be sure to avoid home as much as possible. Though I'm curious, why do you care who visits me? Am I sensing some jealousy?

Mason

I'd stuffed the note in my bag, galled at his audacity. It had taken everything in me not to immediately pen my own note in response. If I wasn't an introvert who preferred just about anything to face-to-face confrontation, I might have even knocked on his door. Instead, I'd decided he wasn't worth the effort and climbed into my car, grumbling to myself about self-important men the entire drive to town. If I took the curves on the drive a little too quickly in my anger, that was no one's business but my own.

When I'd texted the cousin chat about my internet issues once I'd reached the bakery, Lucy had offered once again to book me a new rental, but I'd hesitated. Yes, a new rental would mean internet and a less annoying neighbor. It also meant leaving before I could give Allen my phone number, a thought that left me feeling more disappointed than it probably should have.

I'd settled in at the bakery for lunch and another writing session. And, fueled by frustration, coffee, carbs, and the hint of a promise of seeing Allen again, it had worked. A scene I would have never expected involving Hypatia dragging Petros into a tiny bookstore office to hide from the Fates who were hunting them had quickly populated the page, which had absolutely nothing to do with my similar run in from the day before. At least, that's what I told myself up until the moment when they left the bookstore, and the words stopped flowing. Now I was at a complete loss. I'd been on this trip for two days and all I had to show for it was a handful of chapters, a pastry addiction, and a feud with my neighbor.

Avery was going to kill me.

"Sounds like things are going well over here," Joane observed from where she was wiping down tables following the lunch rush.

"That's an understatement," I said, staring forlornly at my closed laptop. "I wrote some, but it's not nearly enough. If I can't make some solid progress on this book soon, I'm going to miss my deadline. And while my sister's determined and would find a way to still make things work, I know her company would take a major hit with the delay. Not to mention, she's planning on using my popularity to help boost the other authors publishing with Rose & Quill."

So many people to let down, so little time.

"So, no pressure." Joane walked over to my table and stopped with one hand on her hip, the other one waving a cleaning rag at me while she spoke. "Maybe you need to step away for a minute. What do you do for fun?"

"I don't have time to step away," I said, guilt churning in my stomach as I thought about all the writing I should have already finished.

"That's not what I asked. What do you do to refill your cup? To get your creative juices flowing?" Joane asked, sinking into the chair across from me and pinning me with a serious expression. Today her hair was pulled up into another ponytail, and she was again sporting a Salt and Sea Bakery apron like the one I'd seen her in the day before. Underneath the apron, her shirt was covered in bright paisley swirls, reminding me of a similar shirt I'd seen my Grandma Sue wear on multiple occasions.

"I read and write." I knew my response wasn't what Joane was looking for, but it was all I had. When I was in Utah, I occasionally hiked with Hercules, but hiking alone on unfamiliar paths here in Oregon didn't sound like the smartest idea.

"That's it? All you do with your life is read and write?" I felt mild offense at the incredulity in Joane's tone.

"You say it like that's a bad thing," I muttered, self-consciously looking down and tracing a finger along the grain in the wood of my table.

Joane seemed to consider my words a moment before pushing to her feet. Startled at her sudden movement, I looked up to find her gesturing for me to stand.

"That's it," she said. "We're getting you another hobby, something to help you recharge. Otherwise, you're going to burn out, and none of us are going to see that second book."

I hesitantly stood, watching as Joane bustled around the room, flipping the Open sign to Closed and flicking off the lights.

"Why are you closing early?" I asked, packing my laptop into my backpack and waiting to see what Joane would say next. I'd double checked the hours listed on the door before I'd settled in to write, just to be safe, and though the bakery wasn't open for dinner on Mondays, Joane said she typically kept it open a little longer for anyone who wandered in looking for a sweet treat or late lunch.

"Because we're leaving the bakery and you're coming to my house," she said, as if it was the most obvious conclusion in the world. She opened the shop door and waved me through.

"Umm, why?" Honestly, the exchange should have been setting off alarm bells in my head seeing as a near stranger was expecting me to follow her home, but instead of being concerned, I was simply curious.

"Because I'm introducing you to Carl. Though you can't tell Joyce Campbell. If she found out, I'd never hear the end of it."

My mind was spinning as I tried to make sense of what she was saying. "Who's Carl and why does Joyce care?"

Joane let out a huff and threw her hands up in the air, clearly only hearing half of my question. "If I knew why Joyce Campbell cared about anything, I'd fill my shop up with everything she hates and chase her away for good. Unfortunately, I've yet to find the secret to making that happen, so instead I do my best not to tick her off. But trust me, if she knew I introduced you to Carl, let you take a piece of him," she stopped to shake her head, "let's just say, for all of our sakes, it's better if no one from town, least of all Joyce, learns about what we're about to do."

Joane had only answered one of my questions and the fact that she was giving me a piece of Carl had me very confused. Was Carl a person? A pet? Neither option boded well for me or for Carl. Maybe he was one of those plants that propagated ridiculously fast, and Joane was going to try to turn me into a plant lady. Something that would only end in disaster given the number of dead and dying plants that currently dotted my windowsill back in Utah, plants I was just realizing I'd forgotten to ask Avery to water while I was away. The last thing I needed was more plants to murder.

For my own peace of mind, I really needed Joane to clarify who Carl was; however, I didn't dare repeat my question. Maybe if I rephrased it, I'd have better luck.

"So, we're going to meet Carl. And what are we doing with Carl?" I had a writer's imagination and none of the scenarios I was conjuring in my mind were good.

"Giving you a new hobby, of course!" Joane said, as if it was the most obvious thing in the world. But I couldn't, for the life of me think of hobbies that involved pieces of a guy named Carl that didn't end terribly.

If Carl was a pet, maybe Joane made things out his fur. I'd once gone way too far down a social media rabbit hole watching videos of people who repurposed their dog's and cat's fur. And while I found the hobby mildly disturbing, I also had to admire the creator's ingenuity as they somehow turned a tuft of golden retriever hair into a miniature golden retriever.

I studied Joane carefully. She didn't strike me as a cannibal or a swinger, especially given that she'd made it very clear earlier in the day that she was divorced, but what did I really know about the woman? We'd met twenty-four hours earlier and, while I liked her, I technically didn't know her well enough to determine if she was secretly a serial killer or had some kind of fetish involving tourists and Carl.

Lost in my thoughts, I missed what Joane said next. Instead, she just stood next to the bakery door looking at me expectantly.

"Sorry, I missed that," I said sheepishly as I walked to the door, my laptop bag slung over one shoulder.

"I said, go get in your car and wait for me while I finish locking up. I won't be long." She impatiently gestured for me to leave. I had the feeling when Joane got an idea, it took an act of Congress to get her to change her mind.

Deciding it couldn't hurt anything and that I wouldn't win if I tried arguing, I left the bakery and walked around to the parking lot. If nothing else, yesterday's unexpected bookstore interaction had led to inspiration for today. Maybe following Joane home would do the same. Perhaps that's what I really needed, new and unexpected experiences that could force me out of my funk.

Maybe I should have given Allen my number yesterday, instead of playing it safe, though I still couldn't decide if he was flirting or just friendly. But giving him my number would have been an unexpected, new experience on an entirely different level, and I wasn't as alarmed by the possibility as I probably should have been. Possibly a vacation romance without strings attached was exactly what I needed. Perhaps my neighbor with his lothario ways had the right idea. Veronica from the other night hadn't looked the least bit upset when I'd caught the two of them in the driveway. And Tiffany had enjoyed herself enough to plan another trip to this sleepy little town for a chance at round two with Mason. Not that I was about to take Mason up on his offer from Sunday night, but I would consider a similar offer from Allen.

And if Allen was looking just to be friends, I could do that too. Were vacation friendships a thing? It could be worth it to find out.

Shaking myself from my musings involving a certain handsome, clean-shaven man, I unlocked my car and settled into the driver's seat, flipping through radio stations until I found a song I liked.

Not sure how long I'd have to wait for Joane, I pulled out my phone to check for texts. With internet still out at the duplex, I was quickly learning to take advantage of the moments I had reception. While I felt like I was going through a bit of withdrawal from the cousin chat, the limited distractions without a functioning phone were good when I could focus on writing.

Normally, I'd text Sadie my every thought and reaction, but she was currently at a family reunion with her other, less cool, side of the family, and I wasn't sure how responsive she'd be.

With Sadie unavailable, I decided I should update Avery on my plans just in case Joane chose to unalive me, I typed out a quick text in response to her last message requesting a progress report:

Dani:

> If you haven't heard from me by bedtime, I've probably been murdered.

> Or turned into a swinger.

> Or a cat lady.

> Really, anything's possible at this point.

Avery:

> Uh, should I be worried? That doesn't sound like writing, and neither does it sound like you're very safe out there.

Dani:

[Shrug emoji] I mean, how safe are any of us in the grand scheme of things?

Joane declared I need a break from writing to "refill my cup." Whatever that means. So now I'm following her home to be given a hobby that involves a piece of someone named Carl.

Do you think she's about to induct me into a cult? That could lead to some really good book inspiration!

Avery:

Unless you're planning to put a cult in this second book, maybe stay away from whoever Joane is?

Wait, what do you mean, "a piece of someone named Carl?"

Dani! Do I need to call the police? Send an SOS if you're really in trouble.

Motion outside my window had me looking up from my phone to find Joane waving at me as she climbed into her own car, a well-loved white sedan with a Sugar and Sea Bakery bumper sticker proudly sitting next to the license plate. It probably wouldn't hurt to leave Avery hanging until I had more information about Carl and his pieces, so I followed Joane from the parking lot and over a couple of blocks to a cute little green house with thriving flower beds. While dated, the house was welcoming with freshly painted shutters and large windows.

It didn't look like the house of a serial killer or a swinger or a cult leader. Though, I wasn't sure exactly what the house of a serial killer looked like. Probably more red and fewer flowers.

Joane pulled into the garage, and I followed behind her, making sure to park off to the side so she could move her car if needed. I wished Scooter or Tiffany could see me and take notes. It really wasn't that hard!

"Come on in," Joane called, and I followed her through the garage and into the house.

I was immediately greeted by a little dog, its tail wagging furiously as it jumped up on my legs to gain my attention. Maybe this was Carl, and I was about to become an animal fur artist. At least he was a small dog, so there wouldn't be too much fur to work with.

"Down, Franklin," Joane said, trying to nudge the dog away from me. "Let her at least get into the house." There was humor in Joane's voice, and I had a feeling Franklin's enthusiastic greeting was standard behavior for the little dog that looked to be some kind of miniature poodle mix with his curly, caramel-colored fur.

Though learning the dog's name did leave one very important, glaring mystery. Who was Carl? I hadn't seen any plants inside, and there weren't any other animals hanging around.

Deciding I could wait a few more moments to learn Carl's identity, I kicked off my shoes and knelt to give Franklin some attention.

"Aren't you a cutey!" He immediately rolled over to his back on the worn, yellowing linoleum, welcoming belly rubs. I gave Franklin some thorough attention before Joane opened the backdoor and ushered the dog outside to do his business.

"Little attention hog," she muttered affectionately under her breath. "I got him for Spencer when he was in high school to help him navigate the divorce. I always assumed he'd take Franklin with him when he bought a place. Well, Spencer now owns both a house and a bookstore and yet, I still have Franklin."

"Well, I'm glad you still have Franklin. I always need more dogs in my life," I said.

Even though he was significantly smaller, Franklin had me missing Hercules. I'd have to ask Avery to send me a photo when I sent her my all-clear text. Just as soon as I figured out who Carl was.

I pushed to my feet, taking a moment to soak in my surroundings. The entrance from the garage led straight into the kitchen. The room was dated, but clean, reminding me in many ways of my kitchen growing up. The walls were a cheerful blue, the cabinets an orangish brown. The appliances and countertops appeared to be the only things that had been updated with the appliances being stainless steel and the counters being stone, though even those had obviously seen some years.

As if reading my thoughts, Joane waved a hand around the room.

"Before our divorce, my ex-husband tried to update the kitchen in an effort to placate me and save our marriage. He got as far as new countertops and appliances before he realized two very important things. First," she held up a finger to underscore her point, "he hated home renovation and was not, despite the many remodeling shows he watched, cut out to be a handyman. And second," she held up another finger, "he'd rather divorce me than finish the renovation of my dreams. Instead of bringing us together, it just created more fights, including an argument about why on earth he'd buy and install new counters and appliances before painting, the idiot."

"Oh Joane, I'm so sorry!" I said, not really sure how to react to her bland, straightforward assessment of the end of her relationship.

She gave a carefree shrug. "I'm not. I got new appliances out of the whole thing and no longer have to live with the man. Not to mention, the settlement I got from the divorce gave me enough money to open Sugar and Sea Bakery."

She stopped next to the island, looking around the small space. "I probably should spruce the kitchen up a bit more, maybe slap a fresh coat of paint on the walls, but I spend most of my time in the bakery kitchen, which is much nicer and has all the bells and whistles this old lady could ask for."

I joined Joane at the counter, pulling out one of the stools situated there and sinking onto it.

"As long as it works for you, I don't see why you need to update it," I said, loving how, even though this was my first time in this kitchen, it somehow felt comfortable already.

"I like the way you think! But that's enough about me and my kitchen. It's time to give you a hobby," she said this with all the excitement of a daytime television host giving away cars.

"I didn't realize that was something you could just give someone," I said, humor lacing my voice as I watched her, curious to see what was going to happen next.

"Oh, you can. Trust me. Wash your hands and grab an apron," she waved to where some aprons hung on a hook on the wall. "I'm going to grab Carl."

I walked to the sink and turned on the water as Joane disappeared into what I could only assume was a walk-in pantry. Figuring we'd be doing something in the kitchen, I slipped Poppy's bracelet off my wrist and felt guilty over the instant relief at no longer having it pressed against my skin. I had promised the universe I'd wear the bracelet, but I was not a bracelet person. Maybe the next time Poppy wanted to help me with crystals, I'd request something more subtle and less distracting for a writer who was staring at her hands all day, like a simple pendant necklace or a keychain I could keep in my pocket.

"Joane," I called, as I scrubbed my hands, "you still haven't told me *who* Carl is."

I couldn't decide if the fact that we were going to be working in the kitchen was reassuring as I selected an apron from Joane's impressive collection. These aprons were not the tidy, branded pink aprons I'd come to associate with Sugar and Sea Bakery. Instead, they were a hodge podge of colors and styles that I instantly fell in love with, guessing each apron had a story. I picked a purple and white apron with pockets and frills that looked like it belonged in a Doris Day movie and slipped it on over my clothes.

"This," Joane said, as she stepped back into the kitchen holding a glass jar containing a bubbling, cream-colored sludge, "is Carl. He's the best sourdough starter in all of Oregon and the secret to my amazing baking."

Suddenly all of Joane's comments about Carl made sense, and a relieved giggle bubbled past my lips. I wasn't joining a cult today after all, though Joane was making some pretty serious assumptions about my baking ability if she was gifting me part of her prized sourdough starter.

I snapped a quick photo of the jar, sending it to Avery to assuage her worries before returning the phone to my pocket and giving Joane my full attention.

Joane set the jar on the counter, caressing it for a moment before turning to me with an eager grin. "I'm going to teach you how to use Carl. You're going to do sourdough!"

"Joane, that's so kind, but I can't! I only cook for survival. I've never made bread before, let alone sourdough," I said, thinking of my meal from the night before. "Noodles and jarred sauce is about as fancy as I get."

She waved away my concerns before washing her own hands and donning a frock apron made from cow-print fabric that had pink piping along the edges.

"You can absolutely do sourdough! I'm going to walk you through all the steps tonight so that you'll be ready to bake a loaf tomorrow. But don't worry, I already have dough going, so you'll be able to bake a loaf tonight too." She waved to a glass bowl that I hadn't noticed tucked away into a corner of the kitchen. "Sourdough takes time and patience, but there's nothing like making your own fresh sourdough bread. Also, working the dough can be therapeutic. I can't tell you the number of problems I've worked through while kneading Carl."

As she talked, Joane walked around the kitchen pulling out various gadgets and ingredients. Some of the items I'd never seen before, including a device that had rounded metal loops on the end of a wooden handle and some scraping tools.

"Since we're just making one loaf, I'll talk you through what I do when I'm baking at home. Now, do you know if your rental has a Danish dough whisk?" She brandished the tool with the rounded metal at me.

I shook my head.

"Don't worry, you can borrow my extra and I'll add it to the list of things you'll need to buy when you return to Utah." She declared, her eyes sparkling as she added the whisk to the pile of tools we'd supposedly be using as we worked. "Now get over here so we can start. Carl doesn't bite, I promise."

I stepped forward apprehensively, certain this was going to end in disaster, but at the same time recognizing it couldn't hurt anything. I'd tried just about everything to get my writing juices flowing again. Why not making sourdough?

CHAPTER 13
Mason

THERE WAS A MAJOR, gaping flaw in my master plan to befriend Dani. I had no way of accidentally running into her in town without someone blowing my cover.

I'd been all ready to casually run into her at the bakery or bookstore or grocery store. I probably could have even figured out a way to make the thrift store work, but when I'd spotted her through the window of Sugar and Sea, I'd realized there was no way for me to interact with Dani without Joane seeing me. And I knew better than to think Joane would help with my deception.

The struggle followed me home and continued to nag my thoughts as I talked to the internet company (who wouldn't be able to send anyone out until Wednesday) and as I attempted to work on Spencer's commission (which was a terrible idea when I was so distracted). The problem haunted me up until the moment my grandparents knocked on the door of the duplex before letting themselves in.

I'd lost track of the number of times I'd asked them not to walk in, though knocking was at least progress. And I couldn't get too frustrated with them. They did make it possible for me to live on the Oregon coast rent free. I just worried that if I wasn't able to start making a livable wage with my designing, my days on the Oregon coast were numbered, lasting only as long as my grandparents wanted to continue owning the duplex.

I was just grateful they had yet to walk in while I was entertaining any of my female guests. It was better for everyone that they hadn't met any of my tourist flings. Well, any of them except for one. I'd introduced them to Rebecca, before I knew better than to let a summer tourist into my life and heart. It was a mistake I wouldn't be repeating.

"What are you guys doing here?" I asked as I pushed up from the couch where I'd been aimlessly drawing shapes on my tablet, trying to find a solution to my Dani problem.

I hurried to grab Grandma's arm to help her to a seat. Grandpa shuffled in behind her. They both wore blue shirts and matching smiles. The fact that my grandparents wore matching outfits most days had been a source of much entertainment for me and my brother Grey throughout most of our childhood. I'd have to see if I could sneak a picture to send to him before they left. I'd also point out that their white hair was starting to look more and more similar, Grandma's hair seeming to get shorter every time I saw her.

Grandma pulled me into a brief, surprisingly firm hug before releasing me and settling onto the couch. She'd fallen a few days ago, giving us all a scare, though she claimed to be fine despite a slight limp. Grandpa assured me he was watching her like a hawk and had promised to call me if anything else happened, but I still worried. Grandma's fall had brought home the fact that my grandparents were getting older in a way I wasn't fully prepared to grapple with.

What would I do when they were no longer here, stopping in without warning and cheering on my art?

"You cut your hair," Grandma said, giving me a cheeky smile that reassured me she was fine in ways her words never could. "It's about time you listened to me."

"You finally wore me down," I said with a wink, sitting in the armchair across from her. Grandpa settled next to Grandma on the couch, interlacing his gnarled fingers with hers.

My grandparents were the picture of everything a couple should be. Not that I had plans to settle down, but if I ever did, I wanted my relationship to look just like theirs when I was old and gray. It was how I imagined my parents would have been had my dad survived long enough to reach old age, instead of being stolen from our family by an unexpected heart attack.

"What brings you out this way?" I asked, one of my knees bouncing as I waited for their response. While they occasionally stopped by without a reason, more often than not, they came for a specific errand: telling me about the renovations they wanted to do next door, discussing changes to the landscape schedule, dropping off the world's ugliest chair to add to my living room because it fit the aesthetic.

I was currently sitting in said chair and, while the plaid pattern was genuinely one of the worst design decisions I'd ever seen, it was unexpectedly comfortable.

"Can't we just stop in and say hello?" Grandma asked as Grandpa released her hand and leaned forward in what I'd come to identify as his "business" position.

"You're always welcome to stop by," I said, the tempo of my leg increasing as I waited.

"Well, since you brought it up, we just wanted to check to make sure you had everything handled with the current tenant. Where she's staying long-term, we know it's a different scenario and requires a bit more from you than what we've asked for in the past." Grandpa's voice was gruff and serious. Though he'd never say it, I could hear in his tone his doubt in my ability to be responsible enough to keep a guest happy for several weeks as compared to the usual guests who typically only stayed for a week at most.

"I've got it handled, Gramps, I promise," I said, forcing my leg to still as I smiled and did my best to convey calm control. Sometimes I wondered if Grandpa still saw the little kid I used to be when he looked at me, instead of the grown man who was making his way in the world. Or at least trying to.

"Oh, we know you do," Grandma said with a wave of her arm. "But we also know that sometimes it's nice to have additional help and support. You know, your grandpa and I ran this place together. Doing it alone is a lot." She arched an eyebrow, and I read her not so subtle message loud and clear.

They'd feel better about me running things if I had a significant other to help, someone to add what my grandma regularly referred to as a "woman's touch."

"I'm not interested in dating seriously, Grandma," I said, hoping to nip this direction of conversation in the bud before it got out of control.

"I know you say that, but I can't help but wonder. Grey's so happy now that he's got Audrey, and I know there's someone great out there for you. You can't let what Rebecca did—"

"Grandma," I said, cutting her off before she could wander too far down memory lane. Those memories were better left forgotten and ignored, not rehashed and unleashing the loneliness and self-doubt they triggered. "I'm working on my art. I don't have time for a relationship."

"There's always time for a relationship," she muttered under her breath, crossing her arms over her chest.

Grandpa stood, walking over to me and placing a reassuring hand on my shoulder, clearly understanding me better than I realized.

"Your art is important and we're so proud of you for all you've been able to do so far. It would just be a shame if you let what happened in your past keep you from chasing happiness in your future."

"I'll keep that in mind," I said, as I placed a hand over his.

He gave my shoulder a squeeze before shuffling back over to the couch.

"Anyway, tell us about this internet issue? Anything we can do to get it fixed faster?"

Thankful for the change in topic, I quickly jumped into an explanation, realizing as I did that I still needed to write Dani a sticky note letting her know the repair would happen in a couple of days. My stomach dipped at the thought of interacting with Dani again. I really needed to figure out a way to see her again as Allen. My non-romantic future depended on it.

CHAPTER 14
Dani

DRIVING HOME WITH MY unbaked loaf of bread and my own sourdough starter, I felt an odd sizzle of excitement in my stomach. I'd never thought about myself as a sourdough person, but as Joane had talked me through the different steps, I couldn't help but picture myself as a sourdough expert. If nothing else, the kneading of the dough would prove therapeutic whenever I was dealing with writing frustrations, which meant I'd be making sourdough daily at the rate I was going.

I'd have to pick up some bread flour and sea salt at the store. By the time we had finished up, it was late enough that I just wanted to get home and make dinner, though I'd be able to pop the loaf Joane had given me into the oven to go with whatever I decided to make. She had lent me all the tools I'd need to make sourdough while I was here in Oregon, but I'd need to purchase my own ceramic Dutch oven and Danish dough whisk when I got back to Utah, assuming I could keep my starter alive until I left.

When she'd handed me the jar with my very own piece of Carl, Joane had told me I'd have to name my starter, and that Carl Jr. was not an acceptable option. After some pondering, I'd landed on the perfect, eyeroll-worthy name. Avery would hate it, making it even more perfect: Dough-ris Day, after my favorite actress. I couldn't help but think Doris would be pleased to be immortalized this way. Maybe.

My afternoon of sourdough making had had another unexpected side-effect. As we'd worked, I'd started to get ideas for my novel. It wasn't a full outline yet, but I at least knew the next scene I needed to write. I'd even brainstormed a few possibilities with Joane, and she was very much onboard for the direction I was taking Hypatia and Petros's story, even if it was a complete surprise for everyone involved, myself included. My fingers itched to pull out my laptop and get started, as soon as I had the sourdough in the oven.

As I turned the corner to access the duplex, I muttered a curse under my breath. A black car currently occupied the center of the driveway. I wasn't sure which lady friend this car belonged to, but it wasn't the same car I'd seen Tiffany or Veronica drive.

Should I be concerned I remembered the names of Mason's flings I'd met so far? Or should I be more worried that it looked like there was a third woman in the mix? Also, did these women know about the existence of the others?

I parked my car on the side of the road, trying to determine my next course of action as I grumbled to myself about player neighbors. Maybe I should say something about it to the owners. I could only imagine how many times Mason's dalliances had impacted their other renters. They really had a right to know, as it could be impacting their online reviews and income.

I had the garage door opener for my side of the duplex clipped to my sun visor, so I could get inside. I'd just have to balance all of the sourdough supplies Joane had given me or make multiple trips. The other option was to knock on my neighbor's door and ask his guest to move their vehicle. While I was frustrated with the continued battle for the driveway, I couldn't quite bring myself to knock. Maybe I'd write another sticky note.

Walking around to the passenger side of the car, I stooped down, slipping the strap of the reusable shopping bag Joane had lent me over one shoulder, careful to keep the sourdough starter inside from knocking into the other tools and supplies Joane had given me to keep Dough-ris Day happy and thriving.

I scooped up the ceramic Dutch oven containing the unbaked loaf of bread and straightened from the car, using my hip to close the door. The pot in my arms quickly grew heavy and awkward as I headed up the driveaway. The clouds that had moved in this afternoon decided that moment was the perfect chance to unleash a cool drizzle, the rain making me shiver as I did my best not to drop my treasures.

I was nearly to the garage door when I realized I'd made a critical error. I'd forgotten to open the garage door while I was still in the car.

Muttering under my breath, I set the ceramic Dutch oven on the ground next to the garage, hoping the cold and wet wouldn't ruin the bread inside. Yes, the pot had a lid, but I didn't know how waterproof it was, and I'd heard all kinds of horror stories from friends about how temperamental sourdough could be. Had I just ruined the loaf inside because Mason exclusively made friends with people who only parked in the middle of driveways?

It took a couple of tries to get the garage door panel to accept my code. I had just begun to doubt if I had the right numbers when it finally decided to cooperate, slowly opening the door with a gentle whir of machinery.

As I waited, I heard the door of Mason's unit open, followed by voices.

"No, don't follow us out, Mason. It's raining and we'd hate for you to get wet." The voice of an elderly man called before the door closed, presumably with Mason inside.

So, he wasn't entertaining yet another lady friend. That was a surprising change. And knowing the garage was blocked by who I assumed to be the elderly couple that owned this place, my righteous indignation deflated some. Maybe I couldn't blame Mason for every inconvenience I'd experienced since arriving. Just most of them.

Wishing the garage door would open faster so I could slip inside my side of the duplex before I had to meet someone else, I bent down to pick up the ceramic Dutch oven. As I straightened, I saw an elderly couple shuffling their way to the car in the driveway. The woman seemed to be struggling to walk, so the man had her arm looped through his and was helping steady her. They both had white hair and were wearing matching blue collared shirts, though the woman's had small flowers on it.

The man looked up to see me and I gave a small wave around the pot in my arms, wanting to be friendly without encouraging conversation. I just wanted to get inside where it was dry and warm.

Apparently, my wave had been too enthusiastic because the couple changed directions, walking toward me and stopping just inside the garage out of the rain.

"Well, hello! You must be Danielle. We were hoping to meet you when we visited, but no one answered when we knocked earlier," the woman said, her steady voice contrasting with her physical appearance as she leaned heavily on the man who I assumed was her husband.

I wanted to rush her inside and offer her a seat, something that battled with my desire to be left alone so I could make dinner and get back to writing before my inspiration disappeared.

"Hi! Yes, I'm Danielle, well most people call me Dani." I tried to offer my hand to shake but recognized the awkwardness of the gesture with the heavy pot in my arms and returned my hand to holding the pot more securely.

"We're James and Carol Miller, the owners of this place. Sorry we haven't been able to meet you before now. My hip has been acting up with all this rain." The woman gave me a friendly smile, which emphasized the lines filling her face, hinting at a life well lived that included a fair amount of time outside in the elements.

"That and the fall you took while gardening didn't help things," the man said, earning a swat on his arm from his wife.

"It's so nice to meet you," I said. "The duplex is lovely."

Maybe this was my chance to share some of my concerns regarding Mason's social life, though that feedback felt more like something to share in an email and not face-to-face with his grandparents.

"That's what we like to hear," James said, waving at the house behind me. "We bought this place on a whim and haven't regretted it for a minute. We've gotten to meet so many interesting people because of it."

"And it's kept Mason in the area. It's so nice to have at least one of our grandsons close. Grey insists on living in Utah, though I'm so glad he met Audrey. She seems absolutely wonderful."

I nodded, trying to follow their conversation without dropping anything in my arms, even as the Dutch oven grew heavier with each passing moment.

"If we could just find a nice girl for Mason," Carol said, her voice filled with exasperation, "it might encourage him to actually put down roots."

"Now Carol, Dani doesn't want to hear about our woes," James said, patting her hand and starting to steer her to the car.

"Of course not. Where are my manners? It looks like you're in the middle of a project and we won't keep you. Just wanted to say hi and to let you know if you need anything, don't hesitate to ask Mason. He's done an amazing job managing this place. We'd be lost without him."

I forced a smile and mumbled something unintelligible, hoping they'd take it as agreement. I really needed to get inside before I dropped something.

"Oh," Carol said, pausing in her steps and turning to look at me. "I know Mason said something about updating you, but we're so sorry about the whole internet and Scooter cutting the cord issue. I'm so glad the company will be out Wednesday to fix things."

"That's good to know. I hadn't heard from Mason about that," I said, trying not to wince as I considered staying here for two more days without any connection to the outside world. Given my writing goals, that might be an issue. Though it could also lead to some crazy productivity without the "Cheaper Than Therapy" thread to distract me.

"We'll discount your final bill for the inconvenience. We're so grateful for your understanding," Carol said as James patiently waited for her to stop speaking so he could finish helping her to the car.

I exchanged goodbyes with the Millers, making sure they got into their car okay before I entered the house, the ceramic Dutch oven heavy in my arms. I gratefully deposited everything on the counter, shaking my arms out in relief. As I started the oven preheating and got the rest of the sourdough supplies put away, I couldn't help but wonder how my flirt of a neighbor could have come from such nice grandparents.

CHAPTER 15
Mason

WAS I PROUD OF myself in this exact moment? Absolutely not. But was that going to change my current behavior? Once again, absolutely not.

After my grandparent's kindly meant lectures about finding a nice girl and settling down, I'd stayed up far too late working on design projects and concept book covers. My grandparents were my greatest supporters and, while they couldn't quite wrap their heads around making a living off of digital art, they still supported me wholeheartedly. Despite that, though, I could see the worry they tried to hide, etched into the corners of their eyes. Which was why they often gave me kind, unsolicited advice whenever they visited, most of it related to my dating life and their worry about me being alone.

I knew they meant well and that they weren't about to kick me out of my home, but I also knew they worried about what would happen to me when they were gone and I no longer had their generosity to help me. And while I'd like to think my mom and her siblings wouldn't sell the duplex immediately after my grandparents' passing, there was no way my family would want to take on the upkeep with no one else living close.

At times my grandparents were almost as bad as my mother, though they always seemed to sense when they were about to push too hard and would back off. My mother, who'd battled severe anxiety and depression since my father's passing, had no such radar and would push and push until she drove us both insane. There was a reason I lived two states away from her. I could only handle so much before I'd snap.

Despite the late-night work session, I was up early the next morning ready to facilitate a second run in with Dani. I'd realized sometime during my work haze that all the drawing, sketching, and concept art for book covers wouldn't do me any good if I couldn't further my connection with Dani *soon*. Which meant I needed to see her again today.

So now I sat at my window, covertly watching to see if I could catch Dani leaving for the day. I didn't plan to follow her, that would be creepy. However, I hoped her new best friend, Joane, would be able to give me ideas of where Dani might be headed for the day. Assuming she went exploring somewhere instead of staying cooped up all day writing.

Pulling out my phone, I checked the time. It was a little before seven but I knew Joane would be awake, baking pastries and getting ready for the breakfast rush. If I texted her, would she be willing to tell me Dani's plans? I could say I needed to get in contact with her regarding something about the duplex, and she wasn't answering my messages. Though that seemed to veer a little too far into the creepy realm. Also, Joane would ask why I didn't just knock on Dani's door. Like a sane human who hadn't offended her at our first meeting and then proceeded to lie to her at our second.

Deciding it couldn't hurt, I texted Joane, hoping she'd help but knowing it was a long shot.

Given my behavior with Dani over the last few days, I was starting to wonder if I was actually good with the ladies or if they simply took pity on me. Currently I felt like I was writing the book *How Not to Get the Girl: Ten Simple Steps to Ensuring You Mess Up Every Single Time*. Not that I was pursuing Dani for romantic reasons, but still, the concept of "don't lie to her" seemed pretty standard across the board.

I settled in to wait, trying to focus on a sketch on my tablet when really all I wanted to do was pace, channeling my anxious energy into some form of motion. I'd forgone my morning workout for fear that I'd miss my chance to see Dani today, but I was already getting twitchy, wanting to do something to work my muscles and help me clear my head.

A little after seven, I could hear her garage door open. After a moment, her car pulled into the driveway and out onto the road.

I debated what to do. By the time I got in my car, she would be long gone, and I wouldn't have any hope of finding her. I wasn't about to drive around town trying to spot her car. I did have limits. Also, I wasn't trying to stalk or terrorize her. I just wanted to fast-track our friendship into a working relationship. Which really didn't sound all that much better, but there wasn't much I could do about it now. My grandparents' words from the night before about how nice it was to see Grey secure and settled rang through my mind.

I loved my brother but sometimes I felt like I would love him more if he wasn't the poster child of responsibility that my grandparents and mom always compared me to.

As if sensing my inner turmoil, Joane responded to my text.

Joane:

> Why should I tell you where she's headed? I know what you do with that smile, and I'm not empowering you to unleash that weapon on Dani.

Thinking quickly, I responded.

Mason:

> Her garage door opener broke, and I need to get her a replacement, but she's not responding to my texts.

Hopefully Joane would forgive me the little white lie, eventually.

Joane:

> Sounds awfully convenient.

> Mason:
>
> I promise, I'm not trying to play my usual games. I really just need to talk to her.

> Joane:
>
> Why don't you go knock on her door? You do live next door after all.

> Mason:
>
> She's already left for the day, and I'd hate for her to get locked out if I'm not here when she gets back.

If the truth was mixed with a lie, did it make it any less of the truth? I really was headed down a slippery slope. Hopefully, Joane didn't bring up the garage door opener with Dani the next time she saw her, or I'd be in even more trouble.

> Joane:
>
> Fine. I believe she was going to the beach. I recommended a couple of options. Not sure which one she picked, but all the ones I suggested were north of town.

Beaches north of town was a broad list to work with, but it at least gave me a starting point. Grabbing my keys, phone, and water bottle, I headed to the garage where I slipped on a pair of tennis shoes I kept specifically on hand for walking on the beach. I shot a quick *thank you* text to Joane and climbed into my car.

I paused as the garage door opened, wondering if I was making a mistake. But then the comparisons to Grey and my grandparents' worries about my future came flooding back. I reversed out of the garage and pulled onto the road as I pushed any hesitations aside. I was going to build a successful career, no matter what, and I needed Dani's help and connections to make it happen.

CHAPTER 16
Dani

I WOKE EARLY, POTENTIAL story lines a jumble in my head. I'd attempted to write again after the sourdough therapy session and meeting my
landlords, but hadn't found much success. Instead, I'd had a series of
dreams where Hypatia turned Petros into a loaf of bread. Not exactly the
riveting sequel to a romantasy novel Avery was looking for but maybe it
would get traction for its unique, groundbreaking approach?

Yesterday before leaving her house, I'd asked Joane for recommenda-
tions of beaches in the area and this morning I planned to check one of
them out. I couldn't believe it had taken me two days since arriving to
find beach time. What was the point of a trip to the Oregon coast if I
didn't actually visit the coast? It was a travesty that needed to be remedied
immediately.

As I drove, I tried to remember Joane's directions, following a winding
road past restaurants and old houses until the trees cleared and the view
of the ocean caught my attention. It wasn't the spot I was looking for,
but the cliffside overlook was too tempting to ignore.

I found a place to safely pull over and observe the blues and whites
of the ocean waves as they crashed onto the shore, the sound making
the tension melt from my shoulders. Breathing in the sea air was the
most relaxed I had felt since I submitted my final draft of *Of Curses and
Pomegranates* over a year ago.

I took in the initial sensations of being near the ocean before register-
ing the rest of my surroundings. I was standing on an overlook perched

on a cliff above the beach. There wasn't an easy way down to the shore, but up here there was a bench, which could be a promising location to write. I wouldn't be able to dig my toes into the sand, but I would be able to write to the soothing sounds of waves punctuated by the occasional passing car without fear of sand or water ruining my laptop. I also couldn't imagine the random bench on the side of the road being a happening place, except maybe during sunset. From its perch on the cliff, this bench would offer the perfect view of the vibrant hues I was sure filled the sky most evenings over the Pacific Ocean.

I turned to head back to my car to snag my laptop, which I'd stashed in a bag in the trunk, when another car stopped near me, a family spilling out and exclaiming over the view.

Then again, maybe the spot was too visible and too close to the road. While I wasn't looking for a perfectly silent place to work, I'd prefer one that didn't include a small child screaming about how they wanted ice cream at full volume in my ear.

I quickly retreated to my car, determined to find the beach access Joane had recommended. Fingers crossed it came with a beautiful view and a bit more space between me and any other tourist who might also be visiting the beach.

Ten minutes later, I pulled into a nearly full parking lot, managing to snag one of the few remaining spots. While it was still early, it looked like I wasn't the only one who had attempted to beat the crowds. The beach goers at this time of day looked to be of the more active variety wearing sports bras, spandex shorts, and tennis shoes. I could see several figures running on the sand, dogs in tow.

I debated finding a spot to set up writing, but their movement looked inviting. Maybe a workout would jog a few more ideas loose, no pun intended.

Deciding to join the many runners at a more sedate pace, I grabbed my headphones, put my phone and keys in my pocket, and made my way to the beach. Once I hit the sand, I slipped off my sandals, eager to feel the sand between my toes. This would be more of a leisurely walk than a workout. But in my book, exercise was exercise, even if my pace didn't exactly raise my heartrate.

I started off in one direction, walking on the damp sand close enough to the water for the occasional wave to run over my toes without risking the water soaking the bottom of my leggings. The cool temperature was pleasant while still making my breath catch in surprise. As I carefully picked my way along the shore, I scanned the ground, keeping an eye out for interesting seashells or rocks.

After a moment of listening to the waves, I stuck in one of my earbuds and turned on the audiobook I'd started on the plane. I quickly became immersed in the story and my search for beach treasures. I only picked up a couple of shells and rocks here or there, recognizing that I would be here for a while and didn't exactly have the desire or luggage space to bring home an extensive seashell collection. However, I wouldn't mind bringing home a few to remind me of this trip and my time on the coast. I also wouldn't mind placing a few in the kitchen windowsill of my rental, bringing in a reminder of the beach to add a small personal touch to the bright space.

I was so absorbed in my book and the romantic scene that was building between the two main characters that I didn't hear someone approaching until he'd fallen into step beside me.

"Fancy meeting you here," a deep familiar voice said.

I gave a small shriek, throwing my hands up in the air and launching any seashells I'd been holding at my potential attacker, though I somehow managed to hold onto my shoes.

A heart-stopping chuckle and sounds of protest followed the kneejerk reaction and I looked up to find Allen standing next to me, his hands attempting to shield his face from my unintentional projectiles.

"I come in peace," he said, taking a step back from me.

"Allen! I'm so sorry." I quickly took out my earbud and slipped it back into its case.

I attempted to brush off the sand I'd flung his way along with the seashells and rocks. I could feel the heat in my cheeks as I tried to help, running my hands down his arms and chest to chase away the specs of sand I could see dotting his dark t-shirt. I was mortified, though not so much that I couldn't appreciate the well-defined muscles I felt under his shirt as I worked to rid him of any evidence of my freak out.

So much for my carefully cultivated seashell collection or for impressing Allen the next time I saw him. Now the shells were scattered back onto the beach, likely broken, just like my pride.

I'd have to remember this exchange for the autobiography I'd be writing someday: *How Not to Woo a Man and Other Life Advice from Danielle Baldwin.*

"I'm fine, I promise," Allen said, stepping out of my reach and holding up a hand to stop any further assistance I might have offered. "Note to self, don't sneak up on Dani."

I bit my lip and ducked my head.

"It's a lesson most people in my family have had to learn the hard way. My cousin Chloe still teases me about the time I spilled an entire pitcher of lemonade on her in high school when she snuck up behind me at a family party." Chloe had been wet and sticky, and I still cringed when I thought of the photo our cousin Kaden had captured of Chloe's outrage in the moment, splashing it all over social media because Kaden was legitimately the worst.

"Noted. Do you mind if I join you? I don't want to interrupt whatever you were listening to."

Now I really was blushing. Even though my books had a lower heat level, I did occasionally listen to books with more spice than I was comfortable writing, and I'd definitely reached a steamy moment in my book.

"You're—" My voice cracked, and I quickly cleared my throat, hoping my expression didn't reveal the full scope of my embarrassment. "You're welcome to join me. I was just listening to an audiobook."

"Really? What book? I've always wondered what authors read." He fell into step beside me as we started walking, his face full of interest.

"Oh, you know, nothing too special. I like fantasy, young adult, romance." I gestured vaguely, trying for nonchalance while also trying to decide how quickly I could change the topic without coming across as a complete weirdo.

"You okay? You seem tense." Allen's forehead creased in concern, and I felt the unexplainable urge to reach over and smooth away the wrinkles, much like I'd written Hypatia doing in the bookstore scene with Petros from the day before.

"I'm just having a hard time relaxing and letting go of my embarrassment. You know, the usual." I tried to brush away my tension, but I think he could tell it was lingering because he grabbed my arm and pulled me to a stop next to him before releasing me. I registered the gentle warmth of his hand, wishing he would have held onto my arm just a little longer. It had felt nice.

"Let's try this again. I'm going to walk ten steps that way," he waved back the way we'd come, "and come running past you again. Except this time, you'll know I'm coming."

"But I'll still have embarrassed myself epically in front of you. Maybe we just need to walk in different directions and try having this second meeting another time." It wasn't what I wanted, but it seemed like the safest option and the only way to maybe rescue a few fragments of my pride and self-confidence.

"Not in this version of the story. No, in this version you'll spot me running toward you all confident and athletic and you won't be startled, instead you'll acknowledge me with the perfect level of enthusiasm for

a recent acquaintance and we'll have a lovely conversation. Deal?"
Allen held out a hand to shake.

I shook my head. "I'm not sure this is going to work. I'll still know
what happened."

Allen held his hand out toward me even more persistently. "You're
a writer. You believe in editing. So let's edit this meeting into what
we want it to be."

Deciding I had nothing to lose, I gave his hand a quick shake
before essentially sprinting off further down the beach. I knew he
said he'd be the one running, but I could use a moment to gather
my thoughts and try to make the pink fade from my cheeks. I could
write romance with the best of them, but living it was not my forte.
Not that this encounter was necessarily romance. I mean, it could
be. It could also be a really nice guy persistently trying to become
my friend. I'd have to ask the cousins for their opinions later.

After a few more steps down the beach, I felt the tight ball of
anxiety in my stomach ease. I had just begun wondering if Allen was
really going to run past again or if he'd decided to give up on me
when I heard footsteps approaching at a steady pace. Looking over,
I spotted Allen running my way, a smile on his face.

I knew this exchange was planned, but no one should be smiling
that broadly while running. However, I wouldn't protest the view
of him running up to me in his shorts and worn t-shirt. His bright
orange running shoes and confident gait made me think he wasn't
a stranger to exercising on the beach, even if he only visited his
grandparents a couple of times a year. The man was fine, and I
was not above enjoying the view: muscles, short brown hair, and
laughing golden-brown eyes that seemed to drink me in.

Allen slowed as he approached me and, while I did feel some heat
in my cheeks, it was not nearly to the extreme level of embarrassment

from earlier. This was a different sensation, more the heat of interest than mortification.

"Fancy meeting you here," he said, repeating his greeting from earlier, except this time I didn't hurl anything his direction. Progress to be sure. His breathing was slightly labored as he fell into step next to me.

"Well, hello," I said, doing my best to hide the excitement in my voice. I had been kicking myself for not giving him my number after our bookstore run-in and was grateful for the second, well third, chance.

As if reading my mind, Allen gave me a knowing look. "So, do random beach run-ins count as second meetings?"

He really was making this a complete redo, something I was surprisingly grateful for.

"Maybe. That depends," I said, hedging a bit. I reached up to tuck an escaped strand of hair behind my ear, only for the wind to chase it loose again.

"On?" He asked, raising an eyebrow as he waited for my response.

"On if you prove yourself to be a worthy conversationalist on our walk," I said, feeling bold. I didn't need to ask the cousins. Allen was clearly interested, so why not take advantage? If we really were editing our second exchange, I was going to edit it into what I wanted. I knew the power of a good edit to strengthening a story and I was going to make the most of it.

"Is that your way of inviting me to join your walk?" Humor laced his tone.

I had nothing to lose, so I put all my cards on the table. "Absolutely. We've crossed paths twice now. I'd like to see if there's a third interaction in our future."

"In that case, I'd love to join your walk. I was getting tired of running anyway." He gave a casual shrug, hardly the gesture I would have made after running for any period of time, but he seemed unfazed by the effort.

"How far did you go? I mean, before..." I trailed off at his raised eyebrow. He'd promised me an edit.

Squaring my shoulders, I tried again, this time with confidence and curiosity.

"How far did you run?"

The man beside me clearly worked out regularly and I couldn't help but wonder what a normal morning run looked like for him. Not that I minded. I was more than happy to appreciate the effects of his efforts.

He glanced down at his smart watch, fiddling with the dials for a moment. "Well, you know, a good distance."

If I wasn't mistaken, his cheeks flooded with a bit of color, and it wasn't from physical exertion. Interesting.

"And what does a 'good distance' look like for you?" I braced myself, ready to hear some crazy number of miles. A physique like his didn't happen by accident and often involved more hours in the gym than I cared to count.

"Like half," he said, hedging, his facial expression carefully neutral.

"Half of what? A 5k, 10k, marathon?" If this man had run over ten miles already this morning, he was most definitely out of my league, edit or no edit. Also, he was surprisingly not sweaty, even if the morning was cool.

"Half... a mile."

I stopped abruptly, grabbing his arm so he'd stop with me.

"I'm sorry. You've only run half a mile? And here I was ready for some epic double-digit number." I couldn't help but laugh after I'd built up his answer so much in my head.

"Hey now, I had just started my workout when I ran into you," he said, crossing his arms over his chest. "I still have time today to get more exercise in. Unless you had other plans for the day you're hoping for me to be a part of." He quirked an eyebrow at me. It was a very expressive, attractive eyebrow and I wanted to reach over and trace its outline with my finger.

"Well don't let me hold you back. I'd hate to keep you from reaching your mile goal." I jokingly waved in front of us at the open expanse of sand, holding my breath to see if he would call my bluff or if he was as interested in me as I was in him.

He hesitated a moment before grinning at me. "Can I tell you a secret?"

I bit my lip and nodded.

"I was parking my car when I saw you start walking down the beach, so I locked up and ran after you. I couldn't miss my shot at a second meeting, even if it meant I wasn't going to get my full workout today." The smile that man threw my way could end wars. He was that level of pretty, which was probably why I was starting to picture Allen Bradley whenever I attempted to write Petros, even if the character had always had darker hair and green eyes in my head before now.

Did Hypatia and Petros need to have a beach scene? I mean, it would probably devolve into an epic battle with some demigods, but I could build in some incredible chemistry and a few moments for them to check each other out. Possibilities began to fill my mind, and I wanted to race back to the car for my laptop.

Shaking my head, I forced myself to focus on the conversation in front of me. The ideas would hold, I hoped.

"I appreciate your sacrifice," I said, trying to hide my delight at his comment as butterflies danced in my stomach. "Hopefully the conversation proves worth it."

"I'm positive it will." Allen's expression was warm and full of interest. I quickly turned away in an effort to hide the sudden heat in my cheeks.

I spotted an interesting shell and bent down to examine it to give myself a chance to regain my composure. This man was doing funny things to my emotions, and I wasn't completely sure how to navigate it.

"Do you frequently run on the beach?" I asked, determined to lead the topic somewhere other than my interest in him.

I straightened to keep walking, leaving the shell in the sand.

"Since I arrived here, almost every day, weather permitting. Back home in Idaho, beach runs are a bit more difficult," he said with clear humor in his voice. I'd forgotten he wasn't a local. He just seemed so at home here that it was hard to picture him living anywhere else, like the college town in Idaho he'd referenced in our conversation two days earlier.

"I've heard Idaho has some beautiful lakes and rivers. Do you ever run on those beaches?"

I didn't know why I was continuing with this line of conversation. I hated running, but for some reason my brain couldn't think of another topic to talk about. All thoughts in my head were currently limited to running and beaches and running on beaches. There was also a very nice image in my head of what this man looked like while running on a beach. If I asked him to run a bit in front of me so I could experience him running from all directions and angles, would that be weird? It would be for research, obviously. I needed some reference images for writing Petros running on the beach accurately, at least that was the story I was telling myself.

Allen gave a small shrug, tucking his hands into his pants pockets. "I'm sure there are some lake beaches that would be worth running on, but not where I live."

I nodded, at a complete loss for what to say next. I made a living with words and somehow, they'd all deserted me in this moment.

"Are you into running?" Allen asked the only logical next question after my fascination with his running habits.

I vigorously shook my head, sending the hair that had escaped my ponytail flying.

"I don't run. If you see me running, you should be concerned because something's chasing me, and I have no qualms about tripping others in order to aid my escape," I said, completely serious.

"Noted," Allen said with a sage nod as we continued to pick our way up the beach. "But for that to work, you'd have to run faster than me which, given how infrequently you run, I doubt you can."

"You'd be amazed at what I can do with proper motivation."

"I'm not scared."

"Maybe you should be because if I'm getting chased by a chainsaw wielding clown, you're going down." Nice, Dani. Impress the man with your willingness to sacrifice him to a horror movie monster.

"That is one very specific scenario. Do you spend much time pondering things that would motivate you to run? Most people keep initial conversations light with invitations to try the world's best chocolate-filled donut or something. You went straight for the darkest option: murder by creepy circus person."

"Most people aren't published authors who make their living imagining worst case scenarios to inflict upon their characters." I wished that observation wasn't so true but there was a reason Hercules was literally the biggest dog I could reasonably own while living in a townhouse. He was my protector when my imagination got the best of me and I became convinced weird sounds were intruders trying to kidnap me. Forget that Hercules was a bit of a chicken. Potential intruders didn't know that.

Our conversation continued as we wandered a bit further before deciding it was time to turn back. I had a novel to write and a sister who would start texting me in a panic if I didn't message her soon with another progress update. She really needed a hobby or a man or something other than work to distract her from her breakup with Sir Dunce Cap.

Also, I probably needed to break this entire exchange down for the cousins for their full analysis.

When we reached my car, Allen lingered. I hoped he was as hesitant to see our morning together end as I was. It was the best edited second interaction I'd ever had with a guy, and I was hoping he'd ask for my number so we could have a repeat in the near future.

"I don't know about you, but I hate to the see the morning end," he said, leaning in close enough I caught a whiff of lumberjack and bakery again, but this time mixed with a hint of the sea.

"Unfortunately, I do have to get back to my responsibilities. You know, I have a deadline," I said, watching as his face fell at the pronouncement. "But," I hurried to tack on, "I could be persuaded to delay being responsible for the right reason."

CHAPTER 17
Mason

I WAS NOT PROUD about how my heart leapt at Dani's statement, even as my mind scrambled to come up with something to entice her to continue our morning together. I was genuinely having a great time, and I hadn't yet been able to broach my career, starting to hint at the possibility of designing her next cover or at least connecting with her publishing contacts to start my networking magic. I was extending our morning for professional reasons.

"Guess I better come up with something good then." I pursed my lips, pondering.

"Obviously. I can't put off writing for just any old excuse."

I wondered if she knew how much I liked the way she looked with one hip cocked, gazing up at me with challenge and expectation. I wanted to reach over and tuck an escaped strand of hair back behind her ear, letting my fingers linger on her skin.

I shook my head, reminding myself I had to focus. I was looking to connect with her for my career, nothing more. Yes, I wanted to woo her, but more than that I needed to impress her with my artistic ability. I was looking to build a friendship.

Which only worked if I could spend more time with her. While I'd been relieved to find her at the beach, our walk had been too short to really dig into careers and cover designing. I needed to think of something to extend our time together. I racked my brain, trying to think of all the touristy things the women I'd interacted with over the years had raved about.

"Do you like... cheese?" As the question came out, I realized too late it was a movie reference, when I'd genuinely meant the question. I was terrible at trying to be friends with women. I was much better equipped for low stakes, low commitment, flirty exchanges.

She snorted, propping her chin on her hand as she responded. "Why yes, I do. My favorite's gouda." She dropped her hand. "Well, actually I prefer Swiss cheese, but gouda's good too."

I grinned, glad she knew the movie quote. I wasn't ashamed to admit I was a chick flick fan; they'd taught me some of my best moves with women.

"While I appreciate your ability to quote *She's the Man*, I genuinely want to know if you like cheese. There's a local dairy nearby that does factory tours and the connected restaurant makes the best grilled cheese in the country."

She smacked my arm in excitement. "Seriously? Say less! I'm always down for good cheese. Let's go!"

She turned to climb into her car but hesitated before turning back to me.

"I should probably drive myself over, seeing as this is only our second time meeting and these are modern times and safety is important."

"All good points," I said, curious to see where she was going with this line of conversation but also feeling disappointed at the thought of not riding in the same car with her. While the cheese factory wasn't far away, the added drive time would be ideal for shifting our conversation to career-related topics.

"But also," she said, holding up a finger as if asking me to wait, "since we're going to the factory together, it doesn't make sense for us to drive separately. You know where we're going and, really, we should conserve gas and," she paused and took a deep breath before lowering her finger and turning the full force of her brown eyes on me, "I'd like to keep talking to you on the drive."

If that wasn't the greenest of greenlights, I didn't know what was. My mind was already racing, thinking through questions to ask and how to lead the conversation to something more career oriented. Maybe I could learn a bit more about her cover artist search and how that worked with her publisher. I wanted to pull up my website, show her some of my art, but seeing as it was tied to my real name, Mason Stuart, I'd have to remember to download some of my designs to my phone so I could show her my style when the time was right.

"In that case," I said, following her lead, "we probably should drive together. Would you be more comfortable driving with me giving directions or should I drive?" I'd prefer she drive so she wouldn't see my car and then get suspicious if she ever saw it at the duplex, but more importantly, I needed her to be comfortable.

She visibly relaxed as I gave her the choice. She scrunched her face for a moment, thinking before responding.

"I'll drive. That way if you do end up being a creep, I can just leave you at the cheese factory." She said this so matter-of-factly that I couldn't help but laugh.

"Sounds reasonable to me. Just let me grab my water from my car." I couldn't keep from grinning as I walked across the parking lot. Today was going even better than I could have imagined, and it was just getting started.

CHAPTER 18
Dani

"OH. MY. GOSH!" I moaned as I took a bite of the gooey, melty, cheesy goodness in front of me. Honestly, I should have probably been embarrassed by the sounds I was making, but I was too busy falling in love with a sandwich. After touring the cheese factory and reading about the care that went into making the cheese and other products the dairy offered at the different museum-like stations that filled the tour, I knew the food would be good, but I hadn't been prepared for this level of good. I could genuinely move to Oregon for the food alone.

Baked goods and cheese, what more did a girl need?

Of course, the man in front of me watching me eat like an uncivilized animal didn't hurt things either as he laughed and offered me a napkin.

I flushed and accepted the napkin to dab away a piece of cheese stuck to my chin. I also took the time to remind myself to calm down and eat like a proper lady, instead of like someone who'd never seen utensils before.

"I told you it was good," he said with a self-satisfied grin before biting into his own sandwich. "If you're ever in the area around dinner time, there's a restaurant down the street that makes deep-fried cheese curds with this cheese, and they are life changing."

I grabbed his arm, stopping him from taking another bite.

"Seriously? You can't tell me that and then not give me the name of the restaurant so we can plan a day to come back and try it."

It was only when Allen turned to raise one of his very dark, expressive eyebrows at me that I registered what I said. It was a good thing I wasn't trying to play cool or hard to get because I'd just blown that possibility right out of the water.

"Maybe I don't want to give you the restaurant name because it'll give me a reason to text you later, after I ask for your phone number."

Be still my beating heart! The man was smooth, I'd give him that much. Almost as smooth as the scoop of ice cream I'd be getting later once I was done eating this amazing sandwich.

A girl could live on dairy alone, right?

We ate in companionable quiet, both of us enjoying our food. I soaked in the setting with its high ceilings and feel of an upscale cafeteria. The restaurant part of the factory consisted of long tables with wood tops and walls of windows outlined by metal. It was a bright, open space perfect for the many tourists that clearly passed through regularly.

"What was your favorite part?" Allen asked. He finished his sandwich and wiped his fingers on a napkin, his attention trained on me. It was something I'd realized he was very good at on our drive when he'd asked me more about my job as a writer and the dynamics with my publisher. He was such a good listener that I hadn't felt even the least bit self-conscious as I rambled about the publishing process and how I'd ended up at Rose & Quill.

I swallowed my current bite before responding.

"You mean besides this sandwich?" I asked, holding up the last couple of bites that remained. I'd probably have to come back this way just for the sandwich. The factory was a good twenty-minute drive away from where I was staying, but definitely worth it, especially if I used it as bribery to get myself to write.

"Yes, besides the sandwich I'm worried you're going to start writing odes to."

I snorted a laugh. "I'm not that kind of writer. Poetry really isn't my thing; just ask my junior high English teacher." I still cringed thinking about the angsty words I'd penned at the time. "But if I can't say this sandwich was my favorite, then it was definitely the free samples on the tour. I'm going to have to buy some of that white cheddar when I get back to town. It was incredible!"

I'd nearly bought some when we reached the gift store at the end of the tour, but Allen had assured me the grocery stores in this area all carried this particular brand, so I didn't have to worry about the cheese getting warm and going bad while we lingered over lunch and drove back. So instead of cheese, I'd selected a magnet with the dairy's logo on it to take home with me as a token from one of the best days I'd had in a long time.

"I guess I should have seen that coming," Allen said, resting his elbows on the table and leaning toward me. "It's good to know the way to your heart just might be through your stomach."

"I mean, it's not *not* the way to my heart," I said with a shrug that I hoped came across carefree. In reality, my insides were dancing with excitement at the continued interest I saw on Allen's face. It appeared I hadn't scared him away yet, though he still hadn't asked for my number despite hinting at using it multiple times during the drive here and throughout the tour. What was he waiting for?

I finished my sandwich and Allen gathered our garbage, depositing the trash as we made our way past the ice cream counter.

"You still want a scoop?" Allen asked, pausing at the back of the line.

Even though I'd been dreaming of a scoop only moments before, the last couple bites of sandwich had left me feeling full and satisfied. "Unfortunately, I didn't leave room for dessert."

"Then I guess I'll have to bring you back for a scoop of ice cream in addition to those cheese curds," he said as he held the door for me and followed me outside.

The Oregon sun had shown up today, making it the warmest day of my trip so far. It wasn't hot by Utah standards, but I'd had to remove my sweatshirt, leaving me in a worn-out t-shirt with my college mascot on the chest. Not the most flattering attire in the world. I needed to reevaluate my wardrobe if I was going to keep spending time with Allen.

"Where to next?" Allen asked, turning to me with his hands down next to his sides. They seemed to be hanging in invitation.

And while I knew it was bold and he probably was just standing there, I decided to take a chance. Walking past him, I slipped my fingers in his and pulled him to the car, not releasing his hand when he started to follow. Instead, I held fast, enjoying the contact.

"How do you feel about wandering town? Maybe do some shopping?" I knew it wasn't exactly the kind of activity most men dreamed of, but hopefully Allen wouldn't mind.

"Sounds perfect."

CHAPTER 19
Mason

I SHOULD RELEASE DANI'S hand. Professional colleagues and friends did not hold hands. I should put distance between us, recenter this day on my actual goal: connecting with her publisher to further my career.

But even as the thoughts played through my mind, I pushed them away. I'd lost track of the last time I'd just held hands with a woman, no agenda, no expectations, just simple, casual contact. And it felt... nice.

I'd been surprised when her fingers intertwined with mine. She hadn't struck me as the bold type, yet the contact sent electricity zipping up my arm and sending my heart hammering as I caught a whiff of her strawberry shampoo as she tugged me toward a store that clearly catered to tourists.

"I need a new sweatshirt," Dani explained as she gestured to a few hoodies hanging in the window.

"Far be it from me to stand in the way of a woman and a new sweatshirt," I said, pulling open the door and waving her inside.

The bell over the door rang, signaling our entrance to whoever was working the small store. They were nowhere in sight initially, most likely working in the back or tucked in a corner somewhere restocking merchandise.

Dani led the way to a rack of pastel pink, blue, and green sweatshirts with the words *Dreaming of the Oregon Coast* emblazoned across the front. She released my hand as she thumbed through the options, her lips puckering and her face pinched in concentration. I instantly missed the contact and wanted to reach for her hand again, but I hesitated. I wasn't a hand holding kind of guy. It was one thing for Dani to reach out for me. It was something else entirely if I instigated things. I didn't want to send the wrong impression, though I had a feeling I was already doing that.

"I can't decide!" Dani exclaimed, throwing her hands up in frustration after a few minutes combing through multiple racks, feeling the different sweatshirts and commenting on their colors. "They're all so cute. But I don't need five new sweatshirts."

"Do you have a favorite color?" I asked, reaching forward to finger a green sweatshirt that would look good with her skin tone. I wanted to reach for my tablet, try my hand at capturing the colors and textures of this moment.

"Usually blue," she said, waving vaguely down at the blue t-shirt she was wearing, "but I own a *lot* of blue. Maybe I need to switch things up."

She bit her lip, considering her options a bit longer before pulling a yellow sweatshirt and a gray sweatshirt off the rack. The yellow one had a picture of a sunset on it while the gray one sported an image of bigfoot tromping through the woods.

"Which would you pick?"

"Oh no," I said, taking a small step back with a laugh. "I'm a graphic designer, not a fashion expert. I don't do clothing choices for anyone but me."

Dani lowered the two sweatshirt options, seeming to consider me for a moment. "I didn't know you were a graphic designer. You've been so busy asking about my career, I didn't realize I never asked you what you do."

I shrugged, trying for nonchalance now that the cat was out of the bag. This was my chance to start paving the way for conversations about cover designs and connecting with her publisher. And yet, I hesitated. Despite my initial plans in inviting her to the cheese factory, I didn't want today to devolve into shop talk. We'd spent most of the drive here talking about her job and I'd loved watching her light up as she talked about her passion. I wasn't ready to shift the focus to me just yet.

That thought went against my every motivation in getting to know Dani, a fact I chose to ignore for now.

"I was enjoying listening to you talking about the publishing world."

She clutched the two sweatshirts close, looking embarrassed as color crept into her cheeks.

"You must think I'm incredibly vain or terrible company. We've spent almost this whole day talking about me. And—"

"Hey," I took the sweatshirts from her, carefully returning them to the rack before grabbing both of her hands. "I've loved getting to know you, so much so that I agreed to spend the day shopping with you because I wanted to keep talking to you. Trust me, if I wasn't enjoying myself, I wouldn't be here."

"Promise?" She asked looking at me so intently I would have said almost anything to reassure her.

"Promise," I said, my thumb tracing over the bracelet on her wrist. Based on what I'd seen her wear, the colored stones didn't seem her style, and yet I found their smooth, cool texture almost soothing. "Now how about we go back to expanding your sweatshirt collection?"

"On one condition," she said, releasing one of my hands and turning back to one of the clothing racks, my other hand still clutched in hers. I didn't want her to let go.

"What's that?" I asked, curious to hear her stipulation. I liked to think I was an expert on women, but something about Dani kept me guessing.

"You tell me more about you. Your art and your family and your interests. I want to hear all about what makes Allen Bradley tick." The coy look she gave me over her shoulder sent my heart racing.

"I could do that," I said. This was exactly what I'd been hoping and working for, and I should be ecstatic that my plan was going so perfectly.

So why did my stomach twist with guilt as she gave me the perfect opening to talk about my career and my hope of designing book covers?

CHAPTER 20
Dani

THE NEXT MORNING, I woke with bleary eyes and a crick in my neck. After spending the afternoon shopping with Allen, I'd come home full of ideas. As I'd typed, the hours disappeared until the next thing I knew I was waking up on the couch wearing one of the new sweatshirts I'd purchased, a smile on my lips, and Poppy's bracelet digging into my arm, leaving little imprints that would probably take all day to fade. Yet, I didn't mind as the marks reminded me of hours spent holding Allen's hand, his fingers tracing over each stone and sending shivers of attraction up my arm.

Yesterday had been... unexpected.

I had no idea I could have so much fun with a man I'd only just met. Allen was kind, creative, flirty, and outgoing. He'd been endlessly patient with me as I dragged him through multiple thrift stores and tourist shops, looking for more clothes to get me through my time here in Oregon. He'd gone along with it, joining in the fun by trying on some of the crazier items we found, including a jean vest with patches that I was still sad he hadn't purchased. As we'd shopped, we'd held hands, making it clear we were there together, despite the many women who cast interested glances Allen's way.

He'd ignored them all, keeping his attention trained on me.

We'd swapped stories and laughed. I was still embarrassed when I thought about how long it took me to learn he was a graphic designer.

"You know, I've learned the value of a skilled graphic designer," I'd mused as we browsed the jewelry section of one thrift store where I'd spent far too much money.

"I like to think what I do is worth something," he'd said with a laugh, handing me a small bracelet with a heart-shaped pendant to examine.

I slipped the bracelet on my wrist, its delicate chain contrasting sharply with the bulk of the bracelet from Poppy. I took the bracelet off, talking myself out of purchasing any jewelry for now.

"I meant, I couldn't do what I do without incredible graphic de-signers who create covers and promotional graphics. I'd love to see your work some time," I'd said, handing back the bracelet.

"I'd love to show you."

Allen's fingers had wrapped around mine and given them a squeeze before accepting the bracelet and putting it back. And even though it was a perfectly average moment, I couldn't help but feel like something significant had passed between us, like we'd somehow taken a step forward in this undefined, only-just-beginning relationship of ours.

It left me wondering if Petros needed to take Hypatia thrifting. Or maybe he needed to forge her a bracelet from the depths of the underworld. Something a little more in alignment with their story and world.

As I'd dropped Allen off at his car in the beach parking lot, he'd paused and finally asked for my phone number.

I'd rattled it off quickly before remembering my reception prob-lem until the internet was fixed tomorrow, but Allen hadn't seemed worried. Instead, he'd saved my number and made plans to meet up in a couple of days for dinner. It had all felt so easy and simple and wonderful, and I couldn't wait to tell the cousin crew about it. Just as soon as I headed into town to find good coffee and cell reception.

And if cell reception also meant I might hear from Allen today, all the better.

I changed into another one of the sweatshirts I'd purchased the day before, a gray crewneck with a bigfoot graphic on it with the words, *Hide and Seek World Champion* emblazoned at the bottom. I threw my hair up into a bun, pulled on some joggers, and headed to my car. I whistled the entire way to Sugar and Sea, grinning like a fool. Maybe a change of scenery and the fresh sea air really were all I needed to get my creativity going again. Of course, an entire day with Allen Bradley hadn't hurt anything either. I had several thousand words to show for my writing session last night and the ideas were still coming. I'd only stopped writing because of exhaustion.

The bakery was busy when I arrived, so I got in line, pulling out my phone to play a bit of catch-up now that I had cell reception. I had several messages from the cousins but nothing from Allen. Reminding myself I'd been with him just yesterday, I pushed aside any feelings of disappointment. He'd text and, if not, I'd see him at dinner tomorrow.

Once I'd read and responded to all my missed messages, I popped a message into the "Cheaper Than Therapy" group chat, needing to share my good mood with someone:

Dani:

It's official. You all have to pause your lives to come to Oregon. Sadie, you would love the food! And Poppy, there are so many fun thrift stores.

Lucy:

Who are you and what have you done with Dani? Either there's something in the water in Oregon or you're doing more than just writing a love story there...

Chloe:

Lucy has a point. You're only this chipper when a hot guy is involved. Anything you wanna share? Is it your neighbor?

I snorted. If only Chloe knew just how different Allen and Mason were. Though, come to think of it, it had been at least forty-eight hours since Mason had done something to annoy me. He'd been surprisingly helpful with the whole internet situation.

Sadie:

> Food and thrift stores?? Someone is avoiding writing... and why are you so happy about two things you never want to do when you're home?? Answers. Now.

Avery:

> Sadie is right; your whole reason for going to Oregon was to WRITE. [face palm emoji]

I rolled my eyes, shuffling forward in line as I typed.

Dani:

> I'll have you know, I was up all night writing! I have several solid chapters now with plans to write even more today.

> And yes, there might be a guy. But it's only a might right now. [winky face emoji]

"What has you grinning so wide?" Joane asked, making me jump. I'd reached the front of the line and hadn't even realized it. I should have been more focused on my breakfast order than on updating my cousins on my dating life.

"Oh, nothing," I said, tucking my phone into the pocket of my joggers as I perused the menu, quickly selecting the first item to catch my attention. "I'll have the lemon-berry stuffed sourdough French toast please. Oh, and coffee. Lots of coffee."

Joane peered at me from behind the counter, clearly seeing straight through my claims that it was "nothing." She arched an inquisitive eyebrow as she entered in my order.

"You forget, I'm a mother. I know what that look means." She waved accusingly at my face, and I attempted to wipe away whatever expression she was referencing. "You've met someone, and I want to hear all about it!"

The clearing of a throat behind me cut me off before I could protest further.

"Just as soon as the rush is over. We'll talk later." Joane probably meant the words as a promise, but they felt more like a threat as I paid for my food and settled at the table in the corner that I was quickly coming to think of as "mine."

My phone vibrated with thoughts from the cousin crew on my last message.

Poppy:

> You've been wearing the bracelet I gave you, haven't you? I knew those stones would help! But I won't say I told you so. [Two winky face emojis]

Thinking of Allen's fascination with said bracelet had me biting my lip and considering never taking the bracelet off again.

Avery:

> What?!?

Poppy:

> I should have mixed you some oils too. It would seal the deal! What's your address? I'll overnight deliver them to you!

Deciding the cousins could live with a bit of suspense, I switched my phone to "do not disturb," stuck in an earbud, and got to work crafting Petros's and Hypatia's adventure as I waited for my food to be ready.

An hour later, the very loud huff of someone settling into the seat across from me pulled me from my manuscript, and I blinked to focus on Joane, who was grinning at me like the cat who'd eaten the canary. Her hair was once again pulled up, and she was wearing her customary apron over a bright pink floral shirt that I was fairly certain I'd seen the sister of in a thrift store yesterday.

"The breakfast rush just ended, and I have about thirty minutes before I need to work on lunch prep. Spill!"

I leaned back, trying for nonchalance, even as my insides danced and skipped with excitement.

"There's not much to tell. I met a guy at the bookstore the other day and ran into him again on the beach yesterday. We spent the day together and it was... nice." I finished lamely, not sure how else to summarize my day with Allen without it sounding ridiculous.

"'Nice' doesn't put that shade of pink into your cheeks," Joane said, nodding at me. "You've got to give me more than that! What's his name?" Her face scrunched in concern. "Please tell me it's not Mason."

"Why would Mason have been at the beach?" I asked, confused by her concern.

She looked guilty. "He'd asked where you were headed yesterday, something about your garage door opener."

My forehead furrowed as I tried to make sense of what Joane was saying. "There's nothing wrong with my garage door opener. Are you sure it didn't have anything to do with my internet? That's supposed to get fixed today, thank goodness! I need to be able to research when I'm working."

There were several comments in my working document noting places I needed to come back to once I had completed a bit of research. But I'd been too fired up by ideas to let the holes stop me.

Joane shook her head slowly. "No, I'm pretty sure he said garage door opener. Though maybe it was a typo or something."

"Well, doesn't matter," I said, thinking I might need to write a sticky note to Mason to clarify the situation, "I know what Mason looks like, and I definitely didn't see him yesterday. No, my guy's name is Allen and he's," I bit my lip not sure how exactly to describe Allen, "he's kind of amazing."

"Allen? Not on my list of sexy men's names, but definitely better than Gary, my ex's name. That really should have been the first sign." She gave a small sigh, before reaching across the table to pat my hand. "But we're not talking about me and past mistakes. Tell me about Allen! What does he look like? What did you two do after the beach? You have to remember I'm an old lady whose son has the social skills of a tomato. I need to get my romantic excitement somewhere!"

I wasn't exactly sure what a tomato's social skills looked like, but I wasn't going to ask. I'd met Spencer and could acknowledge he wasn't the smoothest individual, and he did tend to turn red when speaking. Though he'd been nice and would likely make some woman a very loyal, kind partner someday.

"Have you tried reading? I've heard it's full of romantic excitement, especially if you pick the right book." I shot back, straight faced. "There's this one called something about pomegranates and curses that I've heard is really good."

"Ha ha. Nice try! Now give me all of the details before I cut off your coffee and pastry supply."

"Okay, no need to be hasty," I said with a laugh, trying to decide where to begin. As I summarized my day, Joane leaned an elbow on the table, her chin in her hand, a slightly dreamy look on her face.

"That right there is better than what you find in romance books because it's real." She gave a big, satisfied smile before glancing at the clock on the wall and pushing to her feet. "Guess it's time to get back to work."

She took two steps before turning back.

"What did you say your man's name was again? If he's from the area, chances are good I know him."

"He's not local. He's just visiting his grandparents. His name is Allen, Allen Bradley."

"Allen Bradley," Joane said, mulling over the name before shaking her head. "Can't say that I've met him. You'll have to bring him to the bakery so I can vet him for you."

It was only much later, after I'd taken a break from writing to visit the restroom that Joane's words registered. The first time we met, Allen had mentioned loving the bakery and visiting it multiple times. With Joane being as friendly as she was, it surprised me she didn't know him.

Pushing away the thought, I finished washing my hands and headed back to my table to keep working. I was reading too much into it. Joane couldn't possibly remember everyone who walked through the bakery doors, even if they visited regularly during the summers.

But maybe I'd take her up on her offer of vetting Allen. It never hurt to get a second opinion from an unbiased party, though I was pretty sure Joane would like Allen just as much as I did.

CHAPTER 21
Mason

I COULDN'T STOP MYSELF from whistling as I parked my car and headed to the bakery. I'd spent the morning getting Dani's internet fixed and squeezing in a home workout. After all the progress I'd made with Dani yesterday, I was in a great mood. I was biding my time before I texted her, not wanting to come across as too eager, but also wanting to let her know I'd had a wonderful time the day before. That's what friends did, right? Though a part of me felt like we'd skipped right past the friend stage into some undefined territory I wasn't quite sure how to navigate.

I couldn't remember the last time I'd had so much fun exploring local haunts.

It had probably been with Rebecca.

I pushed the thought away. I didn't think about Rebecca. She was a mistake from my first summer in Oregon, nothing more. I'd learned my lesson and moved on. She had no place ruining my perfect day.

Deciding I needed coffee and one of Joane's sandwiches, I headed to the bakery. Just as I was about to open the door, a familiar figure caught my eye, and I froze. Dani sat in one corner of the restaurant, typing away furiously on a laptop. I stopped to appreciate her expression of complete focus, her eyebrows pinched together slightly and her lips moving as if she was mouthing the words to herself as she wrote.

Shaking myself out of my surprise, I quickly ducked behind the building before she could spot me. I couldn't risk someone from town, particularly Joane or Spencer, blowing my cover and revealing I was not, in fact, Allen. Especially not now when things were going so well.

Considering my options, I hurried away, hoping Dani wouldn't spot me as I crossed back in front of the bakery window to the bookstore. I'd come to town to show Spencer the concepts for his commission anyway. I'd arrived with time to spare, intending to grab an early lunch at the bakery before our meeting, but it looked like food would have to wait. I couldn't risk Dani finding out the truth, not yet at least. I needed more time to gain her trust and then I'd tell her my real name. Probably.

At the bookstore, it took a moment for my eyes to adjust to the dim light as the chime for the door rang.

"Welcome to Seabreeze Reads! How can I help—" Spencer broke off as he caught sight of me. "You're early. Or did I mix up the time?"

Spencer glanced down at his watch, his lips pursed in confusion as he muttered something to himself about forgetfulness and schedules.

"I'm early." I rushed to reassure him. "The line at the bakery was too long," a white lie I hoped Joane would forgive me for, "so I thought I'd come over and see if you could meet now."

Spencer studied me for a moment before shrugging and waving me back to his office.

"We can meet now. I just might have to step away if there are any customers. My employee isn't here yet to man the cash register."

"That's fine," I said, following him to the office and settling into one of the desk chairs he kept in the small space. As I sat back, I couldn't help remembering the last time I'd been in this room. And while I was happy to spend time with my best friend, I kind of wished I was in this room with Dani again talking about the publishing world or her latest project or her love of cheese. Really anything if it meant I got to be with her again.

"What have you got for me?" Spencer's question pulled me from my thoughts, and I quickly pulled out my tablet, tapping on the screen to open the trio of sketches I'd created with the bookstore's children section in mind.

"You talked about wanting to bring the magic of reading to life, so I wanted to do something fun but also bold." I'd been playing with the idea after our meeting on Sunday, but after spending the day with Dani yesterday, the sketches had taken on new life, quickly becoming one of my favorite projects to date.

Spencer nodded thoughtfully, making the occasional comment as I talked him through each sketch and my vision for the pieces he'd commissioned. As I finished, Spencer settled back into his chair, his hands behind his head, a pensive expression on his face.

"You hate it, don't you?" I asked, my stomach sinking. I'd been so excited about the concept, I hadn't even stopped to think through alternatives if Spencer wasn't a fan.

"No, no." Spencer sat up quickly, waving his hands in a placating gesture. "I love it. I think it'll be perfect for the children's area. It's just, something seems different about you today and I can't quite put my finger on what."

"What do you mean?" My forehead scrunched in confusion as I waited for his response.

"If I didn't know any better, I'd say you're acting like you've met someone. Almost like when you first met R—" He broke off and gave me a sheepish smile. "I'm reading too much into things. You're probably just jazzed about a fantastic idea, which you should be! I'm going to have moms asking me where I got my artwork and looking to buy prints to hang on their kids' bedroom walls at home."

I knew what Spencer was thinking and whose name he'd been about to say. But a woman had nothing to do with my mood. I was making strides in my career and loving life on the Oregon coast. That was all there was to it.

"I'd be happy to sell copies here in the store like we do with the other prints, if you think people would be interested," I said, taking the easy out Spencer offered. "We could probably make a series of bookmarks with these prints too."

My mind reeled with the possibilities.

"Bookmarks would be amazing!"

Spencer continued to ramble as I half listened to him talking about pricing and contracts. My thoughts were stuck on what Spencer had said earlier. I'd only met Dani two days ago. Was that really enough time for my behavior to change? And if so, should I be worried about her ability to get under my skin so quickly?

Deciding I needed a more powerful distraction than children's art prints and bookmarks, I turned the conversation to something guaranteed to take a large amount of brain power: Spencer's love life.

"Have you given any more thought to my offer to help with your dating prospects?" It hadn't really been much of an offer, but there was no time like the present to show up as a better, more supportive friend.

Spencer blinked at me owlishly for a moment, trying to track my change of topic, his glasses sliding slightly down his nose.

"No," he said slowly, watching me like I was a few colors short of a full crayon box as he pushed his frames back up. "I'm looking for something more serious than you typically go for. Besides, you said you wouldn't help me win Danielle Baldwin and she's the only woman who's truly caught my attention lately."

"What about Maisie?" I asked, thinking of the tattooed thrift store owner next door who was an expert at ruffling Spencer's feathers.

"Maisie?" He sputtered, appalled. "What on earth would make you think I was interested in Maisie? That woman exists to get on my nerves and to steal my parking spots."

While the strip mall where both the thrift store and bookstore were located had a decent-sized parking lot, Spencer and Maisie were constantly feuding over what they termed the "best" parking stalls, with both of them claiming the other's customers hogged the prime parking. If they'd asked me, I'd point out that the cars most often in those spots looked an awful lot like the vehicles that belonged to the Gossip Gang who liked to frequent Ed's Barbershop. Up until now, I'd kept my nose out of the argument, content to sit back and watch them clash.

"Okay, so not Maisie, but surely there's got to be someone else besides Danielle Baldwin. She was giving some pretty strong uninterested signals the other day." That and if I could lead Spencer away from Dani, I'd definitely feel less guilty over what I was doing.

Not that I was pursuing her for romantic purposes, but still. I had to remind myself of my own intentions since the handholding from yesterday and my constant thoughts of her had muddied the water.

Spencer shrugged, leaning back in his chair and propping his feet up on the desk.

"No one's caught my interest. But who knows, maybe a tourist will wander in and—"

As if on cue, the chime above the door rang, indicating Spencer had a customer. Taking his feet off the desk, he stood and started walking to the front of the shop.

"Give me just a second to see who this is and if they need help."

"Take your time," I called. Pulling out my phone, I glanced at the time. It was late enough in the day that I could probably text Dani without seeming too eager right? I was going to wait until tomorrow, but all this thinking about her had me wanting to type out a message.

I could hear Spencer greeting his customer. When she responded, I froze with my finger poised above my phone screen to type.

It was Dani. Dani was in the store, and I was currently sitting in Spencer's office with the door wide open for anyone to glance in and see me.

Looking around, I considered my options. I could try to escape the bookstore without Dani noticing, which seemed like the most dramatic option. Or I could close the office door and hope Dani would leave quickly. Seeing as I hadn't said goodbye to Spencer, this seemed like my best option. Just as I was reaching for the doorknob to close the office door, Spencer's words registered.

"I can't believe you haven't chatted with Mason about his art. You guys are next door neighbors. How is that even possible?"

"After our few exchanges, trust me, it's no surprise his career hasn't come up." This came from Dani and my heart gave a small twinge at her dry tone of voice. Hopefully, she felt differently about Allen.

I still gagged a little bit thinking about that name, but desperate times had called for desperate measures.

"Well, he's in my office right now. He just showed me an incredible batch of prints he's working on for the store, and maybe he can tell you more about that print you were admiring."

Spencer was bringing Dani back to the office to meet *me*. Hiding was no longer an option. Moving quickly, I dropped down to all fours and crawled as fast as I could from the office to behind the cash register. I didn't know why I was crawling but apparently I didn't make the best decisions when I was panicking as evidenced by the choice of "Allen" for my fake identity.

Peeking around the corner, I made sure the coast was clear before pushing to my feet and bolting around one of the bookshelves as their voices drew closer. James Bond, I was not, but I could dodge and hide when needed.

Ducking around one more bookshelf, I sank to the floor in an effort to stay even more out of sight, my heart pounding in my chest.

"That's odd. He was just here." I heard Spencer say, his voice carrying through the quiet shop. "Maybe he stepped away and will be right back."

Silently cursing Spencer and his persistence, I pulled out my phone and quickly typed out a text to Spencer. I needed them to move away from the office if I was going to get out of the bookstore without being spotted. While there was a back door near the office, it was alarmed, and I really didn't need to draw added attention my way.

Mason:

> Grandparents needed help with a small emergency. Sorry to duck out early!

Hopefully, Spencer would be satisfied with that lame excuse and send Dani on her way. A short moment later I heard a chime on Spencer's phone.

"Looks like he had to help his grandparents with something."

"Well, that's too bad," Dani said, though her voice sounded anything but disappointed.

"You know, I'm glad you stopped by, Dani. I've been wanting to," Spencer's voice cracked, and he cleared it, making his next words come out even deeper, "to ask you something."

"Oh?" Dani didn't sound excited about Spencer's pending question, and I couldn't really blame her. It didn't take a rocket scientist to guess what was about to happen next. I only felt a little bit bad about witnessing it.

Though maybe I could save Spencer some of the impending pain.

Thinking quickly, I pulled up a text message to Dani and typed:

Allen:

> I had a great time yesterday. Can't wait to see you tomorrow! Would it be okay if I picked you up?

I'd navigate any anxieties about Dani connecting Allen's car with Mason later. Maybe I could borrow a car from one of my buddies or just make sure she never saw Mason's car when she was at the duplex.

Dani's phone chimed and Spencer stopped his rambling build up to a question that would only end in pain.

"Sorry, Spencer. I need to respond to this. It's my date for tomorrow solidifying plans."

"Oh, uh, date? I didn't know you were," Spencer's voice cracked again, "seeing anyone."

"It's a recent thing. I don't know if you'd technically say we're 'seeing' each other, but I'm interested in seeing where things go."

I silently pumped a fist in the air, congratulating myself on saving Spencer from a seriously painful interaction. There was no way he'd continue his line of questioning now, not if he had any self-respect. Now if he could just finish helping Dani with her reason for coming to the store, I could make my getaway while they were both distracted.

Their voices faded until I could no longer make out what they were saying. Assuming the coast was clear, I pushed to my feet and sneaked around the shelves, making sure no one was in sight as I rounded each corner. Finally, I reached the front door and made my exit, only cursing the chime above the door a little bit as it signaled my escape. I just hoped Dani and Spencer were too busy talking to notice.

CHAPTER 22
Dani

AFTER WORKING IN THE bakery for another hour, I needed a change of scenery and to go somewhere that didn't include Joane giving me knowing looks from behind the cash register every few minutes. Maybe I'd take a quick writing break or try writing somewhere else like the bookstore or the bench with a view of the ocean.

Packing up my laptop, I stopped at Retro Rendezvous. After my success at the thrift stores a couple of towns over, I was curious to see what this local shop had to offer. Walking inside, I already loved the vibe as I took in carefully organized bins of vinyl and an entire clothing section that looked like it had come straight from the 1950s and 1960s.

"Welcome!" A cheery voice called from off to the side, and a petite woman with purple hair and tattoo sleeves walked toward me, her arms full of what looked to be vintage coats. "I'm Maisie. Anything I can help you find today?"

Her last sentence was technically a question, but she said it with such confidence that it felt more like a statement, like she knew I'd be leaving the store having purchased something amazing.

"No, just looking. I didn't think I was big into thrifting, but a couple days in Oregon and I'm reevaluating that stance." I joked.

"Oregon will do that to you," she said, depositing the coats on a table next to a stack of hangers. "But if you start thinking you should start a thrift store, run the opposite direction. Trust me." She said this last part cheerfully with a giant grin that told me she loved what she did, despite the warning, which I understood full heartedly.

"That's how I feel about writing. In theory, being an author is an amazing career. In reality, it's a ton of work that I wouldn't wish on anyone. Yet, I wouldn't give up my job for the world." And after the last couple of days where I'd actually been able to make solid progress on my novel, I felt like I was telling the truth with my assessment.

"You're an author? Written anything I've heard of?"

I winced, remembering too late that I was trying not to tell people what I did for a career. And maybe it was the magic of Cascade Harbor or finally finding my groove with writing again or spending yesterday with Allen who made me feel confident and seen, but I didn't really want to hide what I did. I wouldn't be shouting it from the rooftops, but what could it hurt to tell people if they asked? Maybe sharing who I was more confidently would bring me one step closer to banishing the imposter syndrome from my life. Though, I'd felt less like an imposter lately now that I was finally writing again.

"Maybe. Do you read fantasy?"

The woman shook her head, sending her purple curls dancing around her face. "Not really. I'm more of a nonfiction fan, especially if it's true crime or a juicy memoir. I'm here for all the celebrity gossip!"

"Read anything good lately?" I asked, moving to the racks of clothing, looking through the different options as I spoke. A beautiful, deep-green dress caught my eye. It was definitely vintage, the wear around the zipper indicating it was well-loved, but the cut and color looked exactly like something Doris Day would have worn in *Pillow Talk*.

I must have gasped out loud or given some other kind of reaction because Maisie was suddenly standing next to me, examining my find.

"Isn't she beautiful? I picked that one up at an estate sale. The lady it belonged to had made it herself years ago. She had all kinds of gorgeous pieces like it, though I think this might be the only one I have left. Do you want to try it on?"

"Yes please!" If this dress only even sort of fit me, I was buying it. I had no idea when or where I'd wear it, but I'd figure that out later.

"Right this way." Maisie grabbed the dress and led me back to the dressing room, which she unlocked for me.

I quickly changed into the dress, loving how it hugged my curves. The zipper was a bit sticky, but the fit was perfect. All I was missing was a blonde bob and I'd look just like my favorite actress. Even Maisie raved about how I looked in it when I modeled for her.

I purchased the dress, thanked Maisie, and dropped the dress off at my car. It was a completely unnecessary purchase, but I'd find an excuse to wear it while I was here in Oregon, even if I just had a fancy writing day at the bakery.

Deciding I wasn't quite ready to drive back to the duplex, I headed over to the bookstore. I was hoping Spencer would let me work in one of the many armchairs I'd seen dotted around the space when I first visited. Maybe he'd let me use his space in exchange for signing more copies. Though I did worry about him hovering or asking me out. But I didn't want to leave town without hearing back from Allen, and I couldn't spend another minute in the bakery with Joane's knowing looks.

Taking a deep breath, I stepped into the store and was greeted by the cheerful door chime. I took a deep breath of the familiar scent of books as I looked around, trying to remember where I'd seen the chairs.

It didn't take long for Spencer to appear from around one of the bookshelves.

"Welcome to Seabreeze Reads! How can I help," he paused when he saw me before choking out the last word, "you?"

"Hi Spencer," I said with a friendly, but hopefully not overly inviting, smile.

"Hi Danielle Baldwin," he said, and I winced, praying we were the only people in the store. Maybe I wasn't quite ready to share my identity with everyone in Cascade Harbor quite yet after all.

"You know you can just call me Dani, right?" I asked, rubbing the back of my neck. "If you call me 'Danielle Baldwin' every time you see me, the whole town's going to think I'm weirdly conceited or something."

"True!" His voice broke, the word coming out high and squeaky. I genuinely felt bad for the man. He clearly was interested in me, but I had no idea how to tell him that his efforts were having the opposite effect.

Looking around the store for something to talk about, my gaze caught on a framed print I hadn't noticed on my first visit. In purples and blues, a fairy danced from the pages of a book, her wings so delicate they looked almost iridescent.

I moved closer to it, reaching up to brush my fingers along the simple frame.

"This print is gorgeous. Is the artist local?" I asked, wondering if Spencer supported local artists in his shop like his mother did at the bakery.

"Funny you should ask. That was actually designed by your neighbor." Spencer said, this last part coming out almost like a braying, nervous laugh.

"Really?" I was shocked to think the man I'd been doing my best to avoid could produce something so beautiful. The art style reminded me of my book cover. Avery was still looking for another artist to do my sequel and a part of me wondered if I should pass his name onto her, as much as the thought pained me. "You know, I wouldn't mind asking him about his artwork."

I internally flinched, knowing I was potentially signing myself up for an incredibly uncomfortable interaction, but also needing to know more about Mason's work. If I could come back from this trip with both a completed manuscript and a potential new cover artist, Avery might just forgive me for all the stress I'd put on her with how much I'd struggled to write this second book.

"I can't believe you haven't chatted with Mason about his art. You guys are next door neighbors. How is that even possible?" Spencer asked with clear incredulity.

"After our first few exchanges, trust me, it's no surprise his career hasn't come up," I said, my first night in Oregon feeling like a distant memory after everything that had happened since.

"Well, he's in my office right now. He just showed me an incredible batch of prints he's working on for the store, and maybe he can tell you more about that print you were admiring." Spencer waved for me to follow him back to the office where I'd signed a stack of books the first time we met.

When we reached the office, the door was open, but there were no bearded men in sight.

"That's odd. He was just here," Spencer said, looking around as if Mason was going to pop out from behind one of the bookshelves yelling "surprise." "Maybe he stepped away and will be right back."

Spencer's phone dinged with a text notification. He pulled out the device and read something on his screen before giving me an apologetic shake of his head.

"Looks like he had to help his grandparents with something."

"Well, that's too bad," I said, trying to sound disappointed and, while I did want to talk to Mason about his art, I also didn't mind delaying my next run-in with my neighbor for the moment. Though I hoped his being in town meant the internet repairs were finished at the duplex. I missed being able to message people easily at any time of day, even if the social media breaks in the evening had been nice.

"You know, I'm glad you stopped by, Dani," Spencer said, leaning against the checkout counter. "I've been wanting to," here Spencer's voice cracked as his hand slipped out from under him, causing him to topple a bit. He cleared his throat and continued, his next words coming out deeper than his usual register, "to ask you something."

"Oh?" I asked, knowing exactly where this was going and wishing I could stop it. Spencer was nice, but he definitely wasn't my type. Not to mention there was this whole Allen thing that I was much more interested in pursuing.

As if the universe took pity on me, my phone dinged with a text, and I gratefully dug my phone out of my pocket. I didn't even care if it was another check-in from Avery, it was saving me from having to reject Spencer right now, for which I was grateful.

Allen:

> I had a great time yesterday. Can't wait to see you tomorrow! Would it be okay if I picked you up?

My insides did a happy dance at the words, a smile splitting my face. Spencer watched me, hope in his eyes.

"Sorry, Spencer. I need to respond to this. It's my date for tomorrow solidifying plans." I was maybe laying it on a little thick, but I needed Spencer to clearly understand that I wasn't interested, and this seemed easier than rejecting him outright.

"Oh, uh, date? I didn't know you were," Spencer's voice cracked again as he visibly deflated, "seeing anyone."

I did my best to focus all my attention on my phone to give Spencer a chance to regroup. He really was a nice guy. He just wasn't Allen.

"It's a recent thing. I don't know if you'd technically say we're 'seeing' each other, but I'm interested in discovering where things go."

I quickly typed out a response, agreeing to let Allen drive me and giving him my address. Usually, I didn't let a guy pick me up until we'd been on a few dates, but there was something about Allen that I trusted.

I should probably pass his name onto Avery as a potential cover designer as well as Mason's. Though I would like to see Allen's artwork first, gauge his skills. And if it gave me a chance to spend more time with him, all the better.

When Allen didn't immediately respond, I tucked my phone back into my pocket and gave Spencer my best "I just want to be friends" smile. I wasn't sure if that smile was actually a thing, but I really hoped that was what I was conveying as I looked at him.

"So, this date, it's with someone you met while you were in Cascade Harbor?" Spencer wouldn't meet my eye, scuffing the toe of his shoe into the carpet as he talked.

"Yeah. It's pretty new, but he's also visiting the area and has been kind enough to show me some of the sights."

"That's great," Spencer said, nodding like a bobble head going jeeping.

He seemed determined to look at anything besides me, as if searching the bookshelves for what he wanted to say next.

"Anyway," he cleared his throat, "what can I help you with today?"

"I was wondering if I could write in your store for a couple of hours this afternoon? I'm not sure if the wifi is fixed at my place yet and I need a change of scenery from the bakery. Too many pastries tempting me at every turn," I said, trying to keep my tone light. No need for Spencer to know I read every single emotion from hurt to disappointment as it flashed across his face. Dude definitely did not have a poker face. Not to mention his face was turning a shade of red that was a little concerning.

"Of course!" Spencer's face lit up, chasing away at least a little bit of the pain I'd put there. "But only if you promise you'll come do an official signing here after your next book releases. You could tell people you wrote part of the book in the store."

It wasn't a bad idea. Spencer might not have a poker face, but he was definitely a savvy businessman.

"I'll see what I can do, but I'll have to convince my publisher. Thankfully, one of the owners is my sister, so I think I can persuade her," I said, looking around the shop trying to locate an armchair that would suit my needs.

"Really? Because I've been trying to get you out here for a signing and keep hitting a brick wall with some guy named Eric."

I rolled my eyes. Of course, Eric was causing problems. Avery's ex-fiancé had the personality of a marble. And not one of those pretty, colorful marbles. He was just a round piece of glass that looked shiny but really didn't have much purpose beyond that. Eric loved to point out just how shiny he was, touting his connections and advanced degree. How my adventurous older sister had ended up with such a stick-in-the-mud, I'd never know. I had never been more proud of her than when she'd called off the wedding last month.

"Don't worry about Eric. I'll talk to Avery, and we'll get a signing on the calendar just as soon as we can work it into the schedule."

"That would be amazing! Of course you can write here. My bookstore is your bookstore. I mean, for writing. Obviously, if you want to buy a book, you'll have to checkout like everyone else—"

"Can you point me to the nearest armchair so I can get to work?" I asked, cutting Spencer off before he could ramble more.

"Happy to! Right this way." Spencer led the way to the fluffiest reading chair I'd ever seen.

"Oh, this is perfect," I said, as I settled into the seat. I deposited my laptop bag at my feet and retrieved my computer.

I could feel Spencer watching me and finally I paused to ask, "Can I help you with anything else before I start working? Did you get more books that you need signed?"

Maybe he'd take the hint and leave me to work. Instead, Spencer shook his head and bit his lip before blurting out, "You know, Mason says tourists only want one thing when it comes to a vacation romance. You should be careful with this guy you just met."

I flinched at the harsh words, taken aback at their suddenness. My anger began to boil, and I had to remind myself not to snap at the kind, if misguided, bookstore owner in front of me.

"And how would Mason know what Allen wants?"

"Well, he doesn't. I mean, I'm assuming. I haven't asked him about your situation, of course, since I just learned you were seeing someone, but that's what Mason says about all vacation romances. He says tourists just want a temporary fling, nothing serious." All of this spilled out of Spencer in a torrent, without him pausing to take a breath as he wrung his hands as if nervous for my response. He clearly put too much stock in what Mason said, a man who really shouldn't be trusted in the romance department if my observations were anything to go off.

If this was how Mason viewed the world, maybe I didn't want to pass his name onto Avery as a possible cover artist.

"Good thing Allen isn't Mason and is a mature man who's not looking for a temporary fling." I bit out the words, careful to keep my tone pleasant if a bit dry. "Now if you'll excuse me, I have work to do."

Spencer hovered awkwardly for a moment longer, but I ignored him, slipped in my earbuds, and got back to work, channeling my anger into a fight scene with the Fates that would leave readers desperate to get to the end of the chapter.

CHAPTER 23
Dani

THE NEXT NIGHT, I wiped my hands down the front of my dress, trying desperately not to appear nervous as I waited for Allen. I'd had two crazy productive days of writing. Between my growing interest in Allen and my anger and frustration with Mason, I had enough emotions to write five best-selling romantasy series. I still had a long way to go before the sequel to *Of Curses and Pomegranates* was complete, but I was no longer worried I wouldn't be able to write it. Just so long as I didn't think about how the sequel needed to live up the hype of the first book, I could keep putting words on the page.

After my conversation with Spencer, I had almost left another sticky note for Mason, telling him what I thought of his vacation romance theory, but by the time I got home I had cooled off enough to see the note wasn't necessary. Mason had said that to Spencer in general and not specifically about me and Allen. Also, why would I take anything my lady's-man of a neighbor had to say about romance seriously?

Also, I'd just met Allen. Maybe this thing growing between us was destined to stay a vacation fling. Didn't mean I was going to stop getting to know him and enjoying this experience.

A knock on the door pulled me from my thoughts and I hurried to answer.

I was wearing the green dress from Retro Rendezvous and, with my hair styled over one shoulder in soft curls, I felt as elegant as Doris Day heading out for a night on the town.

The look on Allen's face when I opened the door was worth the effort. His expression was filled with appreciation, and I gave him a coy smile, knowing I looked good and fully prepared to use that fact to my advantage.

"Good evening," he said, his voice warm. "I feel like I'm under-dressed."

He gestured at himself, drawing attention to his tan slacks, navy blue button down, and gray jacket.

"I think you look very nice, like you're ready to show a lady a good time." I stepped outside, closing and locking the door behind me. I shivered slightly, my bare arms not prepared for the cool summer air. It was cool enough to need a jacket, but I hadn't had anything that would go with the dress, and I wasn't about to let some silly thing like a cool summer night on the Oregon coast get in the way of impressing this man.

Allen held my door as I climbed into his dark blue SUV, and I enjoyed the view as he walked over to his side of the car to climb in.

On the drive to the restaurant, he asked how my writing had gone, and I told him about the scenes I'd drafted today.

"I probably have about a third of the book written at this point, and I'm hoping to get a good chunk written tomorrow. How was your day?"

"Oh, you know, same old, same old," Allen responded vaguely as he parked the car.

I waited until we were both out of the car and walking to the restaurant before continuing our conversation.

"No, I don't know what 'same old, same old' means for you. You told me you're a graphic designer, so what do you design?" I asked, wanting to know everything I possibly could about this man.

"I design a little bit of everything. The joy and challenge of being a freelance designer is that I can take on any project I want, but it also means I have to attract enough business to earn a livable wage," he said as he held the door open for me.

The restaurant was a seafood place near the beach with views of the ocean. It was nautical themed with tables that had been artfully aged to make them look vintage and worn. On the walls were photos of the ocean intermixed with sailing paraphernalia. It was cozy and quaint, though I hoped it served more than just seafood. I was not a seafood fan.

"That's a lot of pressure," I said as we were shown to our table, empathizing with Allen's struggle to support himself with his creativity.

The waiter handed us both laminated menus and deposited a basket of breadsticks on the table, promising to be back shortly to take our drink orders.

"A pressure you understand," Allen said, giving my hand a gentle squeeze where it rested on the table. The quick, compassionate movement sent sparks dancing down my spine and made me wish his hand had lingered.

"The joys of using our art to support ourselves," I said, feeling a blush suffuse my cheeks at his attention.

Needing a distraction, I glanced down at the menu. Most of the food involved some form of seafood, though I was relieved to see a few chicken options.

"I've heard amazing things about their clam chowder," Allen said, following my lead and reviewing his own menu.

I had to fight the urge to gag, but some of what I was thinking must have shown on my face.

"Not a clam chowder fan?"

I shook my head.

"That is a tragedy! I don't know if you can visit Oregon if you're not going to enjoy a bowl of clam chowder."

I ducked my head behind my menu, not sure if I wanted to see his reaction to what I had to say next.

"It's not just clam chowder," I said slowly. "It's all seafood, if that makes you feel better."

The strangled noise Allen made had me looking up in concern, half expecting to find him choking on a breadstick. Instead, he was staring at me like I'd just declared the earth was flat.

"You don't like seafood?" He asked slowly, each word a staccato beat contrasting with the steady flow of conversation of the diners around us. "I don't think we can be friends."

"That's going to make dinner together really awkward, but I guess I can stop talking to you immediately, really lean into this new dynamic." I quipped, trying to fight back a laugh at how truly appalled he sounded at my food preferences.

"I think it might be for the best," he said, glancing around as if looking for a waiter. "I probably need to ask for separate tables as well."

We both burst out laughing at the absurd suggestion.

"Well, now I feel bad. If I would have known, I would have suggested a different restaurant," Allen said, setting down his menu.

"Don't worry about it," I said, resting a hand on his. "Thankfully, I'm a big chicken fan."

The rest of the meal passed quickly, our conversation easy and natural. My chicken fettucine proved delicious, and I even agreed to try a bite of Allen's shrimp scampi, which wasn't bad, though I definitely wouldn't be ordering it for myself any time soon.

We finished our food, and Allen, mentioning he didn't want the evening to end, suggested we visit an ice cream place a couple of blocks away and I happily agreed to extending our date.

As we stood to leave, I dropped my phone. I bent to retrieve the device, the seams of my dress pulling tight along the side. Not thinking anything of the pressure, I stretched to grab my phone from where it sat under the table. The seams gave a tug and then suddenly released, a popping sound accompanying the change, and I froze.

My vintage, well-loved dress had shown its age, the seam along my right side popping. Based on the air flow I was feeling, I was guessing the hole was currently revealing several inches of skin that likely included a nice view of my very practical, slightly discolored bra.

Grabbing my phone, I quickly straightened, plastering my arm to my side to try to hide the damage. Maybe no one would notice.

"Everything okay?" Allen asked, his eyes wide. He had clearly noticed.

My face turned bright red, and I looked around, trying to find some way to cover up my wardrobe mishap. I had never wished for a jacket more than I did now, fashion be danged.

"Um, yes, but I don't think I have room for ice cream after all." I gave a small, forced laugh, trying to distract from the fact that the whole restaurant was going to see more of me than I was comfortable with if we didn't get to the car soon. I'd worry about finding a way to save things with Allen later. Or maybe I'd book a flight to Utah as soon as I got back to the duplex, run away, and pretend like this was not happening in front of the first man I'd even remotely been interested in in far too long.

Allen continued to watch me for a moment before giving a small shrug and placing a gentle hand on the small of my back to guide me from the restaurant. The gesture placed him on my right side, making it so he helped block my split seam, and I was grateful for his consideration.

I forced my face into a pleasant expression as we thanked the hostess. Reaching the door, I realized we couldn't both fit through, and I steeled myself to walk into the cool evening without a jacket and with my dress falling apart. While I had wanted to show Allen more of myself tonight, I was thinking more along the lines of telling him some childhood stories, not giving him a peek at my underclothing.

Just as Allen dropped his arm and I moved to step outside, I felt the light pressure of Allen draping his jacket over my shoulders. Startled, I glanced over to see him giving me a knowing look.

"You're holding your arm so close to your side, I figured you were cold or something," he said with a wink.

I slipped my arms into the jacket, gratefully accepting its warmth in addition to his discretion. Allen's incredible scent engulfed me, and I gratefully breathed it in as we walked back to the car, the smell both woodsy and sweet.

"I'm so embarrassed," I exclaimed, burying my face in his jacket as we settled into his car.

"Why, because you weren't properly prepared for the weather or because you don't like seafood? Because I'll have you know, neither of those are deal-breakers for me."

Allen pulled the car onto the main road and began driving back toward my rental. I was disappointed that we wouldn't be getting ice cream, but I didn't see a way to keep the night going when my dress was literally falling apart at the seams.

"I know you were cold, but do you mind if we still grab ice cream? The place I'm thinking of has a drive-thru. Then we can find a place to park with a view of the ocean or something. That way you can stay warm and get a sweet treat."

It was like he'd read my mind, and I felt like I was falling maybe just a little bit in love with the man next to me.

"Sounds perfect."

We got our ice cream, deciding to eat it in the car at a nearby park instead of trying to find open parking at the beach.

"You know, I've been here since Sunday and I still haven't seen a sunset on the beach," I said as I took a bite of huckleberry ice cream, savoring the sweet, tangy flavor.

"Now that's just a tragedy! I'd say we should fix that immediately but..." He trailed off and I wondered if he'd finally mention my ruined dress. He'd been so kind not mentioning it before now, but it could only be avoided for so long.

"But walking on the beach in a ripped dress is probably asking for trouble," I finished for him. "Thank you for handling it so well. Leave it to me to split my dress on a first date."

"Believe it or not, this is not the worst wardrobe malfunction I've seen on a date. My brother, Grey, actually split his pants once when we were on a double date in high school. He was hiking and snagged a pocket on a tree branch. We were nowhere near the parking lot, so he'd had to hike back the entire way with his underwear showing." His voice was full of humor as he got lost in the memory, his face growing soft.

"Seriously? You're not just making that up to make me feel better?" I asked, laughing softly at the picture he painted.

"Trust me, it actually happened! And the best part was Grey just rolled with it. Nothing ever seems to faze my brother." His voice held an affectionate note as he talked about his brother.

"Does your brother live near you in Idaho?" Allen hadn't shared much about his personal life or family, and I was curious to learn more.

"No, he's all the way in Utah with my mom. I'm the rebel who lives far away." He took a deep breath, seeming to consider his words before speaking. "After my dad passed away, it was hard to be around them. I needed space to grieve and figure out who I was."

"I'm so sorry for your loss," I said, patting his knee since both of his hands were occupied with his ice cream and spoon.

Allen shrugged, a gesture meant to appear casual, but that seemed to carry the weight of the world.

"It happened a long time ago. My dad was the biggest supporter of my art. His passing was part of why I decided to become a graphic designer, make him proud and prove to the world that I could do it, that I could succeed."

"That's a lot of pressure to put on yourself," I said softly as I watched him use his spoon to draw patterns in his ice cream.

"What's life without a little pressure? I'm sure you understand that better than most." He pointed his spoon at me to underscore his point.

"True, though that amount of pressure's got to be hard and lonely without a solid support system nearby."

"I make it work," he said softly. "And just because they aren't close, doesn't mean Grey and my mom don't cheer me on."

"Tell me about them."

Time passed quickly as Allen shared stories about his family and the trouble he used to get in with his brother. Before I knew it, my ice cream was gone and I was shifting in my seat trying to get comfortable, loath to see the evening end but desperate to get out of my ruined Doris Day dress and into something less restrictive.

"Looks like I'd better get you home, but don't think you're off the hook. I want to hear all about your family too," Allen said as he pulled onto the road.

"Well, the first thing you need to know about my family is that I have an amazing sister and a fabulous group of female cousins who are my favorite people in the world."

The rest of the drive passed quickly, and sooner than I would have liked, we were pulling into the driveway. Allen apparently was also incapable of parking off to one side of the driveway, but I didn't mind. Let Mason get stuck behind us. It would only be fair for him to be inconvenienced by one of my guests for once.

"I had a good time tonight," Allen said as I turned to face him over the console.

"Even with the unfortunate ending to dinner?" I asked as I turned to face him, feeling the fabric around the torn seam of my dress rub against my skin.

"But I would argue it was a very fortunate ending," he said, reaching over to brush his fingers along my cheek.

"Oh?" I bit my lip, my heart racing as I waited for his response.

His gaze dipped down to my lips before he made eye contact with me.

"It meant I got you all to myself while we ate ice cream in the car. I feel like I'm really getting to know you, which means I have no qualms asking you a very important question." He paused, leaning toward me over the console, and my heart pounded in anticipation of his next words as I leaned in too.

"Which is?"

"May I kiss you?" He arched an eyebrow, waiting.

"Yes, you most certainly may," I said in a breathy voice I didn't recognize.

Allen didn't need to be told twice. His hand slipped behind my head, guiding my lips to his in a sweet, gentle kiss. My eyes closed and my world exploded at the contact as I was instantly lost in him, wondering how I'd waited this long to find a man who could make my heart race and dance all at the same time.

All too soon, Allen pulled back, resting his forehead against mine, our breaths mingling as we both processed the kiss.

"I thought talking to you was my favorite part of the night, but that kiss just supplanted it." His voice was deep and gravelly, full of desire.

A simple "uh huh" was all I could manage as I tried to reorient myself to a world where I'd kissed Allen. I opened my eyes to find him studying me, a gentle smile teasing his lips.

"I think I want to do that again," he said.

"Uh huh," I said again, this time adding a nod for emphasis before leaning in closer. Apparently, all it took to turn me from a best-selling novelist into a bumbling teenager was one very good kiss with a man I found highly attractive.

"But I'm not going to," he said, leaning back.

My heart plummeted, and I was not proud of the sound of protest that escaped my lips.

He gave a small chuckle, cupping my cheek with his hand before I could pull away and move back to my side of the car.

"Trust me, I want to keep kissing you, but I can't risk messing this up. I want more than dinner and a good time. I want to see you again."

"I want that too," I acknowledged, leaning into his touch. "Though we can keep kissing *and* see each other again. Just saying."

"Can I walk you to your door?" He asked, choosing to ignore my statement and clear request for another kiss.

"Well, you kind of have to if you want your jacket back," I said, pushing my door open and letting the cool air spill into the car.

Allen followed me to my doorstep. I quickly unlocked the door and turned back to say goodbye. He grabbed the sides of the jacket and pulled me toward him.

"I like the look of you in my jacket. I don't think I want it back," he said, leaning down, his lips inches from mine.

"Well, good news then," I said, pausing with my lips a breath away from his, "because I'm keeping it."

Then, before he could close the space between us, I pushed away, stepping inside and closing the door behind me with a click. From the other side of the door, I could hear Allen's rich, deep chuckle and I paused a moment, leaning against the door, reliving one of the most magical nights of my life, ripped dress and all.

CHAPTER 24
Mason

TONIGHT, HAD BEEN A mistake, yet I couldn't bring myself to regret it.

"What was I thinking?" I asked, even as I replayed the kiss. I'd kissed plenty of women, but there was something about the way Dani's lips fit mine that had me wanting to kiss her again and again until I'd forgotten the taste and feel of every woman that came before.

I was in trouble.

Not wanting Dani to see me pull into the neighboring garage, I pulled out of the duplex driveaway and headed up the coast, stopping at a bench that overlooked the ocean. Sunset would start soon, and, by some miracle, the bench was empty.

I climbed out of the car, welcoming the chill in the air as it cooled my heated skin, though it did little to distract me from the best date I'd probably ever been on. And while I knew Dani was mortified by the ripped dress, I would be lying if I said I hadn't enjoyed the alone time with her in the car after.

But the concern I'd felt at the panic in her eyes when the dress ripped made one thing abundantly clear: I didn't want to be just friends with Dani. I wanted to break my every rule about dating and tourists, and it terrified me. In fact, I had already started breaking the rules by telling her about my dad. But wanting more with Dani meant I had to tell her who I really was and there was no way she'd handle that deception well. Maybe I'd just legally change my name to Allen.

I dropped my head into my hands, groaning, my thoughts churning so fast I didn't hear another car pull up until I felt the presence of someone dropping into the seat next to me.

"Now I'm not an expert, but I feel like you're doing the whole sunset on the beach thing wrong," a kind, feminine voice said. I looked up to find Joane settled into the seat next to me, a soft smile on her lips.

"What are you doing here?" I asked, knowing Joane lived on the other side of town.

"This is my favorite spot to catch the sunset. You can't live on the Oregon coast if you don't occasionally take the time to enjoy the view." She gestured to the horizon in front of us where the sun was starting to paint the sky in shades of pink and orange. "I think the real question is what has you so dejected you're missing this masterpiece."

I leaned back on the bench, debating what to say. I could use Joane's advice, but how could I explain the situation without giving everything away?

"So, there's this girl," I said slowly, choosing my words with care, "and I actually want to see where things go but history has taught me it's easier to avoid relationships."

"Finally!" Joane exclaimed, throwing her hands into the air and causing me to jump. "It's about time someone held your attention for longer than a Friday-night fling."

I scoffed, turning to face her fully, the sunset forgotten. "What do you mean finally? You act as if you've been eagerly waiting for this moment."

"That's because I have been. I think most of the town has been. There have even been bets placed at Ed's about how long it would take you to slip up and turn one of your flirtations with a tourist into something more serious."

I grimaced, not loving being the subject of a bet at Ed's.

"You held out longer than I thought you would, I'll give you that. Cost me twenty bucks."

"You were part of the pool?" I asked, somewhat outraged.

"Of course! I was hoping to beat Joyce Campbell, though we were both wrong." She gave a sigh and shake of her head.

"Sorry to disappoint," I said, pushing to my feet. Maybe I didn't want or need Joane's advice after all. Not if she was going to turn around and share her intel with the Gossip Gang at Ed's and get another betting pool going.

"Oh, sit down," she said, grabbing my hand and giving me a gentle tug back into my seat. "It just proves we care about you. We were all worried about you after Rebecca."

I stiffened. "This has nothing to do with Rebecca."

"Of course it does. That woman ripped your heart out, threw it on the beach, and danced a jig on it. Anyone would be afraid to love again after that experience, especially so soon after you lost your dad."

I held up a placating hand. "No one said anything about love."

I just wanted to get to know Dani better, break out of the "friends" box I'd tried to build our relationship in. But love? We definitely weren't in love territory yet. I'd only known the woman for a handful of days.

"You didn't have to. I know that look. It's the same look I get on my face every time I see George Clooney in a movie. That man." She gave a small growling sound that I wished I could unhear. This was my best friend's mom after all.

"Not to discount your," I searched for the right word, "*appreciation* for George Clooney, but I'm talking about a real woman here. Not a celebrity I have no chance of meeting."

"No chance? Now that's hurtful. But I get what you mean." She took a moment to gather her thoughts, staring off into the sunset a moment longer before turning to face me fully, resting a reassuring hand on my arm. "Since the moment Rebecca hurt you, you've locked your heart away, keeping everyone new at a distance. And maybe it was necessary for a time to allow yourself to heal but Mason, it's been years. It's time to let the past go and allow yourself to be happy."

"I am happy," I insisted, still not willing to admit that my current predicament had anything to do with Rebecca and how she'd hurt me. I *had* moved on. She didn't influence my life anymore.

Joane raised an eyebrow at me and I ducked my head, unable to hold her gaze as I thought about the loneliness that had been creeping in more and more lately.

"Maybe happy is the wrong word. I think you've been chasing moments of happiness, but I don't think you've found joy in your life in a long time, Mason. You've been too busy keeping true connection at arm's length. If my divorce taught me anything, it was life's too short to be settling for temporary moments of happiness when you could pursue lasting things that bring you joy. It's time you took a chance and let someone back into your life again. Give joy a chance."

With those parting words, Joane stood and walked back to her car, leaving me alone with the twilight and my thoughts. Could she be right about giving Dani a chance? And if so, was there anyway I could let her in and tell her the truth without hurting her?

CHAPTER 25
Dani

THE DAYS FOLLOWING MY kiss with Allen passed in a blur. I quickly fell into a rhythm of beach meetups with Allen in the morning, writing in the bakery or bookstore during the afternoon, and outings with Allen to visit one tourist location or another that would leave me inspired enough to keep writing late into the night. Having internet back up and running at the duplex made it easy to coordinate plans, but I didn't spend much time texting my family or scrolling on social. I was too busy writing and enjoying all Oregon had to offer with Allen.

One afternoon, we drove up to a nearby lighthouse. Another evening, we tried the legendary fried cheese curds he'd raved about after the cheese factory tour.

Tonight I was finally getting to see an Oregon coast sunset. We'd come to the beach with a dinner picnic, spreading out a blanket on the sand. Both of us brought devices so we could work after we were done eating. My efforts to be productive had lasted all of ten minutes after dinner was put away. I was too busy stealing glances at Allen as he worked on his tablet, using his stylus to make quick, confident strokes on the screen.

"Stop looking at me and get to writing! Avery's going to hate me if she thinks I'm distracting you from your deadline," he said when he caught me staring once again. To be fair, the man was wearing swim trunks and an unbuttoned shirt, leaving miles of tanned muscles visible.

"Well, if you weren't so distracting," I muttered to myself as I ducked my head and committed to at least finishing the chapter in front of me.

"How am *I* distracting?" Allen asked, pointing his stylus at me. "I'm just working like I'm supposed to be. You're the one who keeps staring!"

"And you're the one putting all of that," I gestured at him, "on display out here in the open. What do you expect me to do?"

"I expect you to hold still and work because that's what I'm doing even though you're putting all that," this time he gestured at me in my floral print swimsuit and shorts, "on display and I'm still focused."

"Oh yeah? Let me see how focused you've been." I reached for his tablet, which he quickly moved out of reach.

"It's not done. I don't like showing anyone my work until it's finished," he said, locking his tablet screen.

"But I'm not just anyone! And you really haven't shown me much of your artwork. I want to see," I said, knowing full well my voice was coming out whiney and not really caring. Over the last few days, this man had seen me hangry, twitterpated, tired, discouraged, excited, and so many other emotions. Why not add exasperated?

"No, it's not ready."

"Please? I'll let you read my first chapter."

"That won't do me any good since I haven't started the first book yet," Allen said with a laugh, leaning away from me as I tried to reach for the tablet again.

"Please?" I asked, this time resorting to dirtier tactics as I leaned in close and pressed my lips to his ear. "I'll give you a kiss." I said this last part in what I'd hoped would come across as sultry and enticing, though honestly I just felt silly doing it.

He turned his heated gaze on me, one of his hands reaching up to cup my jaw.

"Promise?" His voice was a low growl that did funny things to my insides.

"Promise."

He lowered his hand and unlocked the tablet, but hesitated.

"Just keep in mind this is a rough sketch. It's not finished yet."

Allen extended the tablet, and I took it eagerly. He'd mentioned working on a commission for a florist, so I'd expected to see sketches of bouquets. But instead of roses and peonies, I found myself on the screen. Me typing on my laptop. Me in front of the lighthouse. Me eating ice cream in a green dress with his jacket on top.

"Sorry, I should have asked before drawing you, but you're so expressive and I wanted to see if I could capture your emotions and—"

I pressed a finger to his lips, cutting him off.

"They're incredible. How did you even draw these? The only place I remember taking pictures was the lighthouse." I continued to stare at the images, noting a rough sketch down in the corner, this one an outline of our current moment with me wearing a swimsuit, my hair twisted into a claw clip.

"If you think I could forget how beautiful you are at any given moment, you're wrong."

I carefully locked the tablet screen and placed it in his bag before throwing my arms around Allen and all but tackling in him an enthusiastic kiss. We had kissed several times since our first date, but this kiss held something deeper as his lips seemed to answer every unspoken question my lips posed.

As our kisses slowed, we pulled apart and settled back in to work and wait for the sunset, but my eyes were still drawn to him again and again. I could feel myself falling a little more in love with Allen with each passing moment, but I pushed the feeling aside. I lived in Utah. He lived in Idaho. And while both locations were only separated by a state line and a couple hundred miles, I worried what the distance would do once we returned to our homes. It seemed I was headed straight for heartbreak, and I wasn't sure what to do about that fact.

The next day, Allen convinced me to give up an entire writing day for an adventure in Portland. He'd promised it would be worth it, so, much to Avery's chagrin, I'd agreed. I'd kept Avery and the cousins apprised of the situation with Allen and, since I was making good progress on book two, Avery hadn't protested too much when I told her I wouldn't be writing today. I knew she was just concerned I was going to get my heart broken, but I remembered a time before she started dating Captain Vanilla when Avery would have run away on an adventure without hesitation. I hoped she could find at least a piece of that Avery and her happiness again.

As Allen and I walked down the street in Portland, a sign caught my eye and I froze, knowing immediately where he was taking me.

"Seriously?" I looked back and forth between Allen and the red and white sign above the store across the street. "You're taking me to Powell's Books!"

"When you said you'd never been, I knew I had to fix that," Allen said, wrapping an arm around my shoulders as we walked across the street to visit one of the largest independent bookstores in the world.

As we got closer, I hesitated, realizing that I was about to walk into a bookstore without a disguise. And while being a famous author was a level of celebrity that didn't come with much public recognition, being in a bookstore increased those odds exponentially.

"What if someone recognizes me?" I asked, slowing to a stop a few steps away.

Allen stopped beside me, seeming to consider the situation for a moment before taking off his hat and placing it on my head.

"How's that for an instant disguise?"

I snorted a laugh. "Now the challenge is: spot the author in a hat."

Allen paused, studying me before reaching over and tucking my hair back behind my ear.

"Now you're really in disguise."

Rolling my eyes, I took off the hat and, working quickly, tucked my hair up into the hat so that it came through the back. Then I snagged the sunglasses Allen had tucked into the neck of his shirt. I'd feel ridiculous wearing sunglasses inside, but it would have to do.

Even with my disguise, questions continued to circle in my mind, and I bit my lip, hesitating even as other customers passed us to enter the store. Allen watched me expectantly, seeming to sense there was more to my reticence than the need for a disguise.

What if someone recognized me? What if they started asking questions about book two? What if they hated *Of Curses and Pomegranates*?

Yes, I had written the last several days and I was cautiously optimistic that what I'd written wasn't complete crap, but I still felt like a sham. A fake. It was part of why I'd struggled so hard to write book two. No matter how many copies of my book sold, I still vividly remembered the words of my first few negative reviews. There was a reason I didn't read reviews anymore if I could help it. The words "flash in the pan," "overhyped," and "a complete waste of money and time" echoed in my ears if I wasn't careful. It terrified me to think the critics might be right and that I wouldn't be able to live up to the hype with my second novel.

I guess that's what came from being an "overnight" success. Though what the magazines and reviewers didn't see were the years of work I'd put into *Of Curses and Pomegranates*. The late nights writing and revising around my day job. The two unfinished novels that would forever stay buried on my laptop, never to see the light of day. The writing conferences and retreats and forums I'd participated in, trying to hone my craft and learn how to be an author. Yes, some people on BookTok and Bookstagram loved me, but did that really make me an author if all I'd done was publish a single book?

Would my career live past this summer and the initial hype of a book that happened to hit the trends just right?

If I couldn't write a best-selling conclusion to my duology, I had a horrible, sinking feeling that I would fail on a fundamental level to the point that I'd never truly recover.

And yet, here I was, about to walk into this giant independent bookstore with a man I was starting to fall for, pretending like it was no big deal. Yes, he'd seen my books back at Seabreeze Reads, but it wasn't quite the same. For some reason, this felt different. Would I even be able to find my books? Or would they be relegated to a back corner, like some kind of dirty, unimpressive secret?

"You okay?" Allen asked, resting a reassuring hand on my lower back. It was a welcome contact, like he was trying to guide me through this emotional rollercoaster.

I bit my lip before nodding and squaring my shoulders. I could do this.

"I'm fine. It's just always... weird walking into bookstores now that I'm published. Bookstores used to be my favorite places in the world but now..." I shook my head, not fully sure how to finish the thought. "Now it's complicated. There are so many thoughts and emotions every time I walk through the door."

"Tell me more," Allen said, guiding me away from the door and off to the side, out of the flow of traffic going into and out of the bookstore.

"It sounds so stupid to say it all out loud," I said with a self-deprecating laugh, even though I knew I needed to speak the words. "Every time I walk into a bookstore, it's this obstacle course of emotions. Will they have my book? Won't they? If they do, will someone recognize me? Do I want them to recognize me?" I pulled off Allen's sunglasses to rub at the bridge of my nose, trying to relieve the pressure building behind my eyes.

"That's a lot of questions," Allen observed, watching me closely.

I gave a small snort. "That's not even half of them. Those questions are just what run through my head when I go to a bookstore. It's exponentially worse if I'm going to a book signing. Then I add in questions like: What if no one comes? What if hundreds of people come? What if they love it? What if they hate my book?" Here I paused, not wanting to give voice to the last thought that I'd been struggling with since the moment other people started reading my words. Taking a breath, I continued, my voice quieter than before as I finally spoke aloud my biggest fear since I'd started this author journey, my throat constricting around the words. "What if they hate *me*?"

"Oh, Dani." Allen's voice softened and he pulled me into his arms.

I buried my face in his chest, careful to turn my head sideways so as not to knock off my hat, the soft cotton of his sweatshirt brushing against my cheek as I closed my eyes and fought back the tears that wanted to escape along with my confession. I hadn't cried in front of anyone since publishing my book, and I wouldn't start now. I couldn't. Otherwise, I wasn't sure I'd be able to stop.

I'd grappled with these thoughts and emotions since *Of Curses and Pomegranates* hit shelves and the first reviews started coming. I'd heard advice from several author friends to not read my reviews, but I couldn't help myself. That was my book baby people were reading, and I wanted to know what they thought. At the start, the reviews were positive, glowing even. Then the negative reviews had started. One-star reviews questioning my intelligence. Social media posts that tagged me, calling me the bane of the literary world. I'd finally stopped reading the reviews, but the damage had been done.

Each word stung, digging in deep and making me question my abilities and how I could possibly have the gall to write another book.

I didn't tell anyone about the self-doubt that haunted me, not as I quit my day job, not as I flew to book signings and press interviews, not even when I stepped on the plane for Oregon with the goal to write another best-selling novel. I couldn't let my loved ones down by showing them this scared, hurt side of me. Avery's business, Sadie's career as my editor, even Poppy's job selling books in the airport depended on me to a certain extent, and I couldn't let them down.

I was fairly certain Avery suspected that I was struggling in ways I wasn't telling her, but I couldn't find the words until now, in this moment with a man I was coming to care for deeply, standing outside of a bookstore terrified someone would recognize me as romantasy sensation Danielle Baldwin.

"No one in their right mind could hate you, not once they got to know you," Allen murmured into my ear as he smoothed a comforting hand up and down my back.

"How could you possibly know that? You barely even know me." It was true. Even though I could feel myself falling for Allen, we'd only known each other for a handful of days. He couldn't really know me that well.

Allen paused, seeming to ponder his response before finally speaking. "Because what I do know about you is incredible. You're creative and funny and feisty. Based on our conversations and the number of texts you've gotten from your cousin group chat, you're loyal and love your family. And you're a very good kisser." His voice turned sultry and a little wicked with this last comment.

I blushed, remembering our time on the beach yesterday, but pushed away his compliments. Now that I'd started, I needed to get these thoughts and fears fully out into the open.

"What if I'm just a hack, someone who doesn't actually have what it takes to do this author thing?"

Allen released his embrace and grabbed my shoulders, taking a step back so he could see my face.

"I'm a creative too. Trust me, I get it. There's so much fear and worry. What if I'm not actually good enough? What if I can't sustain myself with my art?" He looked into my eyes intently, reading my every reaction.

He'd hit my fear right on the head and could likely see it in every line of my face.

"Dani, I'm just a graphic designer who's barely scraping by, nowhere close to being an internationally best-selling author, but I know how you feel. For every reason there is to create, there are at least five more reasons not to. It's so much easier to take the expected path. To do something without emotional risk, like become an accountant."

I snorted. Clearly, Allen didn't know my ability with numbers. That career would have involved emotional risk of a different variety, mostly the emotionally scarring variety because I would be forced to do something I hated every single day of my life.

"At the end of the day, you have to ask yourself why you're doing this. Are you writing because you want fame, money, love, and notoriety? Or are you writing because, even if no one read another book you wrote, you have stories inside you that need to get out?"

His gaze was intense as he spoke, and I felt each word in my soul.

"You know, for 'just a graphic designer' you seem to know exactly what to say," I said, giving him a half smile. "Are you sure you're not a secret motivational speaker?"

"No, I'm just a guy who sees how incredible you are and wants you to see the same thing."

I ducked my head at the compliment, heat suffusing my cheeks.

"Thank you, Allen."

"You're welcome, Dani."

I took one more deep breath before straightening my shoulders and turning to the bookstore entrance, slipping the sunglasses back in place.

"So, are we going to visit the world's largest independent bookstore, or what?" I asked, trying to push aside any lingering emotions and exude a confidence I definitely didn't feel. Allen had given me a lot to think about when I was alone once more, just me and my laptop.

Maybe it was time I let go of all the expectations and pressures that were holding me back and finally write the story inside of me, not the one everyone else was expecting and hoping for.

If I was being honest with myself, that was what I had been doing since arriving in Oregon with the help of Joane and Allen. Now I just had to keep doing it.

"I thought you'd never ask. This way, my lady." Allen darted around me, opening the bookstore door and ushering me inside. "After you."

He gave a gallant bow, making me snort a laugh, releasing the last of the tension that had settled in my chest.

I stepped into the unfamiliar space and let the wonder of the moment wash over me as a childhood dream finally came true. I was inside Powell's, surrounded by books and standing next to a man who knew how to make me smile, even when I was feeling my most overwhelmed. In this moment, nothing else mattered.

CHAPTER 26
Mason

IF I'D KNOWN THE side of Dani that came to light inside a bookstore when she wasn't signing copies or dodging Spencer's advances, I would have brought her to Powell's sooner. She was fully embracing the moment, flitting between shelves as she perused her options, picking up and replacing books as they caught her attention for different reasons. I hadn't read her novel, but based on how books made her come alive, the woman was born to be an author.

And since it was Portland, no one even gave her a second glance for wearing sunglasses inside. Everyone was content, doing their own thing.

"I've heard amazing things about this one!" Dani squealed, holding up a young adult book with a black cover, the title written in gold type and framed by blue flowers. "And this cover is so pretty."

Her fingers lingered on the cover of a different book, this one a special edition with sprayed edges in a swirling, colorful design. All the cover possibilities had me wishing for my tablet, so I could sketch out all the designs and options, to pull from the inspiration around me. The inspiration that was Dani.

Joane was right. I was falling for Dani, but before it could go any farther, I had to find a way to tell her who I was that wouldn't completely destroy the fragile trust blossoming between us.

It wasn't long before Dani's arms were filled with books. I offered to help carry some or to grab her a bag, but she kept insisting she was fine as she tried to reach for another book, this one a nonfiction title highlighting the benefits of crystals that she said her cousin Poppy would love. I was fairly certain half her stack was destined for various family members. She'd snagged a special edition of *Anne of Green Gables* for her cousin Lucy. There'd also been books for Avery, Sadie, and Chloe, each book carefully selected with the person in mind. The woman in front of me was beautiful, thoughtful, and kind.

And I was the ultimate jerk. My gut clenched every time she called me Allen, a sweet smile on her lips.

I needed to tell her soon. I couldn't keep up this charade. Every moment I spent with Dani showed me just how special she was, and I would never forgive myself if I messed this thing up with my stupid lie.

Outside of the sketches on the beach yesterday, I still hadn't shown her my artwork, but that seemed insignificant compared to the fear of breaking the heart of the woman in front of me. If I couldn't find a way to tell her, I'd be no better than Rebecca: telling lies to get my way and have my fun, while completely disregarding the needs and emotions of the person in front of me.

I turned a corner and spotted a familiar blond head, as if he'd been summoned by my doubts: Spencer. My gut clenched as I realized Dani was coming up behind me, completely unaware of the disaster she was about to walk into.

Thinking quickly, I turned back to her, pointing the opposite direction.

"I think the romances are that direction. You probably need to check those out too."

Her face scrunched for a moment as she looked down at the pile of books in her arms. "How do I have this many books without having even looked through the romance section yet?"

"It's probably a sign that you need a bag," I said, my voice full of humor even as I felt the building worry that Spencer would round the corner and ruin everything.

She sighed, but headed up the aisle, away from where I'd spotted Spencer. "You're probably right."

I watched until she was out of sight before quickly walking to where I'd seen my best friend. If I was lucky, maybe I could get him out of the store before he saw Dani. I briefly considered just hiding from him. Powell's was huge, and I probably could pull it off, but I dismissed the thought, deciding to risk a direct approach for quicker results.

"Spencer! I thought that was you," I said, snagging his arm and dragging him a few steps away from where I'd last seen Dani.

"Mason? What are you doing here?" Spencer asked, stepping out of my grip and looking at me in confusion. "Last time I checked, the only bookstore you visit is mine when we're talking about a commission."

"I'm, uh," I scrambled to think of a reason I'd do something so out of character willingly, "here on a date."

Even as the words escaped, I winced, knowing Spencer would want all the details. Most guys would have patted me on the back, said something like "all right man!", and moved on. Not Spencer. Clearly I wasn't firing on all cylinders tonight. Maybe I should have opted to hide from Spencer, turn this evening into a giant game of bookstore hide-and-don't-seek.

"Dude! What's she like? I've got to see the girl who dragged you on an actual date to Portland. Is she close by?" He stepped around me, looking for my "date" and I hurried to block his path before he inadvertently stumbled into Dani. Even with my baseball hat and sunglasses on, there was no way Spencer wouldn't recognize her.

"Oh, I think she's that way," I gestured vaguely, and Spencer turned just in time to catch sight of a woman wearing all black, her ears gauged, piercings and tattoos covering most of her exposed skin, and her hair dyed jet black.

Spencer's wide eyes whipped back to me. "Her?" He asked in a tone that I would have found humorous in literally any other situation.

"Yep," I lied. "My grandparents met her at church," I scrambled to figure out a story for how I could have possibly connected with the goth beauty in the corner who was clearly the opposite of any woman I'd normally date. "Grandma thought we'd hit it off. It's been... an experience."

I paused and then grabbed Spencer's arm like I'd just had an epiphany.

"You've been wanting to date more, right?" I asked, only feeling a little bit guilty using my friend's lacking social skills against him.

"Yes," he said slowly, pushing his glasses up his nose from where they'd slipped down during our conversation, "but what does that..."

I looked significantly back and forth between Spencer and the woman in the corner and his eyes widened even more.

"Oh no," he said, shaking his head vigorously as he backed away from me, nearly running into an unsuspecting elderly woman headed to the checkout with a cookbook. "Oh no, no, no. I don't think... She's not really..."

"Come on, Spencer, this is the perfect chance to practice. Low pressure, at a bookstore. What more could you want?"

"Maybe a woman who doesn't look like she's going to murder me and use my body parts to cast a spell?" Spencer said, his voice cracking slightly.

"Eustasia's a really nice girl, once you get past her prickly exterior," I said, grabbing his arm and trying to guide him over to my unwitting accomplice.

"You know, on second thought, I have enough books at my own bookstore. No need to shop at the competition," Spencer said, breaking from my grasp. "Enjoy your date."

Spencer fairly ran from the store, nearly bowling several people over in his haste. I fought back my laughter until he was out of the store, relief immediately filling my chest at my narrow escape.

"What's so funny?" Dani asked, coming up behind me with a bag over her shoulder and at least three more books in her arms.

"Oh, just something I saw outside the window. It's hard to explain."

Dani shrugged, accepting my explanation at face value.

"What did you find?" I asked, eager to change the topic and turning to examine her books closer.

She held up two romances and one romantasy novel that looked vaguely familiar. I'd probably seen them around Spencer's shop.

"Aren't these covers gorgeous? I want to read the books, but I'm also going to take them home to show Avery so she can see who the cover designers are. Now that I'm more than halfway done writing book two, we really need to find a new designer."

"Those are nice," I said, grabbing the top book and examining the cover with its bold font and bright colors. It was a beautiful design, but it would clash completely with the current cover of *Of Curses and Pomegranates.* "Though, I'm not sure this designer's style would pair well with your first book."

Dani gasped, grabbing my arm. "How could I forget, you're a designer! What's your style? I mean, when you're working on something besides covertly drawing me."

"It depends on the project," I said, excited but trying to play it cool as I sensed the opening I'd been waiting for since the day I'd officially met Dani in Spencer's store. With that excitement, though, came a sense of guilt that I couldn't ignore. I was coming to know and care for Dani, and I couldn't feel good about using her to advance my career with so many secrets between us.

"You'll have to show me some of your work at lunch! I want to see if you could be a good fit. Not that I have any control over the decision, but if you're good, and I'm sure you are, I'll pass your name onto Avery for consideration."

I followed Dani as she continued to talk about covers all the way to the row of cash registers at the front of the store. Just as we were about to hop in line, a display of books caught my eye. The table was labeled "staff favorites," with Dani's book forming a small stack in the middle of the table.

Snagging Dani's arm, I slowed her dash to the cash register, turning her to see what I saw.

"And you were worried they wouldn't carry your book. Looks like at least three employees are fans," I said as I pointed to comment cards placed next to the stack of her book, each one containing the review of a different Powell's employee.

"Oh, well, that's just..." She stammered, her cheeks turning bright pink as she bit her lip. She reached up to brush at her cheeks, looking suspiciously like she was crying.

"Hey now," I said, pulling her in for a hug. "This is a very good thing."

"I know. I'm being ridiculous. It's just, I feel silly for all my worries, but then there's a voice in my head saying it's a fluke or that—"

I stopped her by pressing a gentle finger to her lips.

"Nothing about this is a fluke. Give yourself some credit and celebrate a win."

"You're right. I know you're right. Why are the negative voices so much louder than the positive ones?" She asked, her voice small and making my heart crack even more for this beautiful woman in front of me.

"I wish I knew," I said, reaching up to brush away a tear that had escaped from underneath her sunglasses and was currently tracing its way down her cheek. "But I'm making it my personal mission to help you listen to those positive voices from here on out."

Biting her lip for just a moment, Dani put down the books in her hands and pulled a pen from her purse before glancing around to make sure no one was paying attention. Once she was satisfied, she grabbed a few of the books, quickly scribbling her signature in the fronts.

Once she was satisfied, she capped the pen and slipped it back in her purse, retrieving the small stack of books she'd been carrying from where she'd deposited them on the table.

"Just celebrating the win," she said, giving me a small, private smile before heading back toward the checkout.

I watched her walk away. This woman was incredible, even if she didn't see it. I hesitated before following her, snagging one of the copies she'd just signed, a small souvenir from this moment. I checked out behind Dani, making sure she didn't see what I was buying.

It was the most sentimental thing I'd done in years, possibly since my dad passed away, and I told myself I bought it for research. If I was going to stand any chance of designing Dani's second book cover, I needed to know what the book was about. But I knew better.

After everything she'd shared with me today, I knew if I wanted to continue getting to know Dani, I needed to read her book. The woman wore her heart on her sleeve, and I had a feeling she'd written a large part of herself into this novel as well.

The question was, if I read her book, would I fall even more in love with this woman who had changed my life in just a few short days? And if I did, would I survive the fallout when the truth about Allen finally came to light?

CHAPTER 27
Dani

AFTER ALLEN'S INCREDIBLE SURPRISE of taking me to Powell's Books, I decided I needed to do something in return. However, instead of finding a museum and taking him to an art exhibit or something equally easy and reasonable, I'd decided sourdough was a good idea. Though it wouldn't quite be ready when he came over tonight, I could still tell him what I was doing, or surprise him with the loaf tomorrow morning.

I'd made sourdough once since Joane's lessons and, while not the best loaf of bread ever made, it had turned out decently. So of course, the next step was to make a loaf for the man I was trying to impress.

Unfortunately, Dough-ris Day had not gotten the memo that we were supposed to be impressing someone. Which probably had more to do with my distracted thinking throughout the day before than it did with my sourdough starter failing me, but it made me feel better to place the blame on someone, or something, that was not me.

But as I'd fed my starter, then mixed up and fermented my dough around writing sprints, I'd allowed my mind to wander back to Allen's words of encouragement, words that had genuinely been fueling my most productive writing day yet. And while I knew I shouldn't depend on outside validation to inspire me, for now it wasn't hurting. Because with each word I wrote, his voice echoed in my mind, cheering me on as I proved to myself that I did know how to do this a second time, no matter what the haters and doubters said.

Unfortunately, this twitter-pated writing haze had resulted in my losing track of the number of times I'd stretched and folded my dough,
making the structure less than ideal as I got ready to shape the dough
before baking. Technically the dough wouldn't be ready to bake until
tomorrow, so maybe things would fix themselves as it fermented one
more time overnight in the fridge.

As I attempted to laminate my dough, it was wetter and stickier than
I remembered. I couldn't get it off my fingers as I attempted to stretch
it across the counter without ripping, the process taking longer than
planned. Muttering to myself, I dipped my fingers in a glass of water I'd
set on the counter to help keep the dough from sticking to my fingers.
When she'd talked me through making sourdough, Joane had taught
me the trick while warning me against adding too much flour to my
dough. The problem was, what was I supposed to do when the dough
was already so wet and sticky?

As the dough became more unmanageable, I decided I needed more
flour, regardless of Joane's warnings.

I washed off my hands, wincing at the large clumps of dough disappearing down the disposal, and grabbed my bag of flour from the pantry.
For some reason, I'd decided I would be so into sourdough that I needed
the biggest bag at the grocery store, a decision I was regretting now.
Hefting the bag into my arms, I walked back to the counter, muttering
to myself about the frustrations of sourdough when my toe caught on
the kitchen rug.

As I tried not to fall, my grip on the flour bag slipped, and the open
bag hit the floor. Flour exploded all over me and the kitchen, dusting
everything, myself included, in a fine coat of white and I bit back a curse.

Flour floated through the air, just as a knock came from the door.

"Just a minute," I yelled toward the front door, then I evaluated my
surroundings. The sink was full of dirty dishes from my bread-mak-
ing attempts. The floor looked like there had been a snowstorm in the

kitchen. And the counter was covered in the sad, sticky remains of dough that looked like anything but a beautiful, appetizing loaf of artisan bread.

I fought back the tears, determined that crying once on this trip was more than enough as I determined the fastest way to get myself and the kitchen clean before Allen saw the disaster. Just as I decided to start by cleaning myself off, I heard the front door open.

"Dani? I thought I heard you say come in. I hope you don't mind—" Allen broke off as he stepped into the kitchen and took in the scene. "Um... wow."

I could only imagine what I looked like in the midst of the chaos of the kitchen: my hair falling out of a claw clip, flour covering my clothes, face, and arms, a look of absolute frustration pinching my features. Needless to say, it was not my finest moment, nor would I have chosen to share this exact moment with the man I was falling for. Especially not after all the vulnerability and emotions of yesterday.

"Surprise," I said, half-heartedly raising my hands in a weak attempt at jazz hands, even as the full force of my failure hit, and tears started to fall.

CHAPTER 28
Mason

IF THERE WAS A more panic inducing sight than a woman bursting into tears, I'd yet to find it.

"Hey, now, it's okay. We can clean up the mess. I promise," I said, picking my way through what appeared to be flour all over the kitchen floor and reaching for Dani.

She backed away, her hands held up to ward me off.

"Don't touch me. I'll get this all over you. This is what I get for trying to do something nice for you and bake. But you took me to Powell's, and I didn't know any cool art museums to take you to, so I thought I could bake you bread. I should have known better, but Joane promised I could do it if I just followed her instructions. Clearly, she overestimated my skills in the kitchen, and now I've probably murdered Dough-ris Day's loaf."

I only followed about half of the words that spilled out of Dani in a torrent of tears. Ignoring her protests that I would get flour on my hoodie, I pulled her into my arms. It only took a moment for her to relax and fully accept my embrace, burrowing in closer.

I rested my chin on her head, letting her cry as I breathed in her familiar strawberry scent combined with the smell of flour in her hair.

"It's okay. I don't need bread, and we can easily clean this up, I promise." I rubbed gentle circles on her back until her tears subsided. "See, it'll be okay."

"I'm such a mess. I've probably scared you away." She gave a pitiful laugh as she pulled back and wiped at the tears and mascara tracks on her face. "Now it's your turn to look a mess in front of me, even the playing field a little."

If she only knew. And she would know, soon. In fact, I'd decided to tell her tonight, rip the Band-Aid off and let the cards fall where they may. But seeing her tears for a second night in a row, I hesitated. I couldn't add to the burden of this moment. Maybe I'd wait, even if it was the coward's way out.

"I'm far from perfect. I have plenty of messy moments, trust me. And it takes more than a messy kitchen to scare me away." I promised, caressing her cheek to wipe away a smudge of mascara she'd missed. "Now why don't you get cleaned up while I take care of the kitchen."

"No, you're my guest! I made the mess. I can clean it up." She went to step around me to the sink, but I blocked her path.

"I've got this. Go take care of yourself and be thinking about what movie you want to watch. I'll order takeout and we can have a quiet night in."

She bit her lip, studying me for a moment. "Are you sure?"

"Positive! Now go." I gave her a gentle nudge out of the room, and she disappeared down the hall.

I looked around the kitchen one more time, hands on hips as I assessed the situation and tried to determine the best plan of attack. As I took in the dough blob on the counter, I couldn't help but feel an odd sense of warmth. Sure, the attempt had failed spectacularly, but Dani had wanted to make me sourdough. It might be the kindest thing a woman had ever done for me.

And I was lying to her face.

I pushed the thought away, grabbing the washcloth from the sink, and got to work cleaning the kitchen. I'd tell her, just as soon as I found a way to prove to her that, no matter how this all started, I truly cared about her.

I hoped it would be enough. It had to be.

Later that night, Dani and I sat snuggled on the couch watching an old movie she'd dug out from my grandma's stash of DVDs tucked into the hall closet. She was almost as excited when she found the DVD as she was when she'd realized I was taking her to Powell's the day before. I might have been offended if it wasn't so fun to watch her face light up as she talked about the magic of *Pillow Talk*.

"Doris Day is gorgeous, and Rock Hudson," here she stopped, shaking her head, "that man *knew* how to play a love interest."

The movie only partially held my attention at first as I took advantage of the opportunity to pull Dani in close, playing with her hair and sneaking occasional kisses.

"You're distracting me," she half-heartedly protested as I nuzzled her neck while Rock Hudson's character attempted to cram himself into a too-small car.

"If you turn your head a little further this way, I can distract you even more," I said, pressing my lips to her ear.

"Shh! Some of the best parts are coming and you're going to miss them," she said, laughing and scooting away from me.

I looped an arm around her waist and pulled her back toward me.

"Fine, I'll be quiet, but you can't sit over there. It's too far away," I said, resting my arms around her shoulders. I hardly recognized the man I was becoming with Dani in my life. I couldn't get enough of her: her smiles, her laugher, her touch. And I was terrified I would mess everything up.

With Dani snuggled in close, the movie began to hold my attention, the conclusion rapidly approaching. As I toyed with Dani's bracelet, an accessory that I had learned was a gift from her cousin Poppy, the plot started hitting a bit close to home. In the movie, Jan Morrow was just finding out the truth about Brad Allen, and my gut clenched as I watched her storm away.

"Would you forgive Brad if you were Jan?" I asked in a whisper, genuinely curious.

"Depends," Dani said, clearly distracted by the movie she'd told me she'd seen more times than she could count.

"On?" I asked, needing to hear her answer and know if she'd ever forgive a man who lied to her.

"How good of kisser he is, obviously," she said with a smirk and a knowing smile.

"I'm serious," I said. I was being ridiculous, but I needed reassurance that I hadn't ruined my chances with Dani completely.

This relationship had gone beyond the possibility of designing book covers to something more. Forget about my past with Rebecca. Forget about rules surrounding summer flings and dating tourists. I was falling for Dani, and I needed to know if we stood even the smallest chance of this becoming something real.

Seeming to sense my desperation, Dani paused the movie and turned to face me fully.

"You know, I've thought about it, and I genuinely don't know. It's easy to cheer for Brad and Jan on the screen, when I have no stake in the game. And I'd like to think that I believe love will win, no matter the circumstances. But I can't deny I'd be hurt if a guy lied to me this much." She bit her lip, her forehead scrunched in thought. "I'd probably forgive him eventually. Though he'd have to earn it."

I opened my mouth to respond, to finally come clean. But the words stuck in my throat.

Instead, I shook my head, mumbling something noncommittal, not ready just yet.

I needed more time. More time to prove to her who I was, regardless of what name she called me. More time to be with her. More time to ease her into the truth.

An idea started to form. Maybe if I could get her away from here, from our easy routine and the familiarity of Cascade Harbor, I could break the news to her, help her see that whether she called me "Allen" or "Mason", I was the same guy who had come to genuinely care for her.

My grandparents had flown to Utah to visit my mom and brother for a week and had asked me to stop by their place to check on things. What if I took Dani with me to their house? We could get away, go somewhere neutral to talk. I could tell her the truth without the constant risk of someone from town blowing my cover. With my grandparents gone, there was no danger of them showing up or of anything else throwing off my plans with Dani.

"Hey, Dani," I asked slowly as she pressed play on the movie and the story in front of us continued to play out. I entwined my fingers with hers, needing all of the physical contact I could get. "How would you feel about an adventure away from Cascade Harbor?"

"Like to Portland?" She asked, her eyebrows pinched together. "Because we definitely already did that."

"I was thinking a bit closer than Portland, like my grandparent's place. They're out of town for a few days, and I need to stay close to keep an eye on things. But I don't want to spend time away from you."

Her face softened at the invitation.

"I don't know. That seems kind of fast."

"We'll have separate rooms, and if you want to come back early, I'll drive you home. I promise. Please, Dani?"

She hesitated a moment longer before nodding.

"Okay, but only if you're the one who calls Avery and breaks the news to her. I'm not telling her I'm skipping another writing day. I'll probably have to kick you out right after the movie to make up for the lost writing time."

I relaxed back into the couch, content to finish the movie now that I had a plan to tell Dani the truth. As the final credits played, she gave a contented sigh.

"There's just something about that movie that makes me happy," she said. "The costuming, chemistry, humor, it's all just so good!"

"Just forget about the parts that don't translate well to our current moment," I said, a couple of scenes in particular coming to mind.

"Hey now, don't be bashing on my favorite movie!" Dani straightened and grabbed a throw pillow, playfully whacking me with it.

"I'm not bashing it. I'm just observing that not all aspects of cinema age the same." I grabbed the pillow, preventing her from hitting me with it again. "The same could be said for most creative endeavors. Things change so fast in the design world that I cringe when I look back on some of my earlier stuff."

She settled back into my side, looking up at me. "Well, if they're anything like the sketches you showed me on the beach, I bet they're still wonderful."

"You're a bit biased," I said, tapping her nose. "But I appreciate the sentiment."

"I'm not biased. Though, I haven't seen much of your work, so I can't really speak to your full skill level. When are you going to show me more? I'd love to see some cover concepts, give me something to pass onto Avery for consideration."

Her question had my conscience twinging, thinking back to the goal that had started this whole deception. As my feelings for Dani had grown, I'd been hesitant to show her my work for fear it would just make things worse when the truth came out.

"I'll show you soon. I promise." Just as soon as I told her the truth and could ensure she wouldn't hate me for the rest of my life.

When I first started designing, chasing this crazy dream of supporting myself with my art, I'd thought there was nothing I wouldn't do or give to succeed. Now, if succeeding meant losing Dani, I wasn't willing to pay the cost. I just hoped I could help her see that.

CHAPTER 29
Dani

I STEPPED INTO SUGAR and Sea and was immediately greeted by the amazing smells of baking bread and cinnamon. I'd arrived a bit earlier than usual, determined to get a good breakfast and at least a little bit of writing done before it was time to leave for Allen's grandparents' house.

While Allen had called Avery and warned her I wouldn't get much writing in today, I was so close to being done that I couldn't not work on the story some. This was the fastest I'd ever written a book, the words flowing at a rate I'd never seen or experienced before. There was something magic about Oregon that had unlocked this story filled with love and magic, and I couldn't wait to see how it ended.

"Don't you look chipper," Joane said as I reached the cash register. Today her shirt was a vibrant purple with white polka dots. It made me feel shabby for wearing a plain blue t-shirt accessorized by Allen's jacket, which I'd yet to return after the mishap with my Doris Day dress.

"It's a good day! What can I say?" I didn't even try to hide the smile that filled my face as I thought about how I'd be spending most of the day with Allen.

I gave Joane my order but waited by the cash register for her to fulfill it instead of going to my table. There was no one behind me in line, and I was in the mood to chat. I'd already texted her about my sourdough debacle the night before, but I wanted to catch up for a bit. We hadn't been able to talk as much the last few days with writing filling my days and Allen occupying my nights.

"Are you still seeing that tourist?" Joane asked, handing me my coffee and a small brown paper bag containing pastries.

"Yes, and he's still wonderful," I said, thinking about our upcoming adventure today, and how we'd snuggled while watching *Pillow Talk* last night.

"I'm glad you've found love on the Oregon coast, though I do wish you'd fallen for one of our locals. I want you to come back and become a permanent resident," Joane said as another customer walked into the shop.

"I don't know that I'm quite ready to relocate for a man," I told Joane, and I started walking to my usual table to squeeze in some writing. Allen would be picking me up from the duplex in a couple of hours, giving me plenty of time to work. "Though I wouldn't say never either. I'm trying to stay open to the possibilities." A part of me still worried that Allen and I wouldn't be able to make a long-distance relationship work, but for Allen I was willing to give it a try.

"Just be careful," Joane called, the whole bakery audience to her parting words. "I know a thing or two about vacation romances, and I don't want to see you get hurt."

"I appreciate that."

As I settled in to write, I did my best to push aside Joane's warning. I knew Allen. In fact, I was fairly certain meeting Allen and allowing myself to fall for him was part of why I'd finally been able to start writing again. His words at Powell's, encouraging me to keep writing, had become a war cry of sorts each time I sat down and felt the imposter syndrome start to niggle at the corners of my mind.

My only regret was that I'd be leaving Cascade Harbor as soon as my draft was done so I could go with Avery to Italy. Though maybe I could fly straight back to Oregon afterward and capture a bit more time with Allen before we both had to return home to reality.

I pulled out my laptop, picking up the story where I'd left off, Hypatia's and Petros's romance calling to me and begging me to reach the conclusion.

But even as I wrote about stolen kisses and magic battles, Joane's words continued to echo in my mind, a warning that I couldn't shake.

I knew Allen. He was kind and genuine. He'd never hurt me, at least not intentionally. So why did Joane's words bring to mind Spencer's warning from Mason about how summer romances never lasted?

CHAPTER 30
Mason

I FOUND MYSELF WHISTLING as I parked my car and headed into Ed's. While my hair wasn't quite ready for a cut, I wouldn't mind a good shave and a chance to catch up on the latest with the Gossip Gang. I had time to kill before I needed to pick up Dani, and I was too anxious to spend the day at home working. Tonight, I was taking Dani to my grandparents' house where I'd come clean and make everything right.

And while a part of me worried what the drive home would be like if she got angry and wouldn't forgive me, I was hoping getting away from Cascade Harbor would give us both a clean slate to build new memories without lies between us.

The bell above the barbershop door chimed, revealing that, despite how much had changed in my life over the last week and a half, everything else in town seemed to have stayed the same.

"Oo, looks like someone got some action last night," Clyde called from his perch next to the window as I walked into the shop. He and the rest of the Gossip Gang watched me expectantly. The trio of elderly men had somehow managed to dress in matching red shirts with jeans, and I couldn't help but wonder if it was by chance or if they got a kick out of being color coordinated.

Art smacked him with his newspaper. "More like someone is *going* to get some action tonight. Who's the lucky gal? I haven't seen you lurking around town wooing the ladies as much as normal. Find a new stomping ground?" Art waggled his bushy white eyebrows in a gesture that should never be made by a man his age.

"That's none of your business," I said, settling in to wait for Davie who was working with another client.

Charlie gave me a sheepish but hopeful look from where he sat in his barber chair, clearly waiting for some work.

"Never again, Charlie," I said kindly but seriously, rubbing the back of my neck. "I don't think I'll ever recover from the last time."

The Gossip Gang chortled at this pronouncement as Charlie blushed a deep shade of red.

"It was an accident," he muttered, looking up at the ceiling and rocking back and forth in his chair.

"An accident that never should have happened," Davie said as he walked past Charlie to ring up his customer before calling me over to his chair. "What are we doing today? If I take any more hair off, you'll be bald. Or are you wanting to rock the hairless look? It hasn't done much good for Clyde over there."

Art and Marty found this hilarious, elbowing Clyde, who took the teasing in stride and laughed along.

"Just a shave," I said as I rubbed a hand along my stubbled jaw. I'd been good at keeping it shaved the first couple of days after Charlie's mistake, but I'd been so busy the last few days with Dani that I hadn't given it much attention.

Davie got to work as I listened to the rambling chatter of the trio of old men. There'd been some kind of drama at bingo night involving Spencer and Maisie, the thrift store owner, that I'd have to ask him about the next time I saw him. I'd just started to tune out the chatter when I heard my name.

"You know that girl staying at Mason's duplex? Apparently, she's got herself a man, but no one knows him or has seen him." I tensed at Marty's casual comment, hoping Davie didn't notice. "Do you know who it is, Mason?"

"Can't say that I do," I said, hoping they'd lose interest in the subject and move on.

"I've seen that girl around town. She's a looker! Told my Benny he should take a crack at her, but you know Benny. If it requires him getting off my couch, he's not moving," Clyde said.

"How do you know she's dating someone?" I asked trying to keep my voice casual as I attempted to ascertain their source of information. If anyone happened to see me out with Dani, everything could come crashing down before I spoke to her tonight. Maybe I should have talked to her last night, risked the explosion without all of my careful planning. "You see her out and about or something?"

"Boy, you need to have Davie clean out your ears while he's shaving your face. Didn't you hear Marty say no one's seen who she's dating? Apparently, he's also a tourist, or at least that's what I heard Joane telling Spencer at the bookstore the other day. Sounds like a recipe for disaster if you ask me. Two tourists sparking up a romance." I could hear Art's disapproval from my spot, tipped back for Davie to work.

"Or it's a recipe for a real *good* time," Marty said, causing the other two to break into laughter and start telling stories about when they were younger and dating.

I relaxed. It sounded like my secret was safe after all.

But glancing up at Davie's face, I caught a disappointed, knowing look that made me think I hadn't been as careful as I'd thought. While I knew Davie wouldn't say anything, I left the barbershop feeling unsettled and determined. I would tell Dani the truth tonight, no matter what. She had the right to know, even if it meant she ended this fledgling romance between us.

As I walked to my car after my shave, I heard my name and turned to see Spencer running my way from the bookstore.

"I was going to call you, but I'm glad to catch you in person. I just scheduled a major children's author for a signing at Seabreeze Reads because her original venue fell through, and I'd like to get your designs printed and hung before she comes later this month. What would you think about upping the timeline on those art prints? I'll pay extra, of course."

I smacked my forehead. I'd been so lost in design ideas for Dani's covers that I'd almost forgotten about Spencer's commission.

"I've been crazy busy with another project, but I'm hoping to work on this the next couple of days. I'll be staying out at my grandparents' with minimal distractions." I hedged. I would be at my grandparents', but the distractions would be anything but minimal, for better or worse depending on Dani's reaction.

Spencer studied me over his glasses for a moment, his forehead creased in concentration.

"You seem different lately," Spencer said, tapping a finger on his chin. "I can't figure out why though."

I ran my hand through my hair. "I mean, the haircut happened over a week ago but I'm still getting used to it."

Spencer shook his head. "That's not it. It's almost like you got a big promotion, which doesn't really work when you're self-employed. Or like you got a girlf—" He broke off, staring at me, eyes wide.

"You've got a girlfriend, don't you? I haven't seen you around town with a different girl every day. In fact, I've hardly seen you around town at all." His words came out in a rush, and he began pacing, waving his hands around as he talked. "The last time I saw you was in Portland with that—"

He stopped and turned to look at me, his face frozen in a look of horror so comical I'd likely be using it for inspiration in future projects.

"Please tell me it's not..." Here he trailed off, seeming unsure how to finish his sentence.

Taking pity on him, I clapped a hand on his shoulder.

"No, I'm not dating Eustasia from Portland. We did *not* suit." He didn't need to know that we didn't suit because we never actually met.

"Oh good." His shoulders slumped in obvious relief. "So, who's the girl then?"

I bit my lip, wanting to tell him but needing to come clean to Dani before sharing my feelings with anyone else.

"She's not exactly my girlfriend, though I have been seeing someone and there's interest there. Let's just say she's a tourist, but there's something different about this one," I said, my voice full of hope as I thought about Dani's heart, courage, kindness, and humor. Things I would have never learned if I hadn't let down my guard to get to know her as a friend, something that had quickly shifted into more almost without me noticing.

"Really? Mason Stuart breaking all the rules." Spencer clapped a hand on my arm before turning to head back to his store. "I'm happy for you, man. Just don't let that woman distract you too much. I need that commission *soon*."

Spencer disappeared into his store, and I walked to my car, praying that Spencer's excitement wasn't misplaced and that I really could make a relationship with a tourist—with Dani—work.

CHAPTER 31
Mason

MY FINGERS WERE INTERTWINED with Dani's where they sat on the center console as we drove along the coast to my grandparents' house, my thumb occasionally flicking over the stone beads of her bracelet. As we drove, she talked through her book, her enthusiasm apparent as she gushed about the scene she'd written earlier and how it would tie into the ending.

"Give me a day, two max, and I'll have a finished draft," she said.

"That's amazing," I said, lifting her hand and quickly pressing a kiss to the back. "We'll have to celebrate."

She threw me a beaming smile, returning to her book talk. I could listen to her discuss her novel forever, falling a bit more in love with her with each word as her passion and excitement shone through.

We stopped along the way to pick up takeout for dinner, ensuring there would be no distractions or excuses for me not to talk to her tonight. I was done giving myself outs.

"I'm still getting used to how beautiful it is out here. One second, I'm soaking up all the forests and greenery and the next it's beaches and ocean views." She gave a dreamy sigh as she looked out her window after our dinner stop.

"It's part of why I love it here so much. You get a bit of everything: forests, mountains, beaches. Really, there's nowhere like it."

"So why do you live in Idaho?" She asked, turning to face me, her head tilted to the side in curiosity.

I'd almost forgotten the lie I'd told her about being from Rexburg.

"It's complicated." I hedged, not ready to tell her quite yet. Once we finished this drive, I'd tell her the full story, come what may.

The drive ended too quickly and soon I was showing Dani to the guest bedroom that would be hers for her stay. I helped her carry her overnight bag into the room where my mom usually slept when she visited, the bed covered in homemade floral quilts and the room filled with well-loved furniture. A print I'd designed that combined pinks, purples, and oranges into a swirling pattern inspired by the sunset hung on one wall, and a window facing the ocean filled another one.

I left Dani to get settled while I finished unloading the car, doing my best to stay in motion to distract myself from my racing thoughts. I also took the opportunity to hide any family photos that could potentially giveaway my secret, only leaving out shots from my early childhood or of extended family members like my aunts, uncles, and cousins.

Needing to do something to channel my anxious energy, I set the table with my grandma's worn white and blue plates that bore more than a few scratches and chips. It wasn't anything fancy, but I hoped Dani would see the effort I was putting in. The table itself was a sturdy thing that my grandparents had picked up on the side of the road a few years back. My grandpa had refinished it, its worn surface fitting perfectly with the lived-in and well-loved feel of their home.

"This looks good," Dani said, coming up behind me and wrapping her arms around me. She gave me a quick squeeze before releasing the embrace and walking around me to fully take in the spread of pasta, salad, and breadsticks I'd ordered for us.

"What was that for? Not that I'm complaining." I asked, still unfamiliar with the type of relationship that lent itself to regular, easy touches. Before Dani, any physical contact I'd experienced of late was calculated, designed to get something. This familiarity was new, and I found myself craving her next touch in a way that was impossible to explain.

Dani shrugged as she snagged a breadstick and took a bite. "Just because I felt like it."

"Well, if you feel like additional hugs or hand holding or more, I'm down," I said, grabbing the breadstick from her fingers and taking my own bite.

"Hey! That was mine," she said with a laugh as she grabbed back the breadstick. "And what do you mean by 'more'?" She quirked an eyebrow and cocked a hip, clearly oblivious to how adorable and inviting she appeared right now.

"You're the writer. Use your imagination." I pulled out her chair and helped her get settled before walking around the table to the place I'd set for myself.

We dug into dinner, falling into the comfortable, familiar conversation that I'd come to associate with Dani. As dinner wound down, I knew it was time. Gathering my courage, I reached across the table to grab her hand. I needed something to ground me in this moment if I was going to come clean and show Dani who I really was.

"Dani, there's something I need to tell you." I took a deep breath and let it out again. "Remember when we first met—"

A knock on the front door interrupted me and I looked toward it, confused.

"Do you need to see who that could be?" Dani asked, looking to the door.

"No. It's someone looking for my grandparents. They'll go away." Or at least I hoped they'd go away. "As I was saying, back at the bookstore that first—"

The knocking came again, this time louder and accompanied by the doorbell.

Dani bit her lip, clearly finding the situation humorous as I let out an exasperated breath.

"I don't think they're going away," Dani said, the corner of her mouth tipped into a small smile.

I sighed and pushed to my feet. "Stay here. I'll see who it is and be right back."

I walked down the short hallway that led straight from the kitchen/dining area of my grandparents' home to the front entry. I glanced through the window set into the door and froze.

Spencer stood on the other side and had clearly seen me walking to the door as he smiled and called through the door.

"Dude! Open up. I brought dinner."

I looked around the hall, decorated with framed family photos mixed with my art, trying to formulate a plan of escape, but there was none.

Drawn by her curiosity to see who was at the door, Dani stood from the table and walked over. "Who is it?"

"Mason?" Spencer called once more, ringing the doorbell again.

I closed my eyes, as it fully hit me. My time had run out. It was too late.

As if reading my thoughts, Spencer took matters into his own hands and opened the unlocked door.

"Why weren't you answering the door? Since you were going to be here alone for the next few days, I thought I could keep you company, and we could discuss the commission. Mom sent me with some fresh sandwiches and—" He broke off, spotting Dani at the end of the hall, her eyes wide. "What's going on?"

CHAPTER 32
Dani

I LOOKED BACK AND forth between Spencer and Allen, unable to make sense of the scene in front of me. Allen was from Rexburg, visiting his grandparents. And while it was possible he'd met Spencer during one of his previous visits, I doubted they'd know each other well enough for Spencer to show up out of the blue to surprise him with food talking about a commission.

"Spencer, what are you doing here?" I asked slowly, my thoughts racing. I felt like I was watching a TV detective show and all the pieces were in front of me, but my brain was struggling to put them all together to explain the events that had led us to this moment. "How do you know Allen?"

"Allen? Who's Allen?" Spencer asked, pushing his glasses up his nose as he looked at me like I'd lost my marbles. "I came to visit," his words slowed, and he turned to look at Allen, "Mason."

"Dani, let me explain." Allen turned away from Spencer and the open front door, taking a step toward me, but I retreated, taking a step back.

"Wait, *Dani* is the girl you were talking about outside Ed's the other day? You're dating *the* Danielle Baldwin?" Spencer's eyes were huge. The look of shock on his face would have been comical if I didn't feel like all the oxygen was being sucked from my lungs. "Mason, how could you lie to me about that?"

"Spencer, just stop talking for a minute." Allen, or, I guess, Mason, stopped Spencer with a hand on his chest and turned back to me, a look of complete panic on his face. "Dani, let me explain—"

I held up a hand, silencing both men.

"Why do you keep calling him Mason?" I asked Spencer. I didn't recognize my own voice. It was stiff and small.

"Because that's his name," Spencer said slowly. "Mason Allen Stuart. Your neighbor and property manager."

With each name he pronounced, I felt the earth shift beneath me as the pieces finally snapped into place. Mason *was* Allen. Allen *was* Mason. Somehow my womanizer of a neighbor and the man who'd made me feel seen and safe were one and the same.

I shook my head, a headache beginning to form. None of this made sense. Mason was an angry, bearded lumberjack and womanizer who left me sticky notes and made my life difficult by ensuring people parked in the middle of the driveway. Allen was nothing like that. He was, kind, sweet, and a great listener. He was clean cut and an incredible artist.

I froze as memories came rushing forward: both Tiffany and Veronica talking about modeling for Mason, Spencer talking about how Mason had done the art prints at his shop. I glanced at the prints lining the wall, prints Allen had mentioned designing for his grandparents. After seeing his sketches of me on the beach, I'd mentioned loving his style and requesting he send samples to Avery for my book cover. A style that was remarkably similar to Mason's.

I suddenly regretted how much I'd eaten at dinner. I was about to be sick.

"Tell me it isn't true," I said, my voice deceptively calm as I searched Allen's face, trying to see the man I'd started falling for over the last week and a half, but only seeing the one who had frustrated me so thoroughly when I first arrived. Then I remembered our conversation from the night before. "Was this why you kept asking me if I could ever forgive a liar while we were watching *Pillow Talk?*"

"Dani, if you'd just let me explain." Allen took a step toward me, his hands extended like he was trying to calm a wild animal.

"I'm listening!" I spat, closing the distance between us and jabbing a finger into his chest.

Allen's words came out in a rush. "I met you in the bookstore and you started talking about your publisher looking for a new cover designer and it sounded like a gold opportunity. But then I realized who you were and that you would never give Mason a chance so—"

"I told you I don't trust easily, that I don't give out my phone number because of how people treat me and use me once they learn who I am. I thought you were different." I felt tears burning the backs of my eyes, but I refused to let them fall where Allen—Mason—could see. "Turns out you're the worst one of them all."

Mason deflated before my eyes, his expression one of complete devastation before he turned his gaze to the floor. "I know."

"Spencer, can you give me a ride to the duplex? I need to leave." I hurried down the hall, reaching my bedroom door as the tears began to fall. Desperately, I shoved everything I'd brought back into my overnight bag, not caring if I forgot anything, just needing to be gone and away from this place.

With my bag in hand, I rushed down the hall and to the front door. As I pushed past Mason, he grabbed my arm, stopping me.

"Dani, you have to believe me. I never meant—"

"I don't have to believe anything you tell me. You lied to me the entire time I knew you. What more do I need to know?" With that, I walked out of the house and to Spencer's car, my head held high even as my chin began to wobble, and the tears gathered again.

Spencer followed behind me, his steps hesitant. As I settled in my seat, I turned away from him and determinedly stared out the window, worried any kindness from him would push my emotions further over the edge. Why couldn't I have been attracted to *him* that day at the bookstore? Everything would be completely different if I'd been interested in Spencer or decided not to open my heart at all. Lesson learned. Life was easier without relationships and vulnerability.

I spent most of the ride back to Cascade Harbor crying so hard I couldn't even see the beaches and forests I'd gushed about during our drive to Mason's grandparents' home. Not that it mattered. I'd never be able to look at Oregon the same.

Spencer attempted to soothe me, but I ignored his kind words, too busy feeling my heart shatter.

When I finally got control of my emotions enough to stop crying, I dialed Avery.

"Hi Dani! How are things going with Allen? I didn't think I'd hear from you at all today." Her voice was chipper, its familiar tone nearly bringing me to tears again.

"Avery."

All it took was the one word and she knew something was wrong. Seeming to sense I didn't walk to talk, she went into full big-sister mode.

"Come home, Dani. I'll book you the first flight. It's time for you to come home."

"Okay," I whispered, the word cracked and broken. Home was exactly where I needed to be right now.

The rest of the car ride passed in silence, Spencer only speaking when we reached the duplex. He carried my overnight bag to the door, but paused before leaving.

"Dani, I'm so sorry. If I had known..." He trailed off, clearly at as much of a loss as I was, his shoulders hunched and his hands shoved into his pockets.

"It's not your fault, Spencer." My voice was rough from crying. I reached up and pulled him into a quick goodbye hug. "Thank you for the ride home, and please tell Joane goodbye for me. I'm going to miss her and her baking most of all."

Spencer gave a nod and a sad smile before climbing back into his car and driving away. Joane would need to stop by the duplex to pick up the sourdough supplies she lent me, but I'd let her sort that out with Mason. I just needed to leave.

I quickly scoured the duplex, shoving everything into my suitcase, muttering to myself as I tried to cram my new sweatshirts and books into the already full bag. Not that I would be able to wear the sweatshirts again. Every time I pulled them out, I would think of Allen or Mason or whatever his name was, and the day we spent together picking them out. The same would be true for the handful of books I'd bought for myself at Powell's. Maybe I'd give everything away once I got home. Or have a cleansing fire. Either option would work, but my thoughts were too tangled to think it all through now. I'd decide once I'd landed in Utah, where I would be with family and friends who actually loved me and didn't lie to me.

After all, if Allen had lied about who he was, what else had he lied about? His feelings for me? My skill as a writer?

At least with that last one, if he was lying, I could prove him wrong. Just like I'd promised to prove wrong every negative review and hater of my first book.

I'd channeled the emotions of falling in love with Allen into my sequel, there was no reason I couldn't do the same with this latest slew of emotions.

As I pushed out of my bedroom, ready to load up my car and leave, my bracelet from Poppy snagged on the doorknob. It was supposed to bring inspiration and good things into my life, but all it had brought was trouble. I slipped it from my wrist, remembering every time Allen had stroked it, sending sparks up my arm. Even though it had been a gift from Poppy, I would forever associate the bracelet with Allen. Anger at him and his lies overwhelmed me and I chucked the bracelet across the room, not caring if it broke as it hit the wall with a satisfying whack.

My phone buzzed when a text from Avery came through with my flight information. Thankfully, she'd gotten me on a flight leaving in a couple hours. I'd owe her for coming through for me.

Typing out a quick email to the duplex owners apologizing for my hasty departure, I left my key on the kitchen counter, loaded my bags into my rental car, and made the agonizing drive to the airport as the light faded from the sky, my emotions transitioning from sorrow to anger to numbness as the miles passed.

Hours later, I arrived in Salt Lake City after a blessedly uneventful flight. It was late, meaning I couldn't stop at Poppy's store to sign book copies, even if I'd had the heart. Instead, I booked it to baggage claim and prayed Avery would be there waiting for me.

When I spotted my sister, I rushed to her, bursting into tears as she wrapped me in a much-needed hug.

"Oh, Dani, it's going to be okay." She soothed as she rubbed my back and held me close.

"Avery, I thought maybe he could be the one. That he actually might—" But the words stuck in my throat, and I couldn't finish.

"Shh, you don't have to say anything. It's going to be okay, I promise," Avery soothed, pulling back to wipe away my tears. Taking control of the situation in her usual big sister way, she grabbed my suitcase and guided me to her car, the only sound between us that of my suitcase rolling behind her.

I was hit with a fresh round of tears when I saw Hercules waiting in the passenger seat, his head hanging out the window. I climbed into the car and pulled my massive dog onto my lap, not caring that it was awkward, but needing his familiar presence as I wrapped my arms around him and held on.

Avery was right. It would be okay. My heart was broken now, but at least Mason had done me the favor of showing me reality before I'd finished my book. Now I could give it the realistic ending it deserved. And then, I'd move on with my life and forget Oregon ever happened.

CHAPTER 33
Mason

THE NEXT SEVERAL DAYS passed in a blur of pain as I tried to figure out how to fix things. By the time I'd made it back to the duplex, Dani was already gone. She hadn't even left me a scathing orange sticky note, letting me know her thoughts, and I felt its absence keenly as I tried to pretend like it didn't matter. All that had waited for me was her orange and green bracelet left forgotten on the floor of her bedroom. I'd slipped the bracelet into my pocket, needing the reminder of her, even if it felt more like a weight than a comfort.

I tried telling myself it was just another failed summer romance. That I'd survived it before with Rebecca. So why did it hurt so much more this time around?

I'd taken to wandering the beach for long stretches of time, lost in thought. Everywhere I turned reminded me of Dani, but at least at the beach I could focus on the sensation of the sand beneath my feet and use the sound of the waves to drown out my thoughts.

One morning after walking for a while, I returned to my car, not really sure what else to do with my day but knowing I couldn't walk forever. I looked up to find a familiar lanky figure leaning on the hood of my car.

"I thought I might find you here," Spencer said as I slowly approached.

"What do you want?" I asked, stopping a few feet away. A part of me wanted to blame Spencer for Dani's departure, but I knew that was wrong. Maybe things would have played out differently if Spencer hadn't sprung the truth on her, or if I could have softened the blow and told her who I really was beforehand. Then again, maybe that would have just made everything worse.

But it didn't matter now since there was no way to know and no one to blame but myself and my own stupidity.

"Initially, I wanted to punch you in the stomach for lying to me and Dani. But then I watched you walking all slumped over, and I realized something."

"What's that?" I asked, crossing my arms over my chest, only mildly curious to hear what Spencer had to say. Mostly I wanted him to get off the hood of my car so I could drive home and get back to wallowing. I'd been wrong before. This was so much worse than when Rebecca had left me all those summers ago.

"You actually love her. Somehow between all the lying and summer romancing, you actually let yourself feel again and fall in love." The shock and incredulity in Spencer's voice were borderline offensive. Though his words echoed the conversation I'd had with Joane shortly after everything had started with Dani.

"You're wrong," I lied. Apparently lying was the only thing I was good at. "I don't fall in love. Or have you forgotten all my summer flings? First rule of dating tourists—"

"Are you really going to keep selling me that BS? We both know you broke every single one of your supposed rules this summer, and you want to know something funny?"

"What?" I snapped, quickly losing my patience with this conversation. If I got in the car and turned it on, would he move? Not that it mattered. If he didn't move when I backed out of my spot, he wouldn't get hurt. Probably.

"That was the happiest I've seen you in a long time."

Spencer's words hit home, and I rubbed at my heart, which hurt more than any of my muscles after a punishing workout. Because what he said was the truth, and, despite my best intentions, I'd once again fallen for a summer fling. Except, unlike with Rebecca, I didn't think I'd be able to move on this time.

"It doesn't matter how happy I was. It's over now. You saw it all implode," I said, finally digging out my keys and unlocking my car.

Instead of taking the hint, Spencer took this as an invitation to climb into my car and continue our talk, folding his frame into the passenger seat as I settled into the driver's seat.

"Yeah, that was painful. Why on earth did you think lying was a good idea?"

"Why do I feel like I'm being lectured by an overbearing parent?" I grumbled as I reached for my seatbelt.

"Because my mother is Joane and if I've learned anything from that woman besides the value of good sourdough, it's how to host a guilt trip. Congratulations, you're in for quite the treat!" Spencer said with far too much glee. "So how are you going to fix things? Because you can't keep moping on the beach. The tourism board is starting to get complaints about a broody man scaring away all the vacationers."

"Ha ha," I said, deadpan. "Very funny."

"I'm serious. You need to do something to fix this."

"Or what? Life goes back to the way it was before, that's what. I hurt Dani so bad she ran away; least I can do is respect her decision." It was the logic I'd been telling myself with every phone call and text Dani refused to answer.

"Are you really okay going back to the way things were, chasing one fling after another, never really caring about anyone but yourself?"

I hesitated, really thinking about my answer.

"No," I said, the single word seeming to contain the weight of the entire world.

"That's what I thought," Spencer said, looking at me with compassion. "Which brings us back to my question: What are you going to do to fix it?"

That night, long after my conversation with Spencer, I found myself back at the duplex, trying to draw. But instead of making progress on Spencer's commissions or any of the other projects that needed my attention, I found myself creating alternate versions of Dani's first book cover. With each rendering, I pictured myself and Dani as the two star-crossed lovers on the cover.

Since Dani had left, I'd binge-read *Of Curses and Pomegranates*, desperate for anything that helped me feel close to her and like our future wasn't hopeless. What I'd found in the pages was a vivid fantasy world covered in Dani's fingerprints. I could hear her voice in the descriptions, see her facial expressions in every character. And instead of it making me ache and want nothing to do with the epic story she'd crafted, it had my fingers eager to sketch and create in a way I never had before.

I was in the middle of a set of monochromatic character sketches when my phone started ringing on the desk next to me. Not bothering to check the caller ID, I answered.

"Hello?" I asked, only half listening as I worked to get the expression of longing in Hypatia's eyes right.

"Where do you get off?"

I froze. I'd only heard that angry voice once before, and it did not bode well for me that I was hearing it again, now.

"Avery, I get that you're upset but—"

"Do I sound like I want to hear your excuses, *Mason*? And yes, I know who you really are you lying turd."

I winced. It wasn't the worst thing I'd ever been called, but it definitely stung more than those other insults ever had.

"I'm going to ask you one question, and you better think about your answer very carefully because if you say one wrong word, I'm flying to Oregon tonight and making you regret hurting my sister."

I already regretted hurting Dani, but I didn't feel like it would do much to help my case to point that out to Avery in the middle of her tirade.

"Do you love Dani?"

The question caught me so off guard, I nearly fell out of my office chair.

"Is this a trick question?" I asked slowly, confused why Avery would be asking me this now.

"No tricks. I just want an honest answer. Do. You. Love. Dani?" This time, she said each word distinctly, as if I were a child.

"Yes, I love Dani." It was the type of declaration I probably should have made to Dani and not her sister, but at this moment, I didn't have much of a choice.

"And are you willing to do anything to make this right?"

This time I didn't hesitate in my response. "Absolutely."

"Then here's what you're going to do." Avery's voice had taken on a clipped, all-business tone and, for the first time since Dani left, I felt hope.

CHAPTER 34
Dani

Herriman, Utah

I WAS GOING TO kill my sister. And probably all of the cousins, minus Chloe, just for good measure. And the only reason Chloe wasn't on my hit list was because she was currently living in a different state. If she still lived locally, she'd also be in my bad books.

Because, despite my heartbreak of the last few days, my family had decided the best way to celebrate me finishing the first draft of the sequel to *Of Curses and Pomegranates* was to host a formal party at my townhome clubhouse with family, friends, my publishing team, and an assortment of bookish influencers.

So, now, instead of celebrating by wearing sweats and wallowing on my couch with Hercules curled up next to me, I was dressed to the nines in a tight-fitting black dress Avery had picked out for me with my hair curled and full makeup on. I hadn't put this much effort into my appearance since I'd worn my Doris Day dress to dinner with Mason, and I was hating every second of it.

Spotting the refreshments table, I snagged a plate and began loading it up with finger foods. If I was going to be forced to socialize with dozens of people, at least I could do it with food in hand. And maybe if I was eating, it would discourage people from talking to me.

Just as I was about to find a table to hide at with my food, Avery's ex-fiancé cornered me.

"Dani, we're so glad to have you back. How was Oregon? It must have been great, since you finished the book! I can't wait to read it. Avery said something about the ending needing some finessing, but I expect it'll be pure gold by the time editing team is done with it." Eric gave me a too-wide, too-white smile and I resisted the urge to simply walk away without saying a word. He did own half of the publishing house that had made my career possible, and I needed to at least be civil. Even if he was faker than the plants dotting the clubhouse shelves.

"She hasn't said anything to me about the ending. I'll have to talk to her," I said with a forced pleasantness that was the exact opposite of how I felt.

I knew what Avery's issue with the ending was, and I was going to stick to my guns with this one. Or at least try to. After getting home from Oregon, I'd channeled all my emotions into the stunning conclusion to Hypatia's and Petros's story. And it was one that would definitely leave a mark. And much like I had with the bookstore scene that unlocked my writing and cured my writer's block in Oregon, I'd decided to pull inspiration from real life because sometimes happy endings were just unbelievable.

I could still picture the final battle I'd written, Hypatia choosing to sacrifice herself and return to the underworld rather than allow her enemies to take over the human realm. As a result, Petros's memories were erased, leaving Hypatia alone to remember their epic love and wonder what could have been.

It was how I imagined my perception of things versus Mason's. Given his history, I figured it wouldn't take him long to move onto the next female to stay in the unit next door. Or at least that was what I told myself to make the separation easier. A small voice in the back of my mind tended to argue with me, pointing out how Mason had gone out of his way to spend time with me and make me feel special, actions that he wouldn't have taken if he was simply looking for a quick fling.

Eric continued babbling beside me—going off about print costs and page counts—and I only half-listened as I scanned the room, taking in the folding tables covered in white tablecloths with floral centerpieces in vibrant hues that reminded me of an Oregon sunset. Avery must have hired someone or recruited the cousins to turn my normally bland clubhouse into a welcoming party.

As if sensing my need for escape, Avery called the room to order. She stood at the front of the room where she'd set up a projector and screen. The room was filled with family members and Rose & Quill Publishing contacts. I'd also spotted a few local authors, many of whom I knew Avery was trying to woo over to Rose & Quill. It was a small group, but the energy was high as everyone turned expectantly to listen to what Avery had to say.

"Welcome everyone! Thank you for joining us tonight to celebrate the next big reveal for Rose & Quill Publishing."

Polite applause filled the room along with a few whistles, and Avery paused, waiting for everyone to quiet down before she continued.

"Now, I know this is a bit unorthodox, but we're so excited about the release of Dani's next book that we decided to do a surprise title and cover reveal here tonight. Please keep in mind, this is for your eyes only until the social media reveal. This cover is an interesting case because we had to switch designers, with our previous designer's blessing of course. We miss her talents and can't wait for her to return from time with her family. That being said, we've hired a very special, new designer, and his work truly deserves a crowd."

I forced down my emotions at the mention of a new cover designer. Not too long ago, I'd hoped my designer would be Mason. Days later and I was still having a hard time with the truth.

"And to make things extra fun, nobody but me has seen the cover. Not even Dani."

I pasted on what I hoped appeared to be an excited smile as all the eyes in the room turned to me. I was puzzled at the unique approach to my cover. Last time, Avery had asked for some cover suggestions and sent me a few renderings for feedback before the cover was finalized. Being shown the final cover, just days after I finished drafting the novel, without having given any suggestions had me more than a little concerned.

Weren't they rushing the cover a bit? What if I hated the design? Though I guess it didn't really matter. As the publisher, Rose & Quill could do what they thought best, and I'd go along for the ride.

I braced myself, prepared to school my features into pleasantly surprised no matter what I thought of the cover.

"If everyone can please help me countdown to the big reveal," Avery requested, sounding like the announcer on a game show.

Poppy and Sadie came to stand next to me, each of them wrapping an arm around my waist as everyone began chanting: five, four, three, two, one.

Excited claps and cheers echoed through the room as the cover appeared on the screen.

The image took my breath away. The design was perfect with its mix of colors and shadow, the silhouettes of two characters embracing, nestled in a tangle of vines. The working title I'd been writing under, *Of Fates and Ruin*, was emblazoned on the front in the same looping font as my debut.

It was everything I'd wanted, the style a familiar combination of whimsical and creative that had first caught my eye in Spencer's bookshop and again on the beach in sketches of myself that I'd cajoled Mason into showing me. How I could have ever thought those pieces could have been created by two different artists boggled my mind. There was only one man who could have created those pieces and the cover everyone in the room was currently gushing over: Mason.

As if summoned by my thoughts, he stepped in front of the screen, shielding his eyes from the projector as he searched the room. He looked good, wearing slacks and a fitted green button shirt. I gave a startled cry, and tried to turn and run, but my cousins held me fast.

"Trust us. Give him a chance," Sadie said softly, gently nudging me toward the man who had completely decimated my heart.

"Hi, everyone," Mason said, clearing his throat to gain the room's attention. "Most of you don't know me. My name is Mason Allen Stuart. I'm a graphic designer from Oregon who royally messed up, and I'm here to try to make it right."

Everyone glanced around, clearly confused by Mason's declaration. I held my breath, curious and terrified to hear what he'd say next.

"You see, I manage a duplex for my grandparents and was lucky enough to be Dani's neighbor during her recent writing trip. However, I didn't exactly give her the best first or second impression." Here he gave a self-deprecating chuckle as he nervously ran his fingers through his hair, the short strands sticking up in contrast with his polished appearance.

"I had a bit of a reputation as a lady's man, a reputation I'd earned, and one that Dani unfortunately witnessed. So, when I was given a second chance with her, and she didn't recognize me as her player neighbor, I lied about who I was because I didn't want to miss my chance with the talented, gorgeous woman we all love. But as you can imagine, my lies came back to bite me, and I ended up hurting an incredible woman, which was the last thing on earth I'd ever wanted to do."

Mason's eyes found mine during his confession, and I felt his words in my soul. My heart began to pound as I saw his sincerity written in every line of his face.

"Dani, I hate that I hurt you because you truly are the most incredible woman in the world. Watching your passion and love for writing amazed me. Reading your words inspired me. And spending those too few days with you in Oregon changed me.

"So, I came here tonight to say I'm sorry and I hope you'll forgive me, whether or not you use my cover. I just needed you to see how I truly feel." He waved vaguely at the cover with its image of lovers embracing. It was honestly the most romantic image I'd ever seen, and my heart pounded double time as I tried to process everything Mason was saying. "I just hope I did Hypatia and Petros justice because their love story, the story you've created, is legendary. The type of love story I hope to have someday."

Mason stepped away from the projector and walked to the door, a sea of whispers following his every step as people turned to watch him go.

"What are you waiting for?" Sadie asked, giving me a gentle shove in his direction. "You've at least got to talk to him."

She was right, so I slipped past people and caught up to Mason just after he stepped outside into the warm Utah summer night. The setting couldn't have been more different from Oregon, and yet, there was a familiarity and comfort in his presence that I couldn't ignore.

"Mason, wait," I called just before he reached the parking lot.

He turned slowly to face me.

"Did you mean what you said in there?" I asked, crossing my arms and hugging myself as I braced for the answer. I needed to know this was real and not another ploy for him to advance his career or add another entry on his list of summer flings.

I knew on some level he must have convinced Avery to trust him, give him a chance, but I wasn't convinced. Not yet.

"It's the most truthful thing I've ever said." Mason took a step toward me. He reached for my hand, a gesture he'd made countless times in Oregon, but he stopped just short of making contact, his hand dropping back down to his side.

"How can I trust you? You lied to me." The words were bitter, but true, ringing with every ounce of hurt I'd been navigating since the second I'd climbed into the car with Spencer.

Mason gave a small, sad shake of his head. "I wish I could say I regret lying, but if it was the only way to get to know you and realize what love really looks like... I can't say I wouldn't do it again. But I do regret hurting you."

"What if I don't forgive you?" I bit my lip. I wasn't one to hold a grudge, but Mason had hurt me, and I couldn't just pretend it hadn't happened.

"Then I'll live my life trying to change your mind. That is," he stepped closer, his hand closing around mine, gently tugging my arm free from its crossed position, "if you'll let me."

I took a breath, considering his words. Could I forgive him? He'd come all the way to Utah, had designed the dreamiest cover I'd ever seen, and he'd shown up for me, even though he didn't know how things would turn out. His actions were speaking pretty loudly at the moment. Our conversation on my couch back in Oregon when he'd asked if I would have forgiven Brad Allen for lying to Jan Morrow came rushing back. I'd told him I would have forgiven Rock Hudson's character. Maybe I should apply the same answer to Mason.

"Only if you promise me a lifetime supply of Joane's sourdough. And countless nights watching *Pillow Talk*," I said softly, a small smile teasing my lips as I stepped closer to him.

"Done and done. Anything else?" His voice was full of hope.

"And trips to Powell's Books, where I can buy all the books I want. And—" I broke off, feeling exposed and ridiculous and vulnerable. It was worse than the jumble of emotions I'd experienced after reading my first hateful review of my book.

But even as I hesitated, all of the love and magic of the cover he'd designed came to mind. A cover that supposedly I'd inspired. Remembering that beautiful cover and the care that had gone into it warmed my heart and reassured me that I was doing the right thing.

"And?" Mason asked, grabbing my other hand and shifting so he stood directly in front of me, leaning close in the late summer sunshine as he waited for what I had to say next.

"And you kiss me senseless whenever I ask."

Needing no further invitation, Mason pressed his lips to mine in a searing kiss that left me weak in the knees and desperate for more.

But he pulled back, resting his forehead against mine.

"I kind of took that as an invitation. Hope that was okay." He whispered, his breath warm against my cheek.

"More than okay," I whispered back, trying to catch my breath. "I think I owe Avery an apology."

"Oh? Because, genuinely, you thinking about your sister is the last thing I was expecting to hear right now."

I gave him an impish grin.

"Well, you might have convinced me that happy endings actually can happen, which means I need to change the end of my book."

"Thank heavens!" A voice called from the doorway, startling us apart.

I broke away from Mason to see the entire cousin crew gathered in the doorway, grinning back at me. I was fairly certain Poppy even had Chloe on a video call watching the whole thing.

"How long were you guys standing there?" I asked, suddenly feeling very self-conscious, even as I leaned into Mason's side.

"Long enough to know that kiss was far too short," Poppy said with a knowing look.

"I concur," Mason said, dipping down to press his lips to mine once more, causing my cousins to whoop and cheer.

And while it wasn't exactly the storybook romance I'd always imagined for myself, it was infinitely better because it was real. Even if it had come with some plot twists I hadn't seen coming.

EPILOGUE
Dani

Cascade Harbor, Oregon

Two weeks later

THE DAYS FOLLOWING THE cover reveal flew by as Mason made it his mission to prove to me his sincerity. During that time, he hadn't lied to me even once. Instead, he'd shown me with both his actions and words just how sincere he'd been on that stage. And while we'd spent some much-needed time in Utah, both of us meeting each other's families and getting to see each other in a new setting, we'd both been eager to board a plane and return to Cascade Harbor, after a stop at the store where Poppy worked to sign some books, of course.

The sound of the waves welcomed me as I stepped onto the beach, soaking in the pinks and purples of sunset over the Pacific Ocean. Hercules fairly danced behind me as he caught his first glimpse of the ocean. After Mason and I had reconciled, we'd decided we needed a redo of my trip to Oregon, this time without any lies between us. And since Avery had headed to Italy for what was supposed to be her honeymoon but had morphed into a solo vacation that she badly needed, I'd decided to bring Hercules with me. I only felt a little bit guilty for bailing on Avery, forcing her to take her trip alone, but I hoped this trip would help her reconnect with the braver version of herself who had disappeared when she'd started dating Eric.

While Mason and I hadn't fully decided where our future would be, I knew the Oregon coast would play a big part in our lives.

"Absolutely stunning," Mason said from behind me.

"I know, right? This is seriously one of my favorite things about Oregon." I looked over my shoulder to find Mason staring at me, not the breathtaking view in front of me.

"I was more impressed with the sight of you at sunset." Mason slipped his arms around my waist as we watched Hercules frolic in the waves, splashing and getting covered in sand.

"I'll have to remember that line for the next book I write," I said. I'd just finished fixing the ending of *Of Fates and Ruin* and I was already eager to start another project. I was considering a complete change of genre, maybe trying my hand at contemporary retellings of favorite old movies. I'd start with *Pillow Talk*, of course, though I could picture my version involving beaches and a sexy artist.

"Only if I get to help with any kissing research you need to do," he said, pressing his lips to my shoulder.

I turned in Mason's arms to look up at him. "I wouldn't have it any other way."

"Promise?" He asked, leaning down, his lips a breath away from mine.

"Promise," I said on a sigh, anticipating the brush of his lips on mine. Instead of making contact, Mason pulled back, and I pouted.

"Before we start any of that research, I have a gift for you," he said, his face filled with the excitement of a kid on Christmas morning.

"You didn't have to get me anything," I said, thinking I'd much prefer the kiss he'd stopped to whatever he was about to give me.

"I guess it's technically more of a return than a gift." Mason held out his hand, a familiar orange and green stone bracelet on his palm. "I found this after you left, and it's time I gave it back."

I gave a small laugh as I slipped it on, the cool stones pressing against my skin as I remembered my distaste for the bracelet when Poppy had first presented it to me. While the colors still weren't my style, the unique piece now held a special place in my heart, and I was grateful to have it back.

"You know, Poppy told me this bracelet was exactly what I needed when I'd boarded that first flight to Oregon. I had no idea just how right she would be."

"You can tell her I'm partial to it," Mason said, rubbing a thumb over the stones before pulling me back in for a hug. "Now where were we?"

"About to conduct some very important book research," I said, my voice coming out husky as I eyed his lips.

"That's right. I think it involved something like this." He bent down, pressing his lips to mine, the familiar pressure making my heart race.

And there on the beach, wrapped in Mason's arms with the sunset behind me and an entire world of possibilities in front of me, it felt like all this moment was missing was the words, "And they lived happily ever after."

The End

Love Dani and Mason? For a FREE bonus epilogue visit
authorhillaryslaughter.com

NEXT UP

I HOPE YOU'RE ENJOYING the Love Connections Sweet Romcom series so far! Up next is Avery's story, *The Fear of Falling* by Dana LeCheminant.

Going on her honeymoon without a husband wasn't the plan, but Avery is desperate for a break from her nonstop busy life working across the hall from her ex. And a no-strings attached fling with the handsome stranger determined to get her to take a different approach to life? That might be the best decision she's ever made.

Too bad fate has other plans.

What happens in Italy follows you home.

Grab your copy today, and be sure to check out the rest of the Love Connections series!

ALSO BY HILLARY SLAUGHTER

ACKNOWLEDGEMENTS

Top of this list will always and forever be my Heavenly Father, who has blessed me with stories and a desire to tell them

Thank you to my family! Thank you for talking me through plot holes, listening to me vent and stress, and cheering me on unconditionally.

To Dana LeCheminant, thank you for being my emotional support human! Your advice throughout this author journey has been invaluable. This book wouldn't exist without all of your help. Not to mention your friendship keeps me sane in so many ways.

To Denae, Amanada, Mak, and Alix, thank you for an unforgettable Oregon trip that laid the foundation for this story. Anytime you want to read books on the Oregon coast, I'm in!

To Nicole Kimzey, thank you for being an amazing support and cheerleader!

To Annie Peterson, thank you for helping me make this story shine with your incredible editing insights.

To Cassy and Rebecca, thank you for being such amazing beta readers.

To the other authors of the Love Connections series, thank you for including me and helping make this story shine.

To Raneé Clark, thank you for your fantastic developmental edits.

To Lindzee Merrill Photography, thank you for the incredible headshots.

To my arc readers, friends, and everyone else who has had a hand in this book, thank you. Your support is felt and greatly appreciated.

Finally, thank you, my readers, for reading Dani and Mason's story! You make what I do possible, and I will forever be grateful for every person who decides to take a chance on one of my books.

ABOUT THE AUTHOR

Hillary Slaughter is a crafting addict, avid reader, and hiking en-
thusiast. Born and raised in Utah, she loves exploring the mountains,
especially if she can bring her dogs with her. She has a Bachelor's degree
in English from Brigham Young University and a Master's of Business
Administration from Utah Valley University. She loves writing sweet
contemporary romance with a dash of humor and is the author of the
Lost Roommates Series and a participant in the Love Connections Sweet
Romcom series. You can learn more about Hillary and her books at
authorhillaryslaughter.com.